GRIN

THE UNAUTHORIZED BIOGRAPHY OF A CHESHIRE CAT

© 2013 by Adam Danielski

Published by BentBeat Productions at Smashwords

All rights reserved. No portion of this book may be reproduced, stored in a retrieval system, or transmitted in any form or by any means—electronic, mechanical, photocopy, recordings, scanning, or other—except for brief quotations in critical reviews or articles, without the prior written permission of the author.

Illustrations/Artwork by Christine Penley

Smashwords Edition

This ebook is licensed for your personal enjoyment only. This ebook may not be re-sold or given away to other people. If you would like to share this book with another person, please purchase an additional copy for each recipient. If you're reading this book and did not purchase it, or it was not purchased for your use only, then please return to your favorite ebook retailer and purchase your own copy. Thank you for respecting the hard work of this author.

# *Dedication*

*To my wife, Elizabeth, for supporting me*

*To Ruth, for encouraging me*

*And*

*To Ms. Pettigrew, who, when I was in the 7th grade,*

*said she would read this*

## *Prologue –*

## *Adapted from Lewis Carrol's "Alice's Adventures in Wonderland"*

Alice strolled down the winding path, and the Cheshire cat followed closely behind. Alice's shiny black shoes with the small strap over the top were quite dusty, as she had kicked up a lot of dirt. The cat was sneaking in the shadows, all the while thinking, wondering, pondering, devising. He leapt up to one of the crooked trees that caused a fork in the path. The cat sat on the branch and wondered, *Is this the girl who called me ugly so many years before, when I was but a small kitten?* He purred as he saw the girl approaching the divider, his claws digging into the wood. The tree groaned in pain.

"Oh, so sorry, Master Tree. I did not realize my own paws were having a feast at your expense. I promise it will most certainly not happen again." The tree rustled its branches, shaking leaves all over.

Alice noticed this event and halted, looking oddly at the tree. "Even the trees are most peculiar here. I swear this one has eyes growing out of its branches," Alice said aloud, now even more convinced that she was indeed seeing a pair of eyes glowing on a lower limb. As she stepped closer, she could now see an outline of a small body and a face. Slowly, the cat came into full view.

"Oh, hello there, Cheshire Puss," Alice said, curtsying and then recoiling a bit, as she was unsure if this name would offend. The cat widened his grin. "Can you tell me which way I ought to go?" Alice asked.

The cat opened his mouth. "Well, that is entirely based on where you want to go."

Alice looked perplexed at this thought. She wanted desperately to go home but also wanted to see more of this strange and intriguing place that afforded speech to cats and other animals in nature. "Well, I don't know," Alice blurted out, without thinking about what she was saying.

"Well, then it does not matter which way you go as long as you go." The cat was now amused at this girl whom he had once considered to be a prospective owner of sorts.

"Well, who lives in these parts of the woods?" Alice was curious as to whether this question would get a direct answer or a questionable riddle.

The furry cat, which Alice had now noticed was a curious shade of lavender, held up one paw and pointed to the right. "If you go that way, you will come across the house of the Hatter." The right paw then went high into the air, swooped down, and now pointed left. "In that direction is a hare, a March Hare to be exact. You can visit either one; they are both mad," he said, grinning again.

Alice's mind drifted off to Dinah at home. *I wonder if Dinah could grin like that?* After pausing to consider what Dinah would be doing at home this very second, Alice remarked to the cat, "I don't want to visit anyone who is mad. I am not accustomed to being around mad people."

The cat looked at her and cocked his head. "Well, you can't help that. We are all mad here." The cat thought he could throw her off if she thought that he was mad, and indeed, *she* was quite mad for even being here. "*I* am mad, and you are *definitely* mad."

"I am not mad, cat. I am just lost," Alice said indignantly.

The cat, however, insisted. "A dog is not mad, correct?" he questioned Alice.

"I suppose not …" Alice replied.

"Well, a dog growls when it is angry and wags its tail when it is happy. I do just the opposite," the cat said, raising one cat eyebrow and winking at the girl.

"I would not call a cat's growl anything but a purr," Alice said, wondering how a cat would even know how to raise an eyebrow; then she thought to herself, *Well, I am talking to a cat, so perhaps it can do a great many more things that I did not think cats could do.*

"Are you playing croquette with the Queen today?" the cat asked, already knowing the answer.

"Oh, I would love to, but I have not been invited. I suppose she just invited the Duchess. Do you think she would let me play if I showed up?" Alice questioned to the cat.

"Of course she would; she loves little girls and would be most happy to see one since there has not been a little girl around here for a long time." The cat knew the Queen disliked pretentiousness almost as much as he did, but he did not care much for the Queen these days, and any trouble he could make for her was worth the trouble being made. "Well, if you do go, you will see me there. I would not miss it for the world." With that the cat vanished into thin air.

Alice looked around to see if it had jumped down or was just running around to the back of the tree. Then before her very eyes, the cat appeared again.

"I almost forgot, what happened to the baby?"

Alice looked back up at the cat. "It turned into a pig, I suppose. It looked very swinish."

The cat looked back at Alice and smiled. "I half expected it to." The cat vanished once again.

Maybe I am going mad. How can a cat disappear and then reappear?

With that thought, the cat reappeared, still sitting on the same branch. "Did you say pig or fig?"

Alice put a hand up and scratched her head. "Pig. I am pretty sure it was a pig. I would appreciate it if you would stop disappearing and reappearing so quickly. You could make a girl quite mad."

The cat took her advice and slowly disappeared from his tail up to his head. His eyes and grin still sat there, but before Alice could turn and walk away, they too disappeared completely.

Alice thought the cat was quite peculiar and wondered if Dinah would be adverse to appearing and disappearing. She had the most curious thought she had ever had…

*How doth the Cheshire cat grin*

*Wide across his face*

*And travel through the worlds*

*Of reality and space?*


*His eyes are wide and glowing*

*Deceptive in his thought*

*Never to reveal his tail*

*Or ever to be caught.*

    Alice shook her head at this thought and began to walk down the path to the left, toward the house of the March Hare. She decided this might have been the best path to take; after all, it was May, and the March Hare might not be too mad. The cat leapt from the branch of the tree and followed after her. He was going to make sure she made her appointment with the Queen one way or another.

    The Hatter and the Hare were sipping their tea as the cat strolled by, invisible to the eye. Knowing he needed a much more direct path to the kingdom gardens, he walked past this revelry to the next path. The cat reached up a tree and drew the outline of a door in the trunk with his claw. This tree was not alive, as it gave no sound or sign of pain. The gold key hanging around his neck lifted itself into the lock as if it had a mind of its own. The door appeared and he sat next to it, waiting for Alice to join him.

## *Chapter 1*

'1'

Many things happen for a good number of reasons, some coincidental, some predestined to shape the future of things to come. The nonsensical ones happen on purpose. This is often the difference between chance and predestination that sets events in motion and changes the course of history. This was the case one fair day in the town of Warrington, England, located within the county of Cheshire.

Willem, an older gentleman from the countryside, sat down in the same shadowed northwestern corner of the quaint village where he had set up shop in for the past three weeks.

A very tall man and a lovely young girl of no more than twelve started to pass by when Willem shouted out, "Afternoon, Doctor Liddell!"

The good doctor spun around on his heels, startled by the lowly looking man in the plain white shirt and blue canvas overalls. "Willem, how many times must I tell you, please call me Henry when I am off duty," Henry said in a harsher tone than he intended.

Willem recoiled a bit. After all, Henry Liddell was an intimidating man. He was a man of great stature at a very thin 6'5". He had a black waistcoat, a dark cloak slung across his back and a tall top hat. His medical bag hung loosely from his hand. Henry was the only doctor in the entire county of Cheshire. Henry turned back toward the young girl just in time to see her remove something from the box Willem had been guarding.

"You are the most curious and ugliest looking little kitty I have ever seen," the young girl said as she held the kitten up to her face, inspecting it as though she were getting ready to research where it came from. Willem turned his head at this point and observed what he thought was a look of insult on the kitten's face.

"I don't want this one, Daddy. I don't! I want a normal looking kitty." She plopped it back down in the small wooden crate. Her blue and white dress flowed in the wind as she stood over the box of kittens, legs straight, bending at the waist. Her blonde hair seemed to shimmer as she bent over to pick up another one.

"I'll take this one, Daddy. He is of proper color, grey and white, like a wonderful day in London," she said, taking the kitten at the back of the box and tucking it under her chin. The kitten purred with delight and batted its paw at the hair flowing in the wind like a serpent.

"Seems your daughter has taken a liking to that one," Willem said.

"Lovely," Henry murmured under his breath with a tinge of sarcasm. "My daughter Alice has been looking for another kitten to dote upon for some time, and this one will do quite nicely." Henry was pouring sarcasm over each word he spoke, glaring at Willem as though it was his fault. "My wife will also be ecstatic for another mouth to feed. Come now, Alice, we need to get home before the sun goes down, and I have many more stops. Willem, you take care."

With an abrupt wave to Willem, Henry grabbed Alice's hand and pulled her along through the small crowd of people who had gathered to see what was in the box. Willem waved back, but by that time Doctor Henry Liddell was just a black shadow in the distance, his top hat shrinking from view.

Willem was hoping that he would be able to get rid of the rest of the kittens before he was to return home at sunset, and he almost had. He had just one more left, but he knew it was almost a lost cause. The crowd around him had dispersed once they saw what was in the box. *No one wants a strange hairless kitten*, he thought to himself as he sat against the wall in one of the busiest areas of the market. The crowd was starting to thin, and he knew it was getting late: The shadows from his corner of the market were beginning to grow and reach ever farther toward the market center.

Willem was a silver-haired farmer and a man tasked by his wife with taking the box of kittens to the market to try to sell them. However, after several failed attempts the previous few weeks, he decided to just give them away. After all, the kittens were not his. He'd just had the unfortunate luck of having them born in his old rickety barn that sat in the countryside where he plowed his fields.

Willem leaned back and remembered finding the kittens that day out in the cold. He probably would not have noticed anything if he had not heard the screams of young, hungry animals. He remembered the shock of looking over the edge of an old wooden crate and seeing five grey and white kittens and one strangely hairless kitten. They could not have been more than three weeks old. The mum, a short-haired tabby, was lying on her side, waiting to feed her young. She looked up at Willem and meowed at him as if to say, *I'd like a little privacy here.* Willem went outside and walked back to the house. He grabbed a large wooden crate and some blankets.

"Martha, come out to the barn and help me for a bit!" Willem yelled up to his wife.

Willem sat there thinking about how his wife had gasped as she saw the little litter of baby kittens.

He laughed and said, "You've never seen a hairless kitten before? It's not the devil, you know. Just a birth defect, I suppose." She looked at Willem and glanced back at the kittens. Five grey kittens and one peculiar kitten, naked as a man on his the day of his birth.

She just looked on without saying a word. Then as if coming out of a trance, she said, "Take these to the house. We'll look after 'em and you can take 'em to the market and sell 'em when they get old enough. We'll keep one of 'em and the mum. The rest you take to the market, though, Willem, or ya be sleeping out here in the barn with your new friends."

When Willem awoke from his daydream, the market was virtually void of any customers. Most of the merchants were packing up to go home early, as the sky was starting to turn grey with what appeared to be rain clouds. Willem figured that he had better give one last push and then head home before it started raining.

"Excuse me, sir, would your daughter or son like a kitten? I have one left and it's getting late. Please do an old man a favor, if you will."

"Let me see what you have," said a young produce seller who was packing up apples into a wooden crate on the back of his wagon. Willem held out the box to the young man. The man looked over the rim of the box and scurried back in fright. "What's wrong with this one? It doesn't look well, sir. It's not infected with the plague, is it? Are you trying to give away plague kittens? Leave, or I'll call the Constable." He pushed Willem in the shoulder with his right hand.

Willem, not understanding what the issue was, looked in the box to see the hairless kitten with a most precocious grin on its face. Willem had the craziest thought that the kitten was laughing at the man's fright.

"It's just a hairless kitten!" Willem yelled at the man as he scurried out of sight.

Willem tucked the wooden crate under one arm and started to walk away when a hand grasped his shoulder firmly. He turned, expecting to see the man who had just accosted him, or worse, the Constable.

"Pardon me, but you say you have a kitten? I am looking for a kitten," said a raspy voice from beneath a hooded brown cloak. The tattered cloak enshrouded the speaker and mostly covered his face.

"You are in luck, sir. I have one left, but I have not had much luck giving him away," Willem explained to the older man.

"Well, if he can't catch mice, then I've got no reason to take him. Is he lame?" The old man lifted the hood of his cloak back, unveiling his face. His hair was white and long, but he looked relatively young considering his age. His face had a wise, elderly look but showed very few signs of wrinkling. The large white beard seemed to Willem to lend the man an air of wisdom.

"I have a rather large library, and the mice damage the books with their chewing. My last cat did a fine job but got too old to chase down the rodents on a consistent basis. I need another to take over for him. Let me see him so I can determine whether or not he can do the job."

Willem lowered the old wooden box so the man could see the kitten.

"He's not much to look at, but he is healthy," Willem said to the old man, who was now stroking his beard. This reminded Willem of the tales of Merlin, a wizard he had read about in books of his youth. Yes indeed … the man was what Willem had imagined the wizard in that book would look like. Not exactly the same, but the same nonetheless. The young kitten reached up to swat at the old man's beard.

"He's feisty. I'll take him. He's a cat and as long as being hairless doesn't affect his hunting abilities, he'll do fine."

The old man picked up the scrawny kitten from the box. The skin was leathery to the touch but felt warm like a spring day. The man, holding him up in the light, lifted his ears, peered inside, turned him around, and then without skipping a beat, looked into his eyes.

"We are in the town of Warrington, right? Well, then, Warrington J. Cat it is." The cat looked back at the old man, and for a moment it appeared to Willem as if the kitten grinned and nodded in agreement.

"Warrington J. Cat, huh?" Willem questioned.

The old man looked away from the newly named kitten for a moment and back at the old farmer. "Animals have their own means of communication, my good sir. A name is a name and without one, there is no identity."

Willem was confused; the man spoke in riddle. Without another word, the old man looked back at Warrington. The brown-cloaked man winked at Warrington and placed him upon his shoulder. Warrington sat there as though it was his throne, and he was king of all he surveyed.

The man then looked up at Willem and asked, "What do I owe you for my new mouser?"

Willem shook his head back and forth. "I won't think anything of your shillings, sir. You have done me the favor of allowing me to go home to my wife with my task accomplished and for that, I am in your debt."

The old man reached out a hand to shake Willem's. Willem, being thankful, did the same. As he did, he felt six cold shillings grace his palm.

"I won't take anything for free; buy your wife something nice." The old man turned and started down the long alleyway from which he had appeared.

By the time Willem managed to say, "Thanks," all he could see was a brown-cloaked figure with a kitten on his shoulder, tail swishing back and forth. Willem stood there until the man disappeared from his sight and then, as if nothing had happened, Willem picked up his empty crate and started toward his buggy as the first drop of rain hit ground.

'2'

Warrington was indeed curious, as the girl in the blue and white dress had stated. The old man walked quickly down the alley. He was spry for an older gentleman, and he walked with an urgent purpose. Warrington's claws dug into the dusty cloak in an attempt to steady himself against the quickening stride and jostling of the man. Without notice to the creature on his shoulder, the man stopped abruptly. He had already traveled some distance down the alley and was out of sight of any patrons of the market.

He looked to his right and then carefully to his left, so as to not knock his new friend from his perch. Warrington looked on curiously as the old man stood in front of a brick wall. The cloaked stranger took out a piece of charcoal and a brass key.

Warrington's eyes opened wide as the man started drawing a rectangular shape along the brick. The black outline was barely visible, as it had gotten quite dark now. After completing the rectangle, which started at the floor and went up six feet to the height of the man, the man took his hand and ran it along the inside of the black line until he reached halfway down. The man then leaned down and drew another rectangle. Within this rectangle, he drew a circle and another shape that was not distinguishable as a shape at all. Warrington looked on as if this man had lost his mind. Of course, this is speculation; kittens probably do not have such thoughts.

The man put the charcoal back in his right hand pocket and took the brass key from his left hand where it had stayed as he'd drawn the outline with his right. The man lined up the key with the indistinguishable shape. To Warrington's amazement—as if kittens needed much to be amazed—the key passed through the brick as though it were freshly churned butter. The brass key turned to the left and then the right. Warrington's ears perked up as the key *clicked* as though unlocking a door.

There was now light illuminating the charcoal outline. The man reached toward the area where he had drawn the circle, grasped, and turned. The brick wall started to move toward them. The loud noise pierced the silence as the sound of brick scraping brick echoed through the alley. The two figures passed through the doorway and into a brightly lit hallway. The door quickly slammed behind them with a crash that echoed twice and then fell silent as if commanded to do so.

The hallway went on as far as the eyes of the kitten could see. Doors dotted the long corridor, with candelabras in between each, lighting the way to the next. Above them, Warrington could see large golden chandeliers burning brightly with a luminous flame on each candle tip. Above the chandeliers were hand-painted ceilings stretching thirty feet into the air. Each had a different scene, but Warrington was uninterested in this, as the man had started to move once again, and Warrington was holding on, readying himself for any sudden changes. Their pace was not as fast as previously, but it was still quick. Each door they passed looked quite different, but they all had one thing in common—each was adorned with a faceplate: some blank, some inscribed. However, Warrington could not make out any of the words, nor did the man care to stop and explain. Besides, this was where the man lived, and kittens probably don't care about such things as these.

After what seemed an eternity to Warrington, the man halted at two large wooden double doors adorned with etchings Warrington could not make out. Gold knockers hung six feet up, held in place by eight golden bolts. The old man grasped Warrington by the nape of his neck and set him to the floor. Warrington looked up more curiously than ever as the man leaned over.

"Curiosity killed the cat, my young friend. You would do well to remember that bit of wisdom as you start your new job."

Warrington once again grinned and nodded. The man unfastened the golden buckle from a leather belt he wore across his chest. He removed a three-foot wooden staff with a knot at the end. He reached out, pulled at both ends of the staff, and before Warrington's eyes, it began to grow ... three ... four ... five... six ... and finally seven feet. The man placed the staff on the ground, breaking the silence as the sound of solid wood on marble echoed twice and was silenced. The old man held the staff aloft and then struck the door with the knot of the staff: once on the left door, once on the right. The staff was held aloft again and came down in the same fashion against the left and right sides. Warrington noticed that these knocks were louder than the staff hitting the marble floor, yet these did not echo. After striking each door six times, the man reached the staff out and tapped four more times quickly on the right. The wood creaked and groaned as the door began to open.

## '3'

Warrington looked on as the door crept slowly toward him. The iron hinges creaked as though they were as old as the man, yet they shone as though they had been molded yesterday. Warrington arched his back and hissed as the door passed and a gust of musty air blew in his face. The man scooped up the startled kitten, who, in his fascination with the unseen force opening the door, had already forgotten about his escort. The man placed the hairless animal back on his shoulder and proceeded through the door.

On the other side of the door, the man took up a lantern that had been hanging on the wall. He turned the switch on the bottom and a bright glow that was flame-like—but lacked the heat or flicker of a flame—arose from the center of the lamp. He held it up, illuminating the path before him. The old man and his companion took five steps past the doors, and just as the door had opened, the door began to close: with no discernible figure pushing or pulling it in either direction. Warrington kept his gaze fixed upon the door, regardless of the continued swaying back and forth of the spry old man. When the door closed with a gasp of air and a large thunderous clap, the cat saw no outline … no hinges … and no handle. The door was gone, as though it had never been there.

In place of the door was a wall with an enormous full-length tapestry of a jester entertaining a king and queen in a large courtyard. The jester was balancing a ball on his head and two large dishes of food in each hand. The king looked pleased with this revelry, while the queen appeared unamused. The embroidered guards that lined the wall looked as though they might arrest the jester at any moment for such a poor performance. It wasn't until the man coughed and brought Warrington's attention away from the tapestry that Warrington noticed they were no longer in a hallway of any sort, but in a room unlike anything he had ever seen.

Oak bookcases stretched fifteen feet into the air and lay twenty feet long. The man walked down one corridor of books and then another. He turned to the left—right—left—left again and continued straight. The bookcases—seemingly endless—continued through the dark abyss. Each bookcase had a multitude of colorful rectangles stacked in order. Many of these were brown and red, but to Warrington they all appeared to be different shades of grey.

The cat put his nose into the air and sniffed furiously at the surrounding space. The scent of this room was dry and odorless, but Warrington smelled something much sweeter coming from another room.

The man noticed Warrington's curiosity. "Ah, I left the kettle on so I could eat when I got back. Guess there will be three for dinner tonight. That is, unless Lord Eldridge III has taken his leave for the evening," the man said with a smile. "I call him Eld for short. You two should get along quite well."

The man passed through a low archway into a room that looked similar to the first, but was small enough that Warrington could see the far wall easily. The man approached the wall, where a standard, man-sized oak door greeted them; he reached out, turned the cast-iron handle, pulled, and opened the door.

## '4'

Before the door had a chance to fully open, Warrington leaned to the man's right side, trying to catch a glimpse of the room beyond. The warm glow of firelight illuminated the dark chamber. The man finished opening the door and side-stepped through it, having to duck, as it was just slightly shorter than he was.

This was *The Western Grand Reading Room*, as a sign on the wall indicated. It was large and filled with the warmth of a fire. The man closed the door and walked into a sitting area with two metal chairs cushioned with burgundy velvet fabric. The metal sides of the chairs rose in a decorative swirling fashion. An old couch in the same color sat across from the chairs but looked much more inviting with its oak frame and soft exterior. The furniture's flickering shadows reached across the room and up the wall as the glow from the fireplace cast its warm light upon them. These disproportional shadows attracted Warrington's attention to the fireplace.

The mouth of the hulking fire pit rose eight feet and could swallow a man whole—if fireplaces were to eat men. The exterior was solid stone. As his eyes traveled upward, Warrington could see that the face of the rock had ancient etchings carved in gold filigree. The etchings seemed to glow in the firelight. Warrington, looking up another few feet, saw a painting, but the fire did not illuminate it enough to make out the subject clearly. This did not worry Warrington, though, as kittens tend not to care much for material objects that remain stationary.

The small cast-iron kettle hanging over the fireplace was what Warrington was really interested in. The smell wafted in Warrington's direction, and he began to lick his chops.

Warrington, in his distraction, failed to see the bearskin rug in front of the fireplace, or its black shadowy occupant sprawled in the center.

The man and Warrington passed through this room and into the next. This room had no fireplace but did display an unnatural light that illuminated the entire space. Bookcases the size of the ones Warrington had previously seen lined all but one of the walls. The man took off his dirty sandals as he crossed the threshold of the great entryway and stepped onto the red carpet. The man moved soundlessly across the soft carpet toward a large desk near the naked wall.

There was a good reason this wall had no bookcases, Warrington noticed. Thirteen six-foot high marble pillars lined the back wall. Each one had a cradle at the top, as if they were meant to hold some sort of artifact. As Warrington scanned them, he noticed that six of the pillars did indeed have strange artifacts on them. Even stranger to Warrington, though, was the presence of color in these round orbs atop the pillars. Warrington was a most curious kitten, as he had never seen color before.

The man approached the large wooden desk and set Warrington down on the top between a bright gold goblet and a stack of books five novels high. Warrington fixed his gaze on the colors; after all, seeing color for the first time is something to be most curious about.

The ancient desk was five feet from the floor, which put each of the marble pillars at a better viewing height for Warrington. The desk was decorated handsomely from the face down to the feet with various carvings. Carvings of animals adorned the four corners of the desk: an elephant on the eastern corner; to the west a wolf. On the southern-most corner was a lion and to the north an eagle. Many objects decorated the top, but Warrington just stared straight ahead at the colorful round objects. The man, looking at Warrington, snapped his fingers twice. Warrington's ears twitched each time, but his gaze stayed forward as though in a hypnotic trance. The man stepped into the path of Warrington's gaze, breaking his line of sight with the round orbs. Warrington cocked his head and tried to peer around the man.

The man looked at Warrington and spoke in a firm tone. "These orbs—balls, whatever you want to call them—I warn you my young friend, those are items I would recommend you touch not. They have brought nothing but misery, grief, and even death to those who have owned them over the years. I have searched high and low in order to relieve the owners of their burden, but seven have eluded me. Put your curiosity aside. I urge you not to touch them. Do you understand?" Warrington shifted his gaze toward the man and stared. "Good," the man said and grabbed the tall leather stool. Warrington's ears flattened at the loud sound of wood scraping rock as the man slid the stool up to the desk and sat down.

The man grabbed an inkwell and a quill from one of the many drawers within the desk and started writing on a parchment that was sitting on the desk. Suddenly, the man looked up at Warrington, who had been lying down on the upper right corner of the parchment.

"My goodness, I forgot my manners, young Mr. Cat—I have told you neither my name nor your purpose here. I suppose your duties can begin tomorrow, but as for introduction, I am Mr. Ias Kindle. I am the caretaker for the Library of Universal Fiction, and while I don't expect you to understand what I am saying, I *do* expect you to understand that you will earn your keep by keeping those accursed mice away from the books. Lord Eldridge will get you started first thing in the morning. You may have noticed him sleeping by the fire as we walked in."

The old man nodded in the direction of the first room and went back to his scrawling on the parchment. He dipped his quill in the ink one last time, made a large gesture on the paper, and put the quill back in the stand.

"Well, now that this is done, Warrington—or do you prefer Mr. Cat? No matter, let's eat and get acquainted with Lord Eldridge." Ias rolled the parchment up and placed it in the drawer, along with the inkwell and quill he had removed earlier.

'5'

Ias walked into the reading room, with Warrington trailing close behind. Ias reached near the fireplace and grabbed a silver rod with a large hook at the end. He leaned the pole into the fire and hooked the handle of the cast-iron kettle, its contents boiling furiously now. Warrington could smell the cooked meat and salivated at the thought of food. After all, he had not eaten since earlier that morning, before Willem left for the village.

Ias set the kettle down in a small cradle to the right of the fireplace. The cradle was just big enough that the kettle fit nicely inside without fear of it tipping and spilling its precious contents. Ias leaned over to the side and took a bowl from the floor. He grabbed a large wooden ladle from the mantle, dipped it into the liquid and brought it back up full. He placed the ladle in the bowl and tipped it over, spilling its contents and filling the bowl. Ias leaned down and set the bowl on the floor. Warrington came over and sniffed. He dipped his paw into the soupy liquid. He then looked up at Ias expectantly, as if to say, *I think you forgot the meat, sir*—but only a small meow came out.

Ias laughed. "All right, no getting past you, huh?" he said, still chuckling. He scooped a small chunk of meat from the stew and plopped it into the liquid with a splash.

Warrington grabbed the meat and tore at it as best he could. While it was not the food he was accustomed to, he thought he could get used to it. After he finished his salted pork, he lapped at the liquid until he was full. He walked over to the bearskin rug, circled around three times, and lay down. It was soft and would take him to places he would never have imagined possible.

Ias sat in one of the metal chairs, his feet perched on a leather ottoman. He watched the two cats as they lay on the rug, and Warrington could hear him slurping his stew. When Ias had finished, he set the bowl to the floor and stretched his feet out, his toes wiggling in the warmth of the fire. Ias looked up at the picture hanging above the fireplace. Out of the corner of his eye, he noticed a shadowy head rising upward from beneath his feet. With a quick leap, the black furry cat was now on the ottoman. Eld climbed up to Ias' groin and lay down in the crook of his lap. Ias reached out a hand and scratched the cat behind his ears.

"Ah Eld, how was your evening? Not too eventful, I hope," Ias said, staring into the fire, one hand stroking the cat's head right behind his ears. Eld seemed to like this, as he pressed his head firmly into Ias' hand.

"No, Master Ias, my evening was most uneventful," Eld said as he lay his head on Ias' leg and fell asleep.

"Good, my friend, there is much to do tomorrow… Much to do."

## *Chapter 2*

'1'

Warrington felt a nudge and stirred on the bearskin rug. He had slept, warm and snug, through the night in what he considered to be his new bed, but somehow it was now nudging him from the back.

"Get up, lazy kitten. We have work to do," a voice boomed from behind him. Warrington rolled over and slowly opened his eyes. He could make out the blurry outline of a shadowy figure with pointy ears as his eyes opened and closed. There was another nudge, this one harder than the first.

"Get up! I will only give you one more chance." Warrington stood up and stretched a large kitten stretch, front paws extended down, posterior straight up in the air. He was startled at who he saw standing before him, barking orders. The beast was large and black as midnight. Warrington thought he looked like a panther, and compared to Warrington's scrawny stature, he was. However, to an average person, he was only slightly bigger than an ordinary house cat. The cat's face was stern and emotionless. Eldridge sported a scar vertically across his right eye, but it appeared that there was no damage to the eye itself. The cat's mouth opened as Warrington stood at attention.

"Good, good, you understand a little of what I am saying. Now let's have a look at you," Eldridge said. Eldridge had a slight English accent, but not like the old man's. Eldridge had the accent of someone who had been in the company of a person with a natural accent for far too long. Eld got up and moved toward Warrington, circling him and hemming and hawing in disapproval.

"You are a scrawny, hairless runt and in need of much training. However, I can get you into shape, and you should have no trouble taking over for me,"

Warrington was still stunned to see this fluffy black cat standing in front of him, using the same words the man had used. While Warrington understood very little of this, he understand enough to know that Eld meant business.

"Warrington J. Cat, huh? The old man has a way with names. Absurd as it is, he feels each creature—man or animal—needs an identity in order to exist. Matters not to me … I am rambling, as old cats do. Now follow me." Eld walked toward the large door that separated the reading room from the main library. "Your training begins immediately."

As they approached, Warrington noticed a smaller door carved within the bottom of the large door. Eld approached and the door swung open, just as the one from the hallway had. It also closed abruptly, almost catching Warrington's tail as he passed through. Eld stopped and turned toward him, his eyes glowing gold in the dimly lit room.

Warrington had not noticed this on the way in, since it was past sundown, but now that it was morning, he observed that there were no windows in any of the rooms.

"Listen to me once, as I will not repeat myself. The mice here are not like the mice you may have chased or caught in that poor excuse of an existence you came from. Here the mice are twice as large and quick. They like to chew on the books, so keep your ears open for any sounds. If you're lucky, the mice won't know you are there until you have already pounced and eliminated your prey. Watch me the first few times, and you'll get the hang of it. You still have much growing to do before you are ready to go out on your own. Understand, kitten?" Eld was staring at Warrington, eyes still glowing brightly and flickering from the candles. Warrington understood little, but nodded anyway. "Good, now let's go."

### '2'

Warrington slunk closely behind Eld, mimicking his every move. They moved in and out of the large bookcases slowly, stopping at any sound that broke the dry air. Eld was an accomplished mouser and could sense the slightest vibrations in the air from even the tiniest pin drop.

Warrington was reminded of home, when he and his brothers would slink through the old red barn looking for mice. He had caught quite a few, and while Willem's wife did not appreciate the gifts left on the kitchen floor, Willem had always praised each kitten for clearing out the pesky vermin. Warrington was not the best mouser of the litter, but he'd caught his fair share.

Eld stopped abruptly behind a bookcase marked with the letters Ga-Ge. Warrington ran into Eld's backside, as he had no warning of any changes. Warrington, now focused, heard why Eld had stopped and peered around the corner. There was a dark animal shape sniffing an unmarked book. Eld's tail whipped high into the air, switching back and forth. Eld was so focused on this enemy, he failed to notice that Warrington had crept alongside him, mimicking Eld's pounce stance. Warrington, not accounting for distance, assumed the animal was a large rodent—not any bigger than he was. He was sure he could dispatch this creature with minimal effort.

Without warning, Eld saw a brown flash dart by him, running full speed down the hallway toward an unsuspecting mouse. The mouse appeared once again to be small enough for Warrington, and he was anxious to prove his worth. Warrington knew he had the drop on his prey and leapt into the dark midmorning air. It wasn't until he landed on the back of this creature that he fully realized the size of what Eld called a mouse.

Warrington hit the back of the large mouse hard, feeling its bristly hairs jab into his naked skin. The coarse hair chafed Warrington's underbelly as the mouse—now aware of the presence of this unknown assailant on his back—started writhing in pain from Warrington's small, dagger-like claws.

Eld took off in a sprint toward the two shadows. The larger shadow was dancing around in circles as the small parasite held on for dear life. As the mouse gnashed his teeth toward the small kitten, saliva sprayed left and right. Warrington dodged away from the large fanged mouth that was trying to get relief from the annoyance on its back. Regaining his composure, Warrington dug in with his back claws for a better grip. Seizing the opportunity to take his prey down, he bit into the back of the mouse. Blood filled Warrington's mouth as the mouse let out a screech that pierced through the dark halls. With this new pain in his back, the mouse darted forward, hitting the wall of books in front of him.

Warrington realized that he was no longer holding on with all four paws and his mouth; he had somehow let go and was currently flying through the air. Time seemed to stand still as the sensation of floating through the air made Warrington drunk with wonder. Warrington felt a sharp pain in his back as gravity took back over, and he fell hard to the concrete. Warrington lay dazed on the hard rock floor as the mouse crept closer toward him, seeking revenge. The mouse snapped its jaws open and shut with each step, as if in anticipation of the taste that would soon fill its mouth. Warrington had finally started to get back up when pressure on his neck prevented him from moving. He could feel the leathery claws of the mouse clamping down on his windpipe as he tried to meow for help. The warm breath from this creature stunk of rotten meat, and Warrington felt alternately warm and cold as the mouse breathed in and out. The mouse—poised to take his prize—opened his jaws wide, ready to engulf Warrington with one bite.

'3'

Eld could see the two creatures moving farther and farther down the corridor as they danced around in circles. Eld was old but had not lost the spring in his step. He was sprinting toward the shadows when he felt a dull bludgeoning pain in his side. The screams of the mouse had alerted another from the Ge-Gi aisle on the other side of the bookcase. Sprinting toward the ensuing battle, the mouse saw Eld through an empty slot where a book should have been. It dashed forward, striking Eld in the side as he crossed the aisle between the two bookcases. The force of the blow sent Eld sprawling, sliding along the cold floor until he came to a stop, dazed. The large mouse gnashed his teeth as he lost sight of the downed cat, and then he scurried off toward the two wrestling figures.

Eld stood up, shaking off the hard hit. He darted back down the aisle just in time to see the mouse still scurrying quickly toward the figures. Eld leapt to an empty shelf and ran swiftly along the top. He could see the mouse gaining on the now stationary figures. Warrington was lying on the ground, helpless. Eld leapt from his empty shelf as it ended and onto the back of the scurrying mouse, sliding across the floor. Eld's sharp grey claws ripped into the back of the mouse, and it screamed but was silenced as Eld's teeth cut into its tender neck, severing the spinal cord. Eld, carried by the momentum of the still-sliding corpse, flew from its back into the air.

Eld landed on the back of the second mouse, claws digging deep into his side, his momentum flipping them both through the air. Eld released the creature halfway through a turn. The mouse flew into the darkness and hit the ground with a large crack. Eld was most certain that the concrete had done his job for him.

"Stupid kitten!" Eld screamed in anger. "You were to observe! Not attack!" Eld gnashed his teeth at Warrington, bringing a paw down across his back and pinning him to the hard floor. "Mice are never alone! They travel in groups of two or more. You must kill before they screech or the others will come. You are lucky—that mouse would not think twice before killing you. You'll do well to remember that from here on out. This is not the world you know.

Things aren't the same here." Eld's voice, in his rage, filled the empty rafters. "You have much to learn in your youth."

Eld released Warrington from the ground. Warrington stood up and shook; his underbelly was bright red and quite raw from the hairs on the mouse's back. Warrington could see Eld was displeased at his unwillingness to listen. What Warrington could not see, though, was Eld's approval of the young kitten's courage—or foolhardiness, whichever it was. It reminded him of when he was a young kitten, eager to learn.

"Come now," growled Eld, "we must take the bodies of those filthy vermin to the fire pit."

'4'

Eld and Warrington walked toward the mouse lying on its side. Dark black blood reflected the candlelight from above.

"Look here, kitten—this spot on the back of their neck offers them no protection from enemies. Their spine does not protect the spinal cord at this small junction in the neck. One quick bite and they are paralyzed from the neck down; you must be careful, though, as they are still very much alive and can still bite. Once paralysis sets in, it is only a short while before they are dead." Warrington smirked while nodding in approval.

Eld pulled the creature by its long tail down the corridor and out into a small grassy courtyard. In the middle of the courtyard was a stone fountain with a statue of a lady holding a book. It appeared as though she were reading. *This statue is very fitting for a library,* Eld always thought when he saw it. She was young and reminded him of his original owner before Ias took him in …

'5'

"Eldridge, supper's ready. Come on, puss, before the flies get it," the woman yelled out the back porch.

Eld came out from between the corn stalks where he had been hunting. The sunlight shone off his black coat. The day was beginning to subside, and his prey would have gone underground, anyhow. Eld strutted up the porch steps and into the kitchen. He climbed up into a wooden chair and placed his paws on the table, peering over into his bowl. Steam rose from the mixture of fresh rice and chicken—warm, but not too hot.

Eld began to eat when something caught his eye—something he had never seen before. There was a bright emerald glow coming from the living room. Eld was amazed, not because there was a glow, but because he had never seen color before. He left his dish at the table and slunk across the floor into the living area. The glow originated from a box on the table. The box's lid was ajar, and Eld could see the round shape glowing from within. His paw reached out to touch the curious object and was not more than a centimeter away when the lid closed.

"Naughty kitty. That's not for you. Mama found it in the fields. She thinks it came from the sky when that last tornado came down. Either way, Mama told you not to touch it. I opened the box 'cause it glowed so pretty." The girl with two brown pigtails stood waving a finger at the cat. Eld swatted at it in a playful gesture, forgetting anything the girl said. The glow was gone and so was his interest in it. Eld returned to his dinner of rice and chicken at the table.

'6'

Warrington was chasing butterflies through the courtyard, dashing here and there, trying to catch the elusive creatures. His kitten instincts had gotten the best of him, and he had forgotten all about the giant mice and Eld for the time being. Warrington climbed up on the small ledge of stone that encircled the statue of the woman reading. He bowed down in the front with his tail high in the air, lashing back and forth. The butterfly hovered just on the other side. Without a moment's notice, Warrington jumped through the air after the butterfly and came down with a huge splash in what he now realized was a fountain. The noise was enough to bring Eld out of his daydream in alarm.

"Warrington, where did you go, you fool kitten?"

Eld saw two paws reaching over the top of the stone ledge. Then he saw a wet head, followed by an even wetter body. Eld laughed a hearty laugh as Warrington shook off. The butterfly whizzed by his head as if to taunt him.

"At least you have no fur. You'll be dry in no time!" Eld said, chuckling a cat's chuckle, which sounds nothing like human laughter but more like a hyena's cackle.

"Come down and let's get this into the fire pit over in the corner," Eld said, still chuckling a little. They dragged the dead mouse, now stiff with rigor mortis, over to the blackened hole in the corner of the courtyard. Rocks outlined the pit, and three small stone benches circled it. They pushed the mouse over the top and hurried off to grab the other body.

When Eld and Warrington passed back through the small door of the reading room, Ias had not yet returned from his errands. Since this was Warrington's first day—and they had already had enough excitement—Eld suggested they rest a bit by the fire and wait for his return.

Eld fell fast asleep, and his previous daydream soon returned to him, for that long-ago day had changed Eld's life forever.

'7'

Eldridge was finishing up his meal at the table when he heard what sounded like a whisper coming from the living room. His ears perked and he cocked his head to the right. A small entryway was all that separated the small downstairs rooms: the living room, dining room and kitchen. Eldridge was curious, but a loud noise from outside pulled his attention away from the living room. Eldridge sat on the wooden chair looking to his left, now waiting for any other noises, when the whisper came again. This time the whisper sounded as though it were saying his name. Eldridge turned his head again to the right. This time he saw the green glow filling the living room.

"Eldridge," the voice whispered again. "Come here, kitty, kitty."

Eldridge was most curious to see the colorful light dancing around the room and the person in dire need of his attention. He jumped down from his chair and made his way toward the living room. Eldridge was crossing through the doorway when another loud noise from outside crashed all around him. He quickly recognized the noise as the counterpart to the lightning that briefly flashed through the room and subsided. Eldridge made his way to the side of the floral print armchair that completed the circle of furniture around the oak table in the middle of the room. Eldridge could see the box was not open, but the green luminescence shone through every crack. The whisper came again into his mind.

"Eldridge," the voice said in a long gasp of air, "release me." The cat, looking curiously at the box, did not understand how he understood, but understood he did.

Eldridge jumped to the table next to the small wooden box decorated with flowers his owner had dried and pressed into the box's exterior. Eldridge lifted up a paw and tucked it under the lip of the box. Though he felt no temperature change, his whiskers could sense the feeling of a cold winter day. His paw tried to open the box further, but the lid snapped shut when he pulled his paw out. He tried again and tucked his head under the lid. His eyes glowed bright in the presence of the emerald ball.

The orb was roughly the size of a ball of yarn, but swirled with green and white clouds. The emerald orb had Eldridge's complete and undivided attention. He moved closer. The top of the wooden box fell backward onto the table, bounced once, and then fell to the floor with a small crashing noise that was drowned out by the thunderous crack from outside.

The room had darkened considerably as storm clouds rolled in quickly from the south. The room now looked as though an emerald river flowed through the center of it. The shadow of a cat was pasted on the back wall.

Patsy came running downstairs to check on her precious kitty and comfort him during the thunder, as Eldridge had been afraid of the crash of thunder since he was a kitten. She reached the bottom of the stairs and gasped as she saw Eldridge with his head in the box and the bright green glow of the crystal ball she had found earlier that day in the barn. It had been sunk into the dirt floor as though it had dug a hole and placed itself there on purpose. Patsy remembered that she had looked up and saw the small hole in the roof and wondered if someone had thrown it, or if it had fallen from the sky during that last tornado.

"Eldridge, get away from there!" Patsy yelled, but the thunder drowned out her voice. The only voice Eldridge heard was in his mind and it came from the orb.

"Jump," the voice said.

It echoed around in Eldridge's head for some time. Eldridge could see a pleasant green pasture in the reflection of the ball. Patsy ran for Eldridge, who was now poised in the pouncing position. Patsy reached out to grab Eldridge, but she was too late. She watched as, with one quick leap, he went into the box and disappeared.

Eldridge could feel his body twisting and turning as the darkness consumed him. Emerald light encompassed his eyes and while he was falling, he was also flying. The experience seemed to go on for days, months, or was it years? He saw everything and he saw nothing.

## '8'

Without notice, he heard the large crash of thunder and sat upright on the bearskin rug. His heart was beating rapidly, and his ears were up and alert. He looked around and saw a shadowy figure walking across the room. Ias had returned and carried with him a leather satchel. He walked directly into the next room, Eldridge never taking his eyes off of him. As Eldridge turned his head, he noticed that he was not alone on the bearskin rug; Warrington was curled up beside him, fast asleep. Eldridge stood up and stretched, his muscles tight from the earlier struggle with the mouse. He walked off the bearskin rug and into the room where Ias now sat at his desk, the six orbs behind him glowing brightly as he wrote on a piece of parchment.

Eldridge jumped up onto the desk, startling Ias as he wrote. "Oh Lord Eldridge, I did not see you there. You gave me a good fright," Ias said, returning to his scribbling.

"Sorry, Master Ias, I came in to see how your errands went today and if you had any news," Eldridge said curiously. His eyes followed the quill as it wiggled in the air; after all, Eldridge was still a cat and it was difficult to resist the temptation to swat at the long quill.

"I did find some information, but nothing conclusive. The Witch's Eye is still out there causing trouble. I found a man who said he had seen it in the possession of an elixir salesman. He said he would not have noticed it except that the salesman held it up to the crowd, and it seemed to hold people's attention until he put it back under his cloak. After that, he remembered the crowd lining up and buying elixir by the case."

Ias looked up at this point and stared at Eld. "How was your first day of training? Uneventful perhaps?" Ias inquired.

Eld recounted the morning and the ensuing battle, forgetting no detail—from Warrington eagerly sprinting at the first mouse to his dive in the fountain. Ias laughed at this portion of the story.

"He reminds me of an eager-to-please cat I took in once. You were always rushing off and getting into trouble. Kittens will be kittens, though. Remember that, please; he has much to learn, but he is also still very young," Ias said distractedly, as he had begun writing again.

"I was never so reckless, Master Ias. Well … maybe once or twice. I was much older than Warrington when you took me in; he is but a quarter my size. He does, however, show the courage and eagerness of the mightiest of beasts." Eld beamed with pride, as though he were the one to instill these values in Warrington.

Eldridge took a swat at the feather of the quill as it passed close to his nose. Ias dipped the quill one last time, made a large gesture on the page, and set the quill in the stand.

"Well, this one is done. We should be much closer to the Witch's Eye. That will make seven of these accursed objects, and one less in the company of the Hunters. You shall see redemption in your older days, my friend. Far too long is your justice overdue. As I promised when I took you in, we shall see your master's death set right." Ias picked up Eldridge and placed him on his shoulder.

"Thank you, Master Ias. I will make sure Warrington is ready for the tasks he has ahead of him," Eldridge whispered as they walked into the reading room. Warrington was fast asleep, dreaming of chasing mice, butterflies, and the elusive white rabbit he had seen in his dreams the night before.

## Chapter 3

'1'

Two winters had passed since that first eventful day, and Warrington's third was about to begin. The days had started growing long, and Eldridge had stopped chaperoning Warrington when he had surpassed Eld in size. Warrington was now a hulking cat, almost twice the size of Eld. His leathery skin gave him the advantage over the mice that were now only slightly bigger than he was. No fur meant those rodents had nothing to grab onto. Warrington would often take on two or three at a time. There was the occasional bite that Ias had to mend, but nothing serious.

Eld would chuckle and exclaim, "I would hate to see what the other guys looked like!" Warrington—although older and wiser—still understood very few of the man or Eld's words. He had gained much knowledge through the past three years, but he still only understood bits and pieces of their language.

Warrington noticed that it was winter once again; the white ice had fallen over the grass. The water from the fountain had become solid and reflected the statue of the woman reading, now wearing a snowy white hat. He pulled his last mouse of the day through the snow and over to the fire pit. The crunching sound of each step reminded him of the noise the mice made as they chewed the books. Warrington had resorted to thinking of them as rodents of unusual size rather than mice, since they were quite a bit larger. The shadows were growing long and Warrington thought it must have been getting quite late. He strolled through the library one last time, looking and listening for any unusually large rodents. As he rounded a corner, he could hear the scratching of an animal against the concrete floor. The candles flickered as a gust of wind blew through the long corridors of the library.

Warrington turned the corner toward the far end of the library. He saw the tapestry where the Jester was still holding court, and the Queen still did not look amused. Warrington slunk along the edge of the bookcase and caught a glimpse of a shadowy tail just drifting out of sight around a bookcase. Seeing an opportunity to rid the library of one more pest, Warrington climbed the bookshelf and walked along the top, leaving pawprints in the dust. Small clouds of dirt, dust, dead skin, and all else that dust is comprised of puffed up around his feet with each step. He observed the shadow moving faster down the corridor and so quickened his pace, now running across the top, jumping the five-foot gaps between each of the bookcases. Clouds of dust were now drifting upward like smoke—the candles lighting each particle on fire as it fell near the flame.

Warrington was almost on top of his target when it stopped. Warrington could hear the sound of a creature sniffing the air. The shadow moved slower, as though it knew Warrington was watching. Warrington—thinking that it would be impossible for the creature to know he was watching as the rodents here were not smart, but rather dumb—continued on his course. Warrington had long ago resorted to using the tops of the bookcases, as this gave him an aerial view so he could see farther than just one aisle. The shadow had now stopped and was looking around, sniffing the air once more.

Warrington poised at the edge of the shelf, both paws over the top of the bookcase, looking downward through the darkness. His intended prey was just below him, seemingly unaware of his presence. Warrington's tail circled the air, making swirls in the dust cloud he had created by stopping abruptly. His eyes widened as his hips moved slowly to the right, left, and then back to the right. Without warning, he dropped through the air, fifteen feet down to the unsuspecting intruder.

He landed on the back of the shadowy figure, knocking it to the ground. A loud yelp rang out through the library. Warrington backed away in shock at this strange sound, as it was nothing like the usual screech of a rodent. The shadowy figure rose up from the ground, high above Warrington. It turned, eyes ablaze with anger. Warrington, seeing this was not a rodent, growled furiously. The shadowed figure—now at his full height, three times Warrington's size—growled in retaliation. The figure started walking toward Warrington, candles illuminating large fangs as the creature snarled. Warrington backed up slowly. The creature became clearer as it moved closer, candlelight showing a muscular frame covered in brown and black fur. The hairs on its back stood straight up while its elongated neck retracted downward to Warrington's height. It stalked closer and closer as Warrington, knowing his job, halted his retreat.

Warrington could see the animal was limping from the aerial attack, but that deterred it very little. Warrington, claws out, hissed a warning at the beast as it advanced. The creature paused, seeming to reconsider its advance, but then forgot about any doubts as it lunged at Warrington, narrowly missing him. Warrington's claws reached out and struck the beast's snout as it passed by. The creature howled in pain as it recoiled from the blow, blood now dripping down the side of its snout into its mouth. The creature's tongue crept from his mouth and licked the wound, and then it growled. It dashed at Warrington, jaws wide open. The creature's jaws snapped shut just before reaching Warrington's body. The creature could feel the leathery skin of its adversary and flipped its head upward. It had caught Warrington off guard as its head lifted him high into the air.

Warrington's feet flailed as he took flight down the corridor end over end and then landed on his feet. The creature darted toward him and lunged again, its head hammering Warrington in his side. Warrington, dazed, went sliding across the floor on his back. He lay there motionless for a moment, thinking about his first confrontation with the mice and how Eldridge had saved his life. At this moment, he wished Eldridge were there, ready to save him from this unknown danger, but Eld had left with Ias, as he had done so many times since his retirement from the great mouse-chase.

The creature reached out, ready to grab Warrington, when it suddenly felt a sharp pain and was blinded in one eye. Warrington had laid still, ready to strike when the creature approached. The creature was not intelligent, Warrington surmised, as it fell for his attack. Warrington's claws had sliced through the creature's cornea and down the side of its face. Blood sprayed the side of the bookcase as the beast flung its head back in pain. Its howl of agony echoed throughout the library, sending mice running from their snack of book pages. Warrington, with a false sense of confidence, thought he had the creature where he wanted it.

The creature was back in its attack posture, injured eye closed. Warrington darted toward the creature, leaping into the air, his claws ready to sink into the beast's skin and finish the job. The air around him seemed to slow down as he flew through it. As he came down, he felt a pain in his back leg and he was suddenly flying again, in a different direction. He crashed hard against the bookshelf. He was now lying on the ground, barely conscious. He saw the creature bearing down on him, blood and saliva dripping from its head. Fearing the end, Warrington struggled to get up but could not. The creature had crushed his leg in its jaws. He fell back to the ground, weak and dizzy. Just as Warrington was drifting into unconsciousness, he saw a flash of blue light illuminate the room, and then everything went black.

'2'

Eld sat on Ias' shoulder as the salesman went about selling his wonderful elixir: guaranteed to make you stronger, more attractive, and even grant magical powers in certain instances.

"Presto magnifico!" the man in the purple top hat and petit handlebar mustache yelled as he waved his hands through the air. A bright green flame appeared out of his shirtsleeve and circled high above his head. The crowd's eyes widened as they gasped in unison. This was all the crowd needed to witness as they lined up, money at the ready.

"Remember—the ability to produce magical powers may take more than one bottle of elixir to develop and is not guaranteed," said the man as he took coin after coin from the eager crowd.

Eld looked on and yawned at the crowd of fame seekers as they clamored up to the wagon to be conned. Ias leaned in close to Eld and whispered, "After all, this time we have finally found the elixir salesman—and it would appear he may have what we are looking for based, on that display of fakery."

Eld licked a paw and said, "I agree, Master Ias."

One of the customers could have sworn he saw the cat cup his paw and whisper something, but shook it off, thinking he was seeing things, since he knew cats did not talk nor cup their paws over their mouth to whisper.

Much time passed, and Ias and Eld proceeded to move through the crowd as it dispersed. There were a few bottles of elixir left on the table, but not many. Ias looked at the man, who was wearing purple pants and a jacket that matched his top hat. The man had a yellow shirt on with a pink bow tie.

"What can I do for you, old-timer? Looking to regain your youth? This stuff will have you as strong as you would have been back in your twenties. Just ten silvers for one bottle of my Magical Miracle Elixir—patent pending, of course. Better yet… I'll give you two bottles for six silvers… or four for twelve. Only got a few left and I would love to see them go to someone in need. Whaddaya say—" his voice trailed off as the old man pulled back his hood.

"Ias. My name is Ias Kindle, and I would be delighted if a man of your stature would have supper with me—my treat."

Ias watched the man's shifty eyes darting back and forth, considering whether the offer was genuine or a ruse to rob him of his money. The man was hungry, nonetheless.

"Oscar Diggs is my name—Wizard and Potion-Maker. Well… I used to be a Wizard, but now I just make potions. Much more lucrative than casting spells and waving a wand," Oscar said through his tight-lipped grin. "Let me grab my cane, and we can head over to the tavern down the street. I just love the skewered pig they have—your treat, of course."

"Oh, of course, I would never think of letting a local celebrity pay for a meal. It's my pleasure to dine with you, sir," Ias said in a very ingratiating tone, building up Oscar's sense of self-worth and importance.

'3'

Oscar and Ias walked into the tavern, the smell of stale ale fouling the air. Footprints of the many patrons that had enjoyed a drink or two that day were outlined in the sawdust spread across the floor. Many of these patrons were still there, sitting at the wooden tables of the tavern's great hall. One gentleman with a feather in his hat lay face down on the table—beer still in his right hand, turkey leg in his left. Beer was not the only thing brewing in this tavern … trouble was afoot as well.

The room was dark and damp as Ias and Oscar proceeded to a small booth in the northeastern corner, where one could conduct business discreetly.

The waitress came over shuffling through the sawdust. "What can I get for you, honey?" the large brute of a woman rasped.

"We'll have two of your skewered pork plates and two of your finest pints of ale," Oscar piped up immediately.

"Don't I know you?" the waitress inquired.

"No, I doubt it, I just have one of those faces that people recognize. I am no one," he said, lying through his teeth. Oscar had changed from his purple elixir sales outfit and was now wearing a black bowler cap with a red band across the top. His pants were white and looked as though they had been used as a ship's sail and then sewn back together after a bad storm. His jacket mirrored the appearance of the pants. His black shirt matched his hat, and his red tie completed the ensemble.

The waitress walked away slowly, turning around and trying to remember where she had seen him. "I try to keep a low profile, or the ladies try to take advantage of me. Better to lay low and stay out of sight," Oscar explained.

Ias looked across the table. "Of course, of course. We wouldn't want a crowd of revelers gathering around interrupting our dinner." Ias was smiling, as he could not remember ever having met a man so full of himself.

"So, Mr. Kindle, what can I do for you? You are obviously a fan of mine, but I know very little about you. Please tell me what I can help you with," Oscar said, looking as proud and arrogant as ever.

Ias was expecting this question and was therefore prepared. "I was wondering about your elixir. I own several wagons and sideshows but have failed to capture the crowd and turn a profit. I need to know how your elixir works. What's in it? Why do people buy it?" Ias said, looking sincere, as it was his turn to tell falsities.

Oscar was about to reply but was interrupted as the waitress dropped two platters onto the table, the pewter plates clanging against the wood. She sloshed two large pints of what the locals called the *Bard's Ale* onto the table, spilling it just slightly.

"Will there be anything else, gentlemen?" the woman asked as she turned away without waiting for an answer.

"If this tastes half as good as it looks, it will be money well spent," Ias said, grabbing the skewer and ripping off a piece of pork. His fingers twirled to infer that Oscar might continue answering his questions.

"Well, Mr. Kindle, that is a trade secret. If everyone knew how I made my elixir, I would be out of business. I can't go around shelling out my recipes to just anyone. Maybe if we had some sort of partnership where I would take, say … seventy-five percent of what you took in at each of your shows—I might then be able to divulge my secret." Oscar's eyes widened in eagerness at the prospect of making money while putting all the risk on someone else.

"Well, Mr. Diggs, seventy-five percent of all elixir sales is a bit much. I would have to think about it," Ias said not unwillingly.

"Mr. Kindle, I was not talking about just elixir sales; I am talking about all profits. After all, my elixir would increase your profits tenfold. I am well-known and my name would sell out every one of your shows," Oscar said, beaming.

Ias looked away theatrically, as though thinking through this proposal.

"So … we would be partners, huh? Kindle and Diggs—Sideshow Emporium," Ias said, almost announcing it across the tavern.

"Well, maybe Diggs and Kindle would sound better," Oscar said, leaning in and whispering. It was at this very moment that Oscar Diggs noticed that something was missing. "You had a cat with you when you were at my wagon. Where did he go? Did he not come in with us?" Oscar questioned.

"I decided to let him roam outside and chase mice. He doesn't care much for taverns or their company," Ias replied in a matter-of-fact way.

In actuality, Ias had left Eld at Oscar Diggs' wagon on the outskirts of town.

## '4'

The sun was now peeking out from behind the trees that surrounded the Magical Mystery Elixir Sideshow wagon. The sign out front read, *Indisposed, please return later. Next show: 10:30am tomorrow*. Eld paid no attention to this sign and strolled through the medium length grass and up to the door of the wagon. The wagon covering appeared to be made of canvas, but was several colors of cloth that had been sewn together. The wagon frame was standard for this type of show, except for the elaborate stage coming off the side, like a mole growing on the side of an old hag.

Eld jumped to the roof of the wagon to inspect it for a way in. The colorful cloth did not give as he jumped up the wooden supports and onto the roof. The cloth was just decoration, as the wagon had a solid wood rooftop. Eld walked along the creases, systematically checking for weaknesses. He was out of luck; he found no discernible weakness within any portion of the roof. Eld walked to the side and jumped down the other wood pole that supported the elixir salesman's wagon and then down into the grass.

Eld walked underneath the wagon to wait for Ias' return, as he had given up looking for a way in. The grass was thick and would hide him well from anyone who might happen by. As he climbed underneath, he noticed light shining though the floorboards, illuminating the grass below. Eld crawled through the grass under the wagon, looking for signs of weakness within the wood. As he reached the back of the wagon, he noticed a small trap door. *Probably an escape hatch for when the mob with pitchforks come to get their money back after they find out the potions are phony,* Eld thought.

Eld stood on his hind legs, front paws on the side of the wood, and pushed the door up with his head. It moved slightly, and he could see inside the wagon. Something heavy must have been on top of the door, because it pushed back against his head. Eld pushed harder and could feel the door give just a bit more, but it still pushed back. Eld put his head against the door and jumped. The door flipped straight upward, and a loud crash startled him as he fell back into the grass.

Eld jumped against the door once again, and it flipped all the way open. Eld leaped through the opening and onto the floor of the wagon. The wagon was quite large inside: shelves lined the interior and a bed was pushed against the edge of the back wall. Eld hopped onto a shelf that held some of this con man's elixir. He looked around for a container he knew must be somewhere close by and large enough to hold the objects he was looking for. Eld's eyes darted around the room, first to the right and then to the left. He walked down the shelf, knocking off a bottle of elixir and sending it crashing to the ground, splashing against the floor and dripping through the floorboards. Eld noticed a chest in the corner with a golden lock hooking through the trap that kept it shut. He jumped down and walked over to what looked to be a pirate's chest embellished with gold flowers and a ruby on top. Eld pawed at the open lock until it fell to the ground with a clank and rolled under one of the shelves.

He pawed at the top of the chest until he got one of his paws under the lip and then slowly nosed his head into the small crack he had created. The box was filled with an emerald glow. Eld slipped his head under the entire lip and pushed the chest open. The metal hinges groaned as it opened. When it reached the ninety-degree angle, it fell away from Eld's throbbing head and crashed into the sidewall of the wagon. Eld looked around as though he was sure that someone had heard him and alerted Oscar Diggs to this intrusion on his property. However, no one was around to hear this sound or see the black smoke that was now filling the inside of the wagon.

'5'

Oscar Diggs could down numerous pints of the *Bard's Ale*. It was his absolute favorite, and he delighted in drinking it—he delighted even more in drinking it when he wasn't the one footing the bill. Ias sat back, nursing his first pint to the halfway point. Oscar was now on his seventh and consequently had no recollection of how many Ias may or may not have had.

Oscar roared loudly as he told stories of how he once ruled a mighty city and all its inhabitants … how he had gotten two very magical artifacts by sending a young girl on a fool's errand that had a slim chance of survival—but she had succeeded.

Ias prompted him to keep talking. "Tell me about these artifacts this girl brought back to you, Mr. Diggs. They may help us in our new business venture." This was, after all, the information Ias wanted to know—and his entire purpose for paying a large bill for a keg of the "*Bard's* best".

"The girl brought me some witch's broom and her glass eye. The Witch was trying to tell everyone I was a fraud. I couldn't let some freak with a skin disease spread rumors that I was a fraud, right? I had the girl go up to her castle and kill her. The girl brought back the witch's broom—which was burned, by the way—not exactly a prized possession. But the Witch's Glass Eye! That was a grand gift indeed. After I left with these items, I started to notice they held power. The broom's power was useless, but the eye made me drunk with wonder. I looked into it and could see lands beyond our own borders.

"I decided to start this sideshow using the Witch's Eye and selling elixir. So far it's been very lucrative for me. The elixir is just cheap rum and grog mixed together. People get drunk and think they are stronger, smarter and even believe they have magical powers. This wears off, though, and they come looking for more."

Oscar was getting quite loud and attracting the attention of the tavern company. The waitress was talking with a few men at a table and pointing in the direction of Ias and Oscar.

"Well … Mr. Ias, I shink we ought to be gonin'. Our time shere hash come to an end," Oscar said slurring every other word. When he stood, he stumbled into the chest of the man who had been face down holding a beer and a turkey leg. Now very much awake, the stench of beer was escaping through every orifice and pore of his body. Oscar stumbled back and waved a hand in front of his face.

"You're that there elixir man, ain't chu? The waitress said your elixir was nuttin' more than rum and grog. We'll teach you to peddle your phony wares in our town, you fraud."

Three other men had joined the confrontation. Ias got up from the table.

"Now, now, gentlemen, violence is not the answer. Let me buy you all a round of ale and refund your silver. I can assure you that this man won't bother you again. He has retired from selling elixir tonight," Ias Kindle said convincingly.

The large beer-soaked man in a golden tunic and brown cloth pants looked at Ias. "How about we'se take that round of ale, take our's refund, and then we'se take a little more for our townsfolk. You can't pay us all back."

Ias took a step back as the man stepped forward, towering over him by at least a foot. Ias unlatched his gold buckle and removed his staff from the sheath on his back. Oscar was still wobbling back and forth, trying to speak, his finger held aloft in a matter-of-fact sort of way.

Seeing the man winding up for a swing at Oscar, Ias poked his cane into the back of Oscar's knee, dropping him to the floor. The punch narrowly missed Oscar and slammed into the face of the man who had held the turkey leg moments before. His friend got up and tackled the large man to the ground, punching him in the face with his iron beer mug and shattering his jaw. The turkey leg drunk went to swing again and hit the waitress in the gut. She doubled over in pain and crumpled to the floor. Her husband—who was a giant in these lands—was tending bar and grabbed his club from over the bar mantle. The earth shook as he stalked over to engage the man who had hit his wife.

Ias took this time to sneak out the front door, dragging Oscar into the street. He propped Oscar up—ale mug still in his hand—against the side of a barrel. The tavern window shattered as the turkey-leg-eating-man left the bar in a most precarious manner. Ias stepped over the man, who was now lying in the middle of the dirt road that led out of town. Ias could see the fight still raging inside. He wished Oscar a good evening—although Oscar would later recount to the local constable that he had no idea what had happened—and Ias headed down the road to the clearing where Oscar Diggs had set up shop in his elixir wagon.

'6'

Eld had turned from the glow of the green orb—which was not as large as he remembered but rather the size of a marble—to see that he had knocked over a small lantern. It had laid smoldering on the floor until Eld had knocked over the elixir; as the elixir dripped through the floorboards, it had also spread down the floor and around the lantern. The fire had then ignited the half grog, half rum mixture and was now burning the old wooden wagon. The mixture had also dripped down into the grass, igniting Eld's escape route. The smoke was filling the wagon interior fast, and he could do nothing to put it out.

Eld climbed into the box with the emerald marble. Inside the box, Eld could see half of a broom, the straw portion burnt. *This isn't much use. Someone already burned the end of it—probably not going to help me in my situation,* Eld thought as the air blackened all around him. *Great ... done in by my own stupidity.*

'7'

Ias could see the glow through the forest in the darkness as he approached the clearing. His staff still in his hand, he began to move faster. The staff barely touched the ground, as Ias was now sprinting and shouting, "Eld, where are you? ELD!" But Eld could not hear him over the roar of the fire inside the wagon.

Ias reached the wagon and shook the locked door. He peered through a glass window five feet from the base of the door. He took his cane and struck it. The glass resisted breaking and the staff bounced off it, flying backward.

"Eld, are you in there?" Ias yelled again.

"Master Ias!" Eld exclaimed. The fire was creeping ever closer toward him, smoke billowing out of every crack of the wagon. "Master Ias, I have the Witch's Eye. My way out is blocked by the fire."

Ias looked through the window but could only see black smoke. "Eld, is the Witch's Broom in there?" he yelled through the door.

Eld looked down and saw the broom that he had dismissed. "Yes, Master Ias. There is a broom here," Eld yelled through the smoke, coughing between each word.

"Take the broom and aim it at the window. Sit on the back and push off. You should be able to ride it through the window and out the door," Ias said convincingly, although he was pretty sure it was not going to work.

Eld took the broom in his mouth and pointed it in the direction he guessed the window would be. The top handle of the broom rested on the lip of the box. Eld placed the green eye in his mouth and pushed off. The broom zipped through the air and straight at the window. Smoke swirled in a vortex as the broom sped through the air. As the broom struck it, each of the window's three layers of glass shattered. Ias watched the broom launch into the night sky.

Eld was flying through the air ... but not with the broom. He had misjudged his grip and flipped backward into the box, the emerald marble still grasped tightly in his mouth. Ias, seeing the broom but no cat, ran to the window and reached through it. The glass shards cut into his arm as he reached for the barricade bar that held the door shut. He pulled up and the door swung open. Smoke billowed out as Ias rushed into the raging inferno, his cloak searing at the edges as the fire lapped the bottom.

Eld was sprawled in the chest, unconscious from the force of the broom knocking him backward against the back of the chest. Ias grabbed Eld and ran out of the wagon just as the rest of the elixir ignited and the wagon exploded into small bits of wood. Ias and Eld lay in the grass, coughing and choking on the smoke. Eld's mouth was glowing green as he came around. He spit out the object and collapsed. Ias could see the small orb lighting the grass.

"Good job, my friend. One step closer," Ias said, picking it up and putting it in a bag made for a much bigger object.

Ias grabbed his staff, which was buried in the tall grass where it fell after it bounced off the glass. He proceeded to walk over to the tree near where the witch's broom had flown. He looked around and saw a long wooden stick singed at one end. He bent down at the knees and picked up the broom. It twitched once in his hand and was dead.

Eld lay limply across Ias' shoulders, feet dangling around his neck, barely alive. Ias, anxious to get Eld some aid, hurried down the road to the next village, where the door home awaited him.

## '8'

The howl of a strange creature ringing through the rafters met Ias as the library door swung open. Ias heard two very distinct creatures scuffling close by. He ran through the doorway and down the first corridor, where he saw two creatures circling in the shadows. One creature was big, the other small in comparison. The smaller creature was holding his own but not by much. Ias saw the large creature advance and then recoil with a howl that echoed through the library.

"Warrington!" Ias yelled, but was too late. Ias watched in horror as the large creature grabbed Warrington and tossed him through the air. Warrington hit the bookcases hard and fell to the ground. Ias rushed down the hallway as fast as an old man with a limp cat on his shoulders could.

The creature started running toward the downed cat that was struggling to get up. Ias reached into his bag and held out the emerald orb. The orb glowed bright as Ias thrust it outward. The orb changed from emerald to a bright blue sapphire. The pale blue light pierced through the darkness. The creature recoiled and stepped away from Warrington.

"Hunters," Ias whispered under his breath. The creature before him was a Jyhena, a dog-like creature that the hunters sent to seek their precious artifacts.

The Jyhena stood paralyzed in the glow of the orb. It snarled at Ias with each step he took closer. The creature, finally aware that this was the target his masters sent him to get, moved forward, breaking the trance. Warrington still lay on the ground, not moving. The Jyhena ignored the small creature as it homed in on its prize. Ias leaned his staff against the nearest bookshelf and grabbed for the witch's broom. He held the broom in his right hand while still holding out the Witch's Eye in his left.

The Jyhena moved closer to Ias. Without warning, the Jyhena yelled out in pain. Warrington had bitten into its back leg. Ias, seizing the opportunity, held the broom aloft and drove it down into the Jyhena's back just as it snapped for the cat hanging onto its back leg. The Jyhena gurgled as it fell over dead.

The glow from the orb slowly subsided and turned to green once again. It glowed brightly and then, like a flame in the wind, was gone. Ias pulled the witch's broom, now red with blood, from the back of the Jyhena. Ias picked up Warrington, who was limping, and placed him under one arm, being careful of his injured leg. Ias went into the reading room and set both cats on the bearskin rug. Ias moved quickly to the next room and placed the green eye on top of the seventh pillar, where it began to grow to match the size of the others. He quickly proceeded to his medicine cabinet, gathering herbs and bandages. He may have been done with this task, but the already long night had just begun.

## Chapter 4

'1'

Green and white clouds swirled around in Warrington's head. He was dizzy, and the emerald fog clouded everything. His mind could only see a long cobblestone road in front of him. He walked past the fields of wheat and over the small stone bridge with the marking *1546 A.D.* on the corner stone. Along the road was a small town with market shops dotting the landscape. The road continued through the center of town and beyond. Warrington could see the edge of town—and farther in the distance, storm clouds rolling in off the horizon above a small castle.

The sky had turned dark green as the yellow edge of the setting sun reflected off the atmosphere and collided with the blue cast of the rising moon. Warrington had not even noticed that the sky was a different color since to him the whole world seemed to be surrounded by a green fog.

Warrington strolled down the streets looking for food, as his stomach was growling, and he was quite interested in any delectable treats he might be able to find. He stopped and put his paws on the side of a very dingy window. It was so dirty one wondered if one could really see anything. Warrington's head darted back and forth, trying to get a view of the display inside. Paw prints were now outlining the bottom edge of the window and then stopped where Warrington had caught a glimpse of the wondrous colors streaming through the panes of glass.

Warrington could see only a few stands with oddly shaped items like the one he remembered seeing on the head of Henry Liddell that day at the market. These, however, were not black like Henry's but an assortment of different colors. Warrington was still unaccustomed to seeing colors outside the usual black, white, and grey. In the display case were thirteen stands set in two rows, and on seven of them were these objects he knew were commonly referred to as hats. The six stands in the back remained empty, but the front seven were a marvel to Warrington's eyes. He quickly forgot about any desire for food, and his curiosity drove him to go in for a closer look. The empty six stands looked naked and out of place, but he thought nothing of it, as hats were meant to be sold.

Warrington heard the small ding of the tiny doorbell, and a shadowy figure walked out of the store and around the corner. Before the door shut, Warrington seized his opportunity and hurried toward it; as with many of the doors back in the library, he just made it through before the infernal contraption closed on his tail. *It's lucky I still have a tail at all,* he thought reflecting over the way doors frequently slammed behind him.

The clothing shop was crowded with dark, shadowy figures that looked like people, but they seemed to ignore him as he wandered about the dusty floor in search of the front display he had seen.

Needing a better look, he leapt onto a table covered with black tunics and a few pairs of canvas trousers. Warrington looked toward the front of the store and saw the display case. He jumped over to the front window display and sat down on the narrow perch that separated the store from the theatrical event that was the hat display. The seven hats seemed to hypnotize Warrington; his head swayed back and forth like swells in the ocean. The green hat in the middle seemed to be slowly turning. Warrington thought it impossible. He looked left to right—red, blue, purple, pink, green, yellow, and black—the green hat was the only one moving. A sense of seasickness washed over Warrington.

The hat finished its slow turn on the stand and was now facing him. A pair of eyes opened wide, as though viewing the world for the first time. They squinted at the bright light, closed shut, and tightened. They blinked open again and looked at Warrington, who arched his back and hissed at this strange creature. The hat was not an inanimate object … nor was it an animal … but it was somehow alive. Warrington noticed that the hat had no arms, legs or body—so how could it possibly pose a threat to him? The hat's mouth opened wide in a yawn, and it stretched.

A voice bellowed deep inside Warrington's mind. *WHOOO ... ARE ... YOUUU?* the hat demanded.

Warrington was perplexed by this thought-provoking question. He had never been asked who he was. In fact, he should not have been perplexed, except that when the hat asked him who he was, he understood the question completely. Warrington opened his mouth and replied to the hat as professionally as possible. "I am Warrington J. Cat, protector of the Library of Universal Fiction." The words came out quickly and startled Warrington. He had never spoken the language of Ias Kindle or Eld.

The hat shook his brim back and forth in disbelief. "Well, Warrington J. Cat, what are you doing in my store?" the hat inquired accusatorially.

Warrington did not know what to say other than *meow*. He opened his mouth to meow and out came, "I don't know. I was just outside and saw these hats. Honestly, I do not know where I am or why I am here."

The hat laughed. "So peculiar—a cat that doesn't know where he is? Do you even know where you are going?"

"I am not sure, Hat. I was just where I was, and then I was here. I do not believe I am heading anywhere." Warrington was starting to get concerned as he realized he had no idea where he was or how to get back to the library.

"Well, Warrington J. Cat, I know where you are and where you are going. You are in the town of Chester and you are headed for the castle. I have seen it with my eyes. You may not know how you will get there, but you will get there. When you get there is another story. Your days at the library are closing. Time to check out, you see." The hat was starting to speak in riddle and pun. "Come see me when you need to find your way, and I will guide you to the White Castle."

The hat slowly started to turn around to face the front window.

"You mean the castle at the end of the road? I don't think I would need your guidance to find that castle," Warrington replied.

The hat, having already turned almost completely around, looked out of the corner of its eye at Warrington.

"No, the White Castle. The castle here has no importance to you. The White Castle is where you are going. The White Queen awaits your arrival." The hat continued his rotation. The other hats glowed brightly, illuminating the store in their glow. The rain outside had broken, and a rainbow was coming in through the glass.

"I don't understand what you mean, Hat. Why must I go to the castle, and who is this White Queen?" Warrington pleaded. Warrington loved the library and felt that it was his home. The hat gave no heed to his pleas and continued to turn on its axis until it was facing directly away from him.

"Hat!" Warrington yelled. His cries fell on deaf ears. Warrington reached out his paw and slapped the hat on the brim. It spun in circles on the stand and fell over. The eyes and mouth were gone—the hat was inanimate once more. The other hats had returned to their previous shade of grey.

From behind him, Warrington heard a shout. "Hey cat, get out of here!" Warrington could see another shadowy figure coming after him with a large stick with straw attached to the end. The man swung the object, and Warrington felt it pass through him and come out the other side. The object came down once more and Warrington felt a warm breeze.

"You don't belong here, you ugly cat, get out." The voice seemed to change from a yell to a whisper. The object now felt furry and warm. He closed his eyes, flinching as the strange object came down toward him again.

'2'

When his eyes opened, he could see the glow of the fire. Ias saw Warrington's eyes open, glazed over from sleep.

"Ah, Mr. Warrington, I see you are awake. I had begun to worry. You had quite an ordeal. Most cats would not have survived a Jyhena attack. They are the scouts of the dark ones from the east: the hunters who search for the orbs in order to gain an advantage in their fight over the land of Terra-Mirac," Ias commented, smoking his pipe in the chair. "You have proven to be one of the most courageous cats I have ever had the pleasure of keeping company with."

Warrington looked up at Ias and meowed as if to say, *Thanks, I think. What exactly happened?* However, Warrington was surprised that no words exited his mouth, unlike his previous conversation with the hat.

Ias looked down at him curiously and somewhat in awe. "How you survived is beyond my knowledge, but you did. Nothing short of a miracle, I suspect. You'll have to stay off that leg for a while until it heals properly. Eld will take on your duties until you are fully capable again. You've been asleep for three weeks, you know. I'd almost begun to wonder if you were coming back." Ias smiled and took another puff on his pipe.

'3'

Eld had spent the weeks after the fire in the wagon recovering with Ias in the study next to the reading room. No matter how hard he tried, he could not see what he'd seen many years before in the emerald orb that was now perched in its place on the seventh pillar behind Ias. Eld lay on the desk staring, but no voices came … no visions … and no swirling green clouds intermixed with a white ribbon. The life of the emerald orb had no purpose for him, it would seem.

Eld stared at the orb, thinking of the day he had first encountered it …

He could hear nothing except the sound of the orb telling him, *Jump, jump, Eldridge. Quick! Before the woman gets to you.* Then darkness had enveloped him and twisted him as he fell through the abyss of time and space. Knowledge of the human world came to him as he fell farther and farther. Time seemed to stop when his speed reached maximum velocity. Cats are one of the few creatures of this world with a non-terminal velocity, so when he hit the ground, he was shaken but not dead—indeed, far from death was Eldridge.

He was looking at a large field of bright green grass that swayed in the wind. Eldridge saw thick waves of stalks as far as he could gaze and wondered how he got there, and what he was going to do about getting home. This was Eldridge's first coherent thought and he began to worry. The tall grass seemed to weave back and forth to the rhythm of the breeze. Bounding along, trying to look as he jumped over each grassy section, he came upon a path made of clear stones with a slight yellow tint. The path seemed to glow under his paws with each step.

Eld came to a fork in the road where three most curious gentlemen stood. The man in black stood in the middle of the left path, while the man clad in white stood to the right. The man in grey stood in the middle, scrutinizing the cat from a tall podium. The man wearing grey had a face that was old and wrinkled—most likely from standing out here in the sun too long. Eld began to ask the men what they were doing when the man in grey interrupted him.

"Sir Cat, you seem lost. I am—or should I say *we are*—the Farseer. From what I can tell, your problem has but a simple solution. You need to take the right path in order to go where you need to go. The left path is correct if you are going left, and the right path is the right one if you are going right. Be warned, though—the wrong path is neither right nor left, but right and left."

Eld looked at the man, confused. "How do I know which path will take me back home?" Eld asked, cocking his head. He wondered why the man didn't seem more confused that he was indeed talking with a cat. *Cats don't talk*, Eld thought, yet he was talking to this man. It was not too far out of the realm of possibility to Eld, the more he conversed with the man, that maybe he was not the first talking cat this man had met.

"Well, Sir Cat, the correct path is as easy as asking a simple question. The question, however, is not as easy as it could be," the man in grey replied cryptically.

"Well, my lord, please tell me what I must do to gain knowledge of the correct path," Eld requested, then added, "I am all ears." Eld chuckled at his little joke and twitched his ear. The man, not chuckling, looked at Eld. His eyes were bright green.

"These two men you must ask, Sir Cat. Each one knows the correct path you must take. You can ask each one a single question, but no more. I must warn you, though: One man will surely tell you the truth; while the other lies through his teeth. I do not know which one is which, since they are twins, and I have never been very good at telling them apart," the man presented the pair to Eld.

Eld looked at each man strangely, as they all looked very much alike—the only difference was the color of their suits. Eld looked back at the man in the grey suit in bewilderment.

The man in grey continued, "I almost forgot, Sir Cat; you must ask each man the same question. Ask the right question, and you are free to go down the right path—ask the wrong one and you will wander about these parts for eternity, looking for the way home."

Eld was ready to get on with this test of wits. However, he was unsure of what question to ask. He looked at the man in the grey suit. "Has anyone gotten this correct?"

"To be honest with you, Sir Cat, no. Many have come through here, but we have sent many down the wrong path, I am afraid."

Eld sat there, thinking of what question he could ask that would allow him passage. *The question*, he thought, *needs to divulge which path is correct or which path is wrong.*

Eld looked at the man in the grey suit who was growing impatient. "Do you have a clue for me? I am still new to this thinking and talking."

"Sir Cat," the man groaned, "we do not have all day to stand here. We have other things we could be doing. Just don't think too hard over this question—it's as simple as asking the right one."

Eld cocked his head at the man, reflecting that he looked very much like a door-to-door salesman. Eld replayed the words in his head... *Ask the right one ... Which path is the right one? Which path would these men take? What path would they say the other would take?*

"I have my question, sir," Eld said with confidence.

The man looked up from the podium he was standing behind. Eld had not noticed this structure in the middle of the field at the fork in the road. "Ask each man, then. Be quick, though; I have places to be and I don't want to be late."

Eld looked at the man in white, who had one hand on a gold pocket watch and the other on the inside collar of his jacket. With a commanding voice, Eld asked, "What path would your brother tell me to take?"

The man looked at the cat and arrogantly replied in a high-pitched English accent, "My companion in black would tell you to take the path to the right because it is the correct path to take."

Eld turned to the man in black. "Sir, what path would your brother tell me to take?"

The man in black looked nervously at the man in grey and the man in white. Beads of sweat ran down his forehead. Eld was not sure this dramatic interpretation was for his benefit.

The man in black opened his mouth and whispered, "The man in white would tell you to take the path to the right ... Sir Cat." He stuttered as he got the last word out.

The man in grey looked at Eld. "Well, Sir Cat, it looks like you will be going down the right road, then?" the man in grey said, grinning from ear to ear.

"Au contraire sir, I will be taking the path to the left. The question was asked what path the other man would say to take. The liar would say that the man who tells the truth would take the wrong path because he is deceitful. The man telling the truth would say that his companion would tell me to take the wrong path because the man of truth knows the liar would not tell me the truthful answer. They both said that the other would tell me to go down the right path. Thus, the right path is actually the wrong path, and I shall be on my way down the left."

The three men stood at the fork as Eld trotted past them. Eld had begun to walk down the path to the left when he noticed the path start to swirl about in circles. Eld saw the eyes of the grey-suited man in the sky glowing green.

The man spoke clearly in the rustling of the world. "You have released me, Eld, and enclosed another in my stead. Go now and be free of this place."

The path became like a wave and the world grew dark. Eld was now flying into the air wriggling about. His eyes were shut tight, as he was unsure where he was going to land. When the world ceased its circular movement, he opened his eyes.

Eldridge was sitting on the table looking at a large woman who had her mouth open as wide as anyone could open it. She rushed over and grabbed him. She squeezed Eld hard against her chest. He squirmed uncomfortably in her arms as she suffocated him against her bosom. She was awoken from her excitement at seeing Eld by a knock at the front door. The sound of knuckle on wood rang clearly throughout the country house.

Patsy put Eld back on the table and thought, I must be going crazy. I did not just see a cat disappear and then reappear. It was just the lightning making me see things, that's it. Patsy opened the door to see a man in a brown cloak standing there, drenched from the rain.

"Good day, madam. I was at the market today, and your daughter told me that you might have found an item that belongs to me," the old voice said clearly.

The large woman was skeptical of the old man on her stoop. "Can you tell me what it looks like?" she inquired.

"Of course, madam. Where are my manners? I am Ias Kindle, and the item I am looking for is a round glass ball—green in color, but it may not always stay that color." Ias was still hooded and looked very suspicious. He drew back his hood and revealed a young face and a long grey and brown beard. Eldridge remembered this clearly, as he had watched Ias' beard go white through the many seasons.

"I am sorry, sir, but I have not found any such item," the woman lied. She had seen the ball and thought she could get a fair price for an artifact like that. She had found it in the barn on *her* property. It was hers—she did not have to give it back. Her mind saw green flashes and she focused on its wonder.

"You know the object the man seeks," the small, but deep voice spoke. Patsy turned around to see only Eldridge standing behind her. Patsy thought she was hearing her conscience, but ignored it as she had no intention of telling the truth.

"Ma'am, this item is very dangerous, and I must insist on taking it. Your cat has confirmed you have it," Ias replied.

"Don't be silly, cats simply cannot speak. Have you gone mad? Leave, or I will call the sheriff. They are just right down the road and would be here soon."

Ias, not wanting trouble, held up his hand and waved it back and forth as if to say never mind.

"I'll be on my way. If you do happen upon this object, please let me know. I must remind you that it's a very dangerous object and could cause harm to any who come in contact with it," Ias said as he turned and started walking down the steps of the porch. "Have a nice day, ma'am."

The woman closed the door and placed her back against the thick oak, the brass handle digging into her hip. "Well now, let's take a closer look at this dangerous object. It must be worth a fortune," Patsy said, excited that it must be worth more money than she originally thought—the depression in the country had hit their farm hard.

"We need all the money we can get, Eldridge. With Ted gone, I can't support us. This may bring us a handsome price."

Eld looked up at the woman. "You heard the man. It's dangerous. We should give it back. We'll find another way to survive."

Patsy's jaw dropped opened and then closed. Patsy wobbled back and forth on her feet as she almost fainted. "I must be going crazy," she said as the initial shock wore off. "The cat is talking, and I know cats just can't talk."

Patsy walked into the living room but was interrupted by another knock on the front door. She was paranoid that the old man had come back, convinced she had the object. The voice in her head told her she must not give it back. She walked slowly to the front of the house. Her hand reached for the doorknob, her sweaty palm making it hard to grip the brass handle. She opened the door to see the brown-cloaked man standing there silently before her. "I told you, sir; I do not have your green crystal ball. Now, go away!"

The hooded figure slowly lifted his head. The face was not that of the man she had seen before, but rather a silver mask shining in the glare of the light from inside the house. Eld arched his back and hissed as he looked on through the doorway.

The voice growled, "I'm not here to ask for the ball. I know you have it. I am here to take it under the authority of the Dark Queen of the Eastern Keep. You can hand it over, or we can take it."

Patsy looked at the masked man. "Like I told your friend that was just here, I'm not giving you anything. Leave, or I will call the police."

"I have no friends," the voice said.

Turning to close the door, the woman was suddenly gasping for air as yellow light surrounded her body. Eld looked on in terror as the woman shrieked in pain, and then she was gone. Black dust swirled about the air. The man stood there holding a yellow orb much like the green one.

"Come here, kitty, kitty," he said, holding out the ball. Eld began to run. A beam of yellow light shot out of the orb and struck the floor where Eld had been, igniting the floor into flames as Eld ran toward the back of the house. The man walked forward, his metal boots striking the wood. The metallic sound of each step echoed throughout the house. Light from the yellow ball shone through the dark rooms.

The mask smoked under the hood as the ball reflected off the shiny metal. Eld heard footsteps entering the living room, where he had taken up residence under the couch. The man lifted the golden orb high into the air. Eld could feel the heat from the ball radiate throughout the room and could smell the smoldering wood as the heat grew more intense.

The sound of metal on wood halted at the living room table. The heat in the room was dissipating, and Eld no longer felt the need to run for a cooler place to hide. The man was now standing over the coffee table, looking down at the small cedar chest with the crushed flowers. The green orb glowed brightly as the man lifted the cover off the box. There was a hearty laugh as the figure lifted the box into the air with his free hand. The golden light that illuminated the room disappeared from sight now, and all that was left was a faint green glow. This too dissipated as Eld watched the man slip the ball into the black velvet sack he had pulled from a satchel around his shoulder where he kept the yellow ball.

"Your lucky day, felis catus. Guess I won't need to rip the whereabouts of the ball from your memory."

With those words, Eld heard the man's boots smashing down on the floor as he walked to the front door. It was promptly slammed shut, and the man was gone. Eld walked around looking for Patsy, even though he knew she was gone. Eld was walking toward the front door when he heard scuffling. Two voices were coming from outside, and Eld saw a bright flash of yellow light. The front of the house was suddenly engulfed in flames.

'4'

Ias had been walking down the road thinking of how he could get into the woman's house and get the Emerald Eye. He knew it was there but needed to convince the woman she was in grave danger. He thought perhaps the woman's daughter might listen to reason and retrieve the object for him. She seemed quite sensible … and was very lovely.

Ias was halfway down the dirt road leading into town when he heard a shrill cry behind him. He quickly ran back to the house, mud sloshing up on his cloak. A bright yellow light flashed through every window of the house. Ias sprinted toward the house, climbed the front steps and grabbed the handle of the white door leading inside. The door was ripped out of his hand as the brown-cloaked man was exiting. Shocked to see this small figure standing in his way, the masked man stopped, looking at Ias.

"Out of the way, caterwauler. There is nothing you can do to stop us—you've been lucky in the past, but the Dark Queen will have the Creator's Gifts." He moved towards Ias, but Ias stood his ground. The masked man grabbed Ias by his cloak and effortlessly tossed him out of the way. Ias landed in the mud, tumbling end over end.

The figure pulled the yellow orb from its satchel. Crouching, he held it up in the air and pointed it towards the house. The yellow orb reflected the small ray of sunlight shining through the clouds, and the beams supporting the front porch suddenly glowed bright red. With a crackle of wood, the beams exploded in flames.

Ias got up quickly and threw his cloak to the ground. Pulling his staff from the sheath on his back, he extended it outward, twirling it in his hand. Ias circled around the figure, which was remaining stationary, waiting for Ias to strike, as the house burned brightly in the background.

The man held the orb up, firing a yellow beam toward Ias, who raised his staff to deflect the beam—but the sun disappeared behind the clouds just in time, and the power of the orb was gone. Ias pointed his staff at the cloaked figure; a bright white beam of light shot from the crystal encased in the swirled wood at the top of the staff. The beam hit the man in the chest, engulfing him in flames. The yellow orb fell to the ground and sank into the mud as the man flung off his cloak, screaming in agony as his flesh burned.

"We, the Dyhedral of the Eastern Keep, who serve the Dark Queen, will not allow a mere peasant to disrupt this task. You shall die here, old man, for your interference."

The Dyhedral got up and removed his mask. His skin was leathery and scaled—black birthmarks covered his face. Ias had never encountered a Dyhedral before. He only knew what he had read in books at the library.

The Dyhedral were an ancient race of half men and half lizard that once lived between this world and the next. They were thought to protect the central angle between the arterial plane. The Dark Queen found them and used her powers of persuasion to entice them to do her bidding. They agreed to serve her in repayment for releasing them from the world between this and the next. Dyhedral were murderous creatures who had turned the tide of the war in the favor of the Dark Queen against the armies of the Duchess.

The creature's flesh was still smoldering from the fiery blast; the Dyhedral looked around carefully. The yellow ball lay cradled in the small crater it had made when it hit the ground drying the mud into clay. The Dyhedral picked it up and wiped the orb with a piece of burnt cloak. He held up the glass as it reflected the sun, which had broken through the clouds again. Ias stood, staff at the ready. The traces of mud, though, created a layer that blocked the orb from gathering the reflection of the sun's rays. The Dyhedral wiped furiously at the orb.

Ias was focused on the Dyhedral when out of the corner of his eye, he saw a small animal fly through the air from the porch roof onto the Dyhedral's back. The Dyhedral screamed, its soft leathery skin on fire as Eld clawed at his back. The Dyhedral ripped Eld off his back and threw him at Ias. Ias sprinted toward the flying creature and caught him with one hand. The Dyhedral flung his cloak over his back, turned, and ran toward the cornfield.

Ias set Eld to the ground and sprinted after the Dyhedral. The Dyhedral dug a scaly hand into its satchel, drawing out a key, which it then flung to the ground. The key stuck straight up in the mud. Light created a door-shaped rectangle on the ground, and a black hole appeared as the door swiftly fell open. The Dyhedral stood over the door, ready to exit when Ias threw his staff. It whirled through the air, end over end. The crystal at the end of the staff shattered against the chest of the Dyhedral, shards burying deep into its leathery flesh.

This unexpected attack knocked the Dyhedral to the ground. The claws clutching the golden orb fell open and it rolled into the mud, disappearing from sight. The satchel around the creature's chest burst open, and the Emerald Eye sailed straight up into the air and fell back toward the open doorway in the ground. Ias reached out to grab it and could feel the cool glass brush his fingertips as it rolled off his hand. The green orb flashed brightly and then disappeared into the doorway in the ground.

The Dyhedral was regaining consciousness. Its claws dug into the mud and it pushed itself back up. Glaring at Ias, it roared in anger. Ias stood defenseless, his staff lying in the mud at the foot of the Dyhedral. The creature stalked toward Ias but suddenly roared in pain once again. Eld had jumped onto the back of its legs and was climbing toward its head. The Dyhedral spun around, slashing at the cat. Ias ran forward, shoulder lowered, and rammed into the creature's rib cage. Ias felt the ribs give way as the creature fell backward and slid into mud just feet from the open door. The Dyhedral saw his chance to escape and crawled toward the door. Ias was busy looking for the small cat, as he'd lost sight of him when the Dyhedral fell. The creature grabbed the edge of the door, pulled himself over, and disappeared from view. The door slammed shut and was gone.

"Cat, where did you go? Are you okay?"

Eld came walking out from between the corn stalks, where he had landed on his feet, licking his paw where he'd been scratched. "I am fine, sir."

"Well, my friend, looks like we lost the battle today. He won't be coming back here, though. He got what he was looking for and more. I must be getting back home, though—I need to figure out where that green orb went."

"I have nowhere to go, sir. That thing killed my master. I am now bound to you, as you have saved my life. I am in your service, master; I only ask for the chance to seek revenge for my owner. That creature has left a young girl without a home or a mother. It was a good thing she had left to go into town for the day and wasn't here to see the demise of her mother, but what will become of her?"

"I am sure she has other family that will take her in, and with this fire, the Sheriff is sure to be here soon—he'll take care of her," the man said. "Ias … my name is Ias. If you can catch mice, I have work for you. You will need to earn your keep, though—I don't take in freeloaders." Ias bent down and stroked the cat's head. He picked Eld up around the waist and put him on his shoulder, muddy paws and all.

Ias walked over to the corn that had began burning and picked up the gold orb that lay on the ground. "The Yellow Sun of the West. I have been looking for this one for some time. We will seek out the Emerald Eye when we can locate exactly where it went. Judging from what I saw before the creature escaped, he didn't make it back to his original destination."

With that said, the old man walked past the house, now fully engulfed in flames and sending smoke billowing high into the air, and toward the small town five miles west of the rural farm, where his doorway waited patiently for him.

The Dyhedral would not be so lucky, as the door had opened to a different world than he was expecting; he would be captured, tried, jailed, and executed for being of the Animal species.

'5'

Eld sat up, thinking about that day as he watched Ias polish the Witch's Eye (as Eld and Ias had taken to calling the green orb since the Witch's passing). Ias recounted to Eld the story that Oscar had told him … The mysterious emerald ball falling into the heart of the city, the curious green-skinned girl who found it, and the Animal known only as *The Dyhedral*. Oscar did not know how the witch made the magical sphere, but he did know she was able to use it to make normal animals into Animals and to see far off into the distance of space.

Eld sat on the desk and put his head down. His flashback had made his eyes heavy and tired. His eyes closed and he returned to the dreams of the small farm in Kansas where his owner gave him rice and chicken each night for dinner and doted upon his needs. He thought of the poor young girl who had rolled the ball of yarn for him. She would have no explanation of why her mother was gone or why she would have to go and live with her aunt and that wretched little dog. He wished he could go and explain to her what had happened. Through half-open eyelids, he saw the glowing Witch's Eye, but he was no match for his exhaustion and his lids dropped closed as he drifted off to his dreams.

'6'

Warrington hobbled into the study where Eld was sleeping and Ias was scrawling on his parchment, as he often did after a trip outside the library. Eld was fast asleep, as he had been out hunting mice all day, and in his older age, just catching a few often wiped him out.

Ias looked up from his parchment. "Warrington, you should be resting. You are healing nicely, but your wounds still need more time."

Warrington was feeling much better. He had been asleep off and on for three weeks, dreaming and not remembering much. As Warrington entered the study, he noticed the Witch's Eye glowing brightly in pronounced contrast to the rest of the orbs.

"I have limited the access to the library since our Jyhena visitor a few weeks ago," Ias said. "There won't be access to the outside until we find out how he got in. We wouldn't want a repeat event. He appeared to be scouting the area, so when he does not return to whoever sent him, we may almost certainly expect another visitor. We need to be on guard. Once you are healed, you can go back to your duties. Eld, I am sure, will be most happy to turn them back over to you."

Ias dipped his quill in the ink, made a large gesture on the page, and returned the quill to its place. Warrington was in agreement with the thought of returning to his duties, but the cast on his leg was a burden. He could not jump or run with it. The heavy weight of the molding was anchoring him down. Warrington turned and started heading back to the bearskin rug when he heard the familiar voice of the green hat whisper, *Warrington, the time draws near.* Warrington turned to see if the emerald hat was there, but saw nothing but the emerald glow of the Witch's Eye.

## Chapter 5

'1'

Another winter had passed, and the summer sun had begun melting the snow in the courtyard. The fountain lady was a dark grey from the slow wet melting process. Warrington, who had gotten his cast off just a month before, was outside enjoying the sun. Ias had allowed the courtyard to be open to ensure that the mice were not decomposing in the furnace downstairs, as the smell permeated the entire library in the evenings when the furnace was full. Warrington sat by the fountain, enjoying the warmth as the sun beat down on his naked skin. He had put in a full day's work and was entitled to a small break.

Ias and Eld were off on their first trip since returning with the Witch's Eye. They had gone to investigate a black orb that had been uncovered in the rubble after two large castle towers had collapsed. Warrington remembered the story Ias had told one night by the fire …

"This story was told to me by the previous librarian many years ago, and now I pass it on to you two," Ias had said.

"Many years before the current world formed, there were many great battles. The race of elves made many Palantirs or crystal balls. Many different sizes were made, but most have passed from the world. Thirteen of them are known to remain, granting sight for most, but some have power over the others. The Witch's Eye had been granted the power to bestow thought and speech upon animals. (This power had been granted to Eld upon exiting the orb.) All but the blackest of the thirteen orbs were lost during the third age. When the age of elves had passed through the third age and the age of men began, the black orb was lost from memory until a few hundred years later, when it appeared again. It disappeared and reappeared at will, corrupting the hearts of those that used it."

Ias had looked ahead with a blank expression as the story finished. He'd stood up from the desk. "No matter, my dear Warrington and Eld—it will soon be here with us and protected from those who would use it for evil. Warrington, Eld and I will be back before supper. Take the day off if you like." Ias had grabbed his cloak, put Eld on his shoulder, and left the library.

Warrington had had enough of the warm sun and cold breeze and retreated back inside to see if any mice had decided to snack on their favorite treat. The mice had been a rare sight since the Jyhena had showed up, but a few had come out to meet their fate at Warrington's claws.

The naked cat slunk his way back toward the reading room. The candles burned brightly, flickering as a slight breeze drifted through the library. Warrington's ears perked at the unmistakable sound of gnawing coming from the aisle where he had had his first mousing encounter years before. His eyes glowed in the candlelight and his body was low to the ground as he turned the corner. His head crept slowly around the corner. Two mice had dragged a book to the middle of the floor and were happily gnawing on it, unaware of their impending fate.

Warrington's hips were shifting side to side. Faster and faster they swayed. He bent down into his sprinter's stance, now fully visible down the corridor of bookcases. Before the unusually large rodents knew what was happening, Warrington had flown through the air, tackling one of them. It slid across the floor, getting up quickly. *Not quick enough,* Warrington thought. The mouse lay dead on the floor before *What was that?* could even cross its mind.

The other mouse was hastily beating a retreat down the long hallway. Warrington sprinted after him. Turning a corner, the mouse headed directly for the reading room. Warrington scurried up a bookcase and ran across the top, leaving a fresh dust cloud in his wake. Warrington, seeing the mouse running toward the reading room door, leapt from the bookcase, crashing into the mouse. The two shapes, intertwined, slid across the floor and through the door into the reading room. The mouse quickly recovered and took off toward the study. Dazed, with his back leg hurting, Warrington tried to get up. As he got to his feet and tried to push off his back leg, pain shot through his body and he stumbled.

Warrington, seeing the rodent heading toward the back wall where a hole had been covered up, ignored the pain and went after him. Trying to dodge Warrington, the rodent scurried up Ias' desk and across the top, sending the contents crashing to the floor. Warrington cut off the rodent at the edge of the desk, before it could reach the hole between the pillars holding the pink and yellow orbs.

The rodent, desperately trying to survive, backed up, looking for another way out and gnashing its teeth at the cat standing between him and freedom.

The mouse, fully in the grip of desperation, did something Warrington had never seen a rodent do. It charged full speed across the desk toward Warrington. The mouse rammed Warrington, and both flew through the air. The mouse fell to the floor as it hit Warrington and tumbled off the side of the desk. Warrington sailed through the air, expecting to hit the floor ... the wall ... *something*. Instead, the study, desk, and mouse faded into darkness. The mouse looked at him and waved a solemn good-bye as Warrington floated off... at least this was what Warrington imagined.

'2'

As Warrington fell farther and farther through the darkness, he could see sunlight ahead of him. Warrington felt the warm sun on his skin. When he came to a sudden halt on the earth, he saw the familiar cobblestone road with the bridge crossing the river and heading into town. He could see the castle in the distance at the end of the road. *I must be dreaming,* he thought. *Well, let's see if it goes any better this time.*

He walked down the street, stopping when he recognized the clothing shop with the dirty windows. He crawled to the window, put his little cat head right up to it, and peered in. There were thirteen stands still, but this time there was only one grey hat. The store was dark and deserted.

Warrington, seeing that he was obviously not getting in, decided to continue down the street. A woman stood outside her shop, using the large wooden object with straw at the end to brush debris from the front of her doorway. Warrington sat and watched the woman meticulously sweep one side and then the other.

He was so mesmerized by her sweeping he was almost stepped on by the man in the lavender suit with green trim. He walked with his head held high, his black cane with a silvery head cracking down on the stone floor with each step. Atop his head sat a green hat with purple ribbon around the base.

Forgetting all about the woman, Warrington got up and followed the man. The man's pace quickened, and then he suddenly stopped. He put his hand beneath his freshly shaved chin in contemplation. "One couldn't hurt," the man whispered to himself and spun on the heels of his dark black boots towards the last doorway he'd passed.

Warrington followed him into the dwelling. The man took off his hat and walked to a long desk, asking the man behind it, "Can I get a pint of ale, barkeep?"

The bartender put his elbow down on the desk and dropped his chin, resting it on his hand. "Ya think that be a good idea, Theo? Ya know how angry ya get after ya have a drink," the bartender lectured in his Irish accent.

"I think I can handle just one, sir. Cut me off after that." Theo put six shillings on the bar that encircled the room. Warrington saw Theo's hat sitting quite still on the counter, giving no signs of movement or animation. Warrington walked over to the counter and looked up at the hat. He then jumped to the barstool directly above him, where he sat and waited for the hat to talk.

"Does your hat talk, sir?" Warrington asked in a clear voice.

Theo looked over, but saw no one. He looked down and scowled. "Good Lord, what a hideous looking cat."

"Well, you aren't much to look at, either," Warrington replied sharply.

Theo jumped back, gasping, "Good lord, a talking cat! Away, devil cat!"

Theo was backing away from the cat as the bartender came back with his stein filled with ale, the head overflowing and running down the sides.

"Amos ... this cat ... talks," Theo said, pointing a shaky finger at Warrington.

"Now, now," laughed Amos, "apparently you have already had one too many of these. You best get on now, Theo. I won't be serving you tonight." Amos pulled the stein back and took a sip of it himself.

"Yes, yes ... I do believe you are right. I'll be going now. I should be getting home right away," Theo said, backing toward the door.

"Don't forget your hat, sir," Warrington sneered.

Theo turned and leaned over, as far away from the cat as possible. He gingerly reached his hand out and grabbed the brim with his index finger and thumb.

Warrington, noticing the man was susceptible to scares, stared at Theo wide-eyed, slapped at his hand, and yelled, "I'll take your soul!" as loudly as he could.

Theo screamed and ran out of the tavern. Warrington sat on the stool chuckling. The bartender, who had turned away to empty the stein, came back to see Warrington sitting there, still laughing.

"Go on cat, scram! This isn't no place for animals. Ye'r scaring off my customers," he said, making a shooing gesture with both his hands. "Talking cat, that'll be the day," he mumbled under his breath, turning away from the cat on the stool.

Warrington looked back at him, laughing deviously. "Well, I guess today is that day, Master Amos," Warrington said as he turned. The man spun back around, but Warrington had already jumped down and was on his way out to follow a frightened patron down the narrow walkway.

Theo was striding down the road, continually glancing furtively over his shoulder, as if he expected his soul to be snatched by the demonic cat at any moment. Warrington was entertained at how badly the sight of the talking cat had frightened the man. *Devil cat*, Warrington mused as he walked down the street, *that is the most absurd thing I have ever heard. Maybe a satyr cat, but devil? Never.*

Theo reached the edge of town and turned to go inside a small tan brick building across from the wooden amphitheater. Warrington jumped up to a flower box and peered through the four-pane glass window. The dirt covering the window made it hard to see, but it appeared to Warrington that Theo was lounging in a robust purple velvet chair in front of a crackling fire. The chair-back was at least six feet high, though, and blocked Warrington's view as to whether or not the man was there. *It could be anyone sitting there*, Warrington thought, peering through the murky glass. On the back of the chair, Warrington could see the outline of something small, stitched in black thread; he did not recognize weaving patterns. Warrington could see movement as the hatless silhouette in the chair leaned over and placed a large teapot shape over the fire.

Warrington jumped down and walked around the house, looking for a way in. After all, he needed to speak with the hat, as crazy as that sounded. However, Warrington figured that since cats did not talk—and *he* was obviously talking—that it was not out of the realm of possibilities that hats could also speak.

Warrington walked around the side of the house toward a window that was propped open while a pie cooled on the ledge. He jumped up, knocking the fresh blackberry pie off the ledge and into a steaming mess on the grass below. Although he was hungry, he ignored the pie and dropped down to the floor inside the house. The wood creaked with each step he took as he looked for the hat—but he saw none. He walked around to the side of the purple chair where the man named Theo was sitting, now sipping at a cup of tea in a mug that looked as old as some of the leather-bound relics in the library. Looking around the room, he spotted the shape he had been searching for. The hat was sitting precariously on the end table beside the chair. Warrington was mesmerized by the hat when a rap came at the door.

'3'

Theo put his cup of tea down next to the green hat. Warrington slinked out of sight under the chair as Theo walked briskly to the door. The quick rap on the door had grown into a constant pounding.

"Theo! Theophilus Hatmaker! You open the door this instant, or I will break it down!" the voice yelled, putting a strong rolling sound on the "r" in break.

"Calm down, Marchavious. I'm coming—calm down," Theo said, fumbling with the latch. He stood at attention and organized himself. He slowly unlatched the door and turned the iron knob. Warrington saw the outline of a man, short in stature compared to Theo—or Theophilus, as the man named Marchavious had just called him.

"Amos said you came into the tavern jabbering on about a talking cat. Are you out of your mind? You are lucky the constable is not the one banging down your door and hauling you off to the sanitarium," Marchavious muttered, his hands and arms flailing wildly.

"Please come in. It's six o'clock and I would quite enjoy some more tea. We can sit by the fire, and I'll explain the whole situation," Theo said calmly.

Marchavious nodded and stepped through the door and into the firelight. The sky had grown dark as twilight approached, and the only light in the house came from the hearth, where the fire burned. Warrington could now make out a young blond-haired gentleman with buckteeth wearing a burgundy cloth vest that was in sharp contrast to his yellow undershirt. His brown canvas trousers were adorned with dark patches on the knees, and the cuffs were tucked at his calf into burgundy and white striped knickers.

The two men walked over to the sitting area that was the main stage for the fire. Theo grabbed the teapot and poured a cup for himself. He then lifted his hat to reveal another floral print teacup. This one looked newer than the one he'd just drunk from. The teapot's brass exterior shone in the firelight as Theo tipped it over, filling the second cup.

"Now," said Marchavious leaning back, curious to hear about Theo's strange happenings. "Let's discuss this talking hallucination you had."

Theo was known to spin a tale or two about strange goings-on after he had a few too many drinks. The local regulars at the tavern considered him the Don Quixote type and would sit as Theo spun a tale or two about his latest adventure. Theo had also spent many nights in the town lock-up for disturbing the peace. Once he had even gone as far as to proposition the constable's daughter, who was very fond of hats, but not very fond of men groping her. It was after this event that Theo had vowed to quit drinking and decided to go into business making hats for a living.

"I had just walked in, Marchavious, and ordered a drink. I knew I could have just one and be fine. When Amos turned to pour the drink, I looked at the stool next to me, and there was a hairless cat. The cat asked me a question and I just yelled 'Devil Cat!' and got out of there. The cat even reached out to try and grab me. He yelled, 'I got your soul!' when I went for my hat." Theo leaned in and whispered, "But this was not the strangest thing, Marchavious—I could've sworn the cat was laughing at me as I left the tavern."

"And you'd had nothing to drink?" Marchavious said, raising an eyebrow.

"NO! I hadn't even gotten the chance to grab my cup yet," Theo said, leaning back in his chair and again bringing his teacup to his lips to sip the now lukewarm substance.

"Well, maybe it is the chemicals used to make your hats that are causing these hallucinations. I have heard rumors of other hat makers going insane after many years of work. They say the chemicals can drive one mad …"

"No, Marchavious! I can tell you that when I saw the cat and heard him speak, I was quite sane." Theo was now scratching his head.

Warrington had lain down and was listening intently to this conversation, amused, when he spied something moving across the floor. The dark shadow moved slowly and then stopped, moved again, and then stopped once more in front of the fireplace. Warrington instinctively homed in on it. His tail shot up into the air, and before he could even think to remain hidden, he was dashing forward.

Startled, Theo and Marchavious jumped up in their chairs as the brown creature streaked across the floor. The mouse that had been nibbling on a piece of crumb looked to his left just in time to see a small black abyss filled with sharp teeth heading toward him. The mouse darted forward, trying to escape this certain doom. Warrington skidded on the smooth wood as he narrowly missed the tiny mouse. He had forgotten what it was like to catch small rodents of the usual size.

The mouse scampered quickly across to the dining area, with Warrington just steps behind. The chase continued around the dining room and into the kitchen. Warrington hit a chair and knocked it over with a crash. The broom leaning up against it spun around in circles, hitting the edge of a pan and sending its watery contents through the air and onto the floor. Making a wide turn, the mouse quickly sped toward the living room. Warrington could see the mouse heading for a quick getaway as it scurried toward a hole in one of the floorboards. He was almost on top of his prey when the hat jumped in front of him, covering the mouse.

"Good throw, Theo!" Marchavious said.

Warrington skidded to a halt as the hat stood there in his path. No eyes were looking at him and no mouth spoke to him.

Theo looked at Marchavious. "It's him, Marchavious. The talking cat—he has come for my soul indeed."

"Good gawd, Theophilus, get a grip. It's just a cat. A curiously hairless cat, but not a devil cat, from what I can see."

Warrington stood at attention, looking at the hat and awaiting the hat's removal in order to claim his prize.

"Cat! You ... cat, do you talk?" Marchavious asked.

Warrington might have responded to this, but he was so focused on the hat that he heard nothing. Theo walked over and slowly lifted the corner of the hat to see if the mouse was still underneath. Curiously, he looked from one side to the other. He picked up the hat and looked inside.

"No mouse in here. Guess it wasn't that good, Marchavious," Theo said with a grin, putting the hat on his head.

"Looks like your aim was good; it's your floor that needs work." Marchavious pointed to the hole that the mouse had originally been running toward.

"Well, I guess he followed you home to finish the job," Marchavious said, chuckling now. "Talking cat ... you must have been hearing someone else."

"No, he heard me correctly," Warrington said, looking at Marchavious, who had opened his mouth to speak, but no words came out.

Marchavious shook his head quickly left and right in disbelief. "Did you just say something, cat?" Marchavious inquired.

"My name is not cat; it is Warrington, Warrington J. Cat. I presume you are Mr. Marchavious?"

"Why yes, Master Warrington, I am Marchavious Harbinger." Marchavious forgot he was talking to a cat for a moment. "How did you come here and what can we do for you? I assume you need something from Theo, since you followed 'im and snuck into his house."

"My business is not with Mr. Theophilus, but with his hat. I assume I was sent here to seek his counsel," Warrington said.

"Well, Master Warrington, as you can see, the hat does not desire to hold counsel with you, does it? How can a hat with no eyes, nose, mouth, or body hold a conversation with you?" Marchavious said, putting his psychology background to good use.

"That truly is a riddle for the ages. However, I have held counsel with this hat before in the hat shop down the road—just the other day, in fact. It told me to come see it when I was beginning my journey to the White Castle … I guess I have not begun my journey yet," Warrington said, confused.

"Well, maybe this is the beginning, but the hat seems to have brought you to us. Maybe this is where you begin your journey, but I would not want to go there. As I recall, that is where the White Queen resides," Marchavious said.

Theo was still stunned at the thought of this cat talking in his living room.

"Well," Warrington said, "you know of this White Castle with the White Queen, then?"

"Yes, but-—well Warrington, what I say is only conjecture. I say conjecture because she does not exist. It is only a fairytale that has an unhappy ending.

*Across the Terra-Mirac*

*Her kingdom to the west;*

*No man the path will lead*

*But to his certain death.*


*Follow the shore of light;*

*Upon the hill so grey*

*Lies the castle of the white,*

*Held at stormy bay.*


*Up the darkened path,*

*Down the lightened road,*

*Past the ocean of her wrath,*

*Down the Moors of Toad.*


*The White Castle rises into the run*

*And falls under the moon*

*Reach this castle not, my son*

*Or her madness come over you.*


*If the castle you must reach,*

*Take the stairs around;*

*Before the White Queen you come,*

*Kneel six feet in the ground.*


"You see, Warrington, it was just a poem we were taught as young children. I don't quite remember the rest of it, but she is apparently feuding with a dark witch who lives to the south of Terra-Mirac. Each is said to claim ownership of this land, but it's nothing more than a fairytale told to children."

Warrington listened intently, wondering if this was what the hat was talking about or if it was something else, some other castle, perhaps, and not some made-up fairytale. He had no clue how he could even get to this White Castle, as he was not adept at solving children's fairytales—if that was indeed what the hat was speaking of.

Theo looked over at Marchavious. "Are you two done talking? I really still don't believe there is a talking cat. We are both just hallucinating. I spiked the tea; that must be it. Marchavious, you probably are not even here."

Warrington suddenly began to feel very strange as he sat by the fire. Marchavious' eyes widened as he watched Warrington start to grow dim. Warrington felt a pulling at the nape of his neck.

Theo looked at the cat and rubbed his eyes. "Is it just me,

Marchavious, or is the cat fading away? All I can see is a pair of eyes."

Theo rubbed his eyes once more, and Warrington was gone.

### '4'

Warrington felt his body being pulled from behind, like when his mother had carried him around by the nape of his neck. He could see darkness envelop him as he traveled past the teacup, the teapot, the green hat, and Theo's chair. The green hat circled around him twice and disappeared. Warrington noticed a bright light up ahead. Faster and faster, he approached the small but rapidly growing dot of light. Warrington looked around, searching for something to stop him. Anything. But there was nothing. Seconds went by, and the dot was now a bright, wide circle. Minutes seemed to fly by now, and the circle became a lake. Warrington closed his eyes to brace for the impact.

Warrington felt a slight gust of air as he smashed through the bright circle, glass shattering into the darkness behind him. Warrington opened his eyes and found the pool he had crashed into was just his entry back into the study.

The rodent he had been chasing around the study was gone. He wondered how long he'd been gone. He felt like he was gone for hours, but from the looks of the study, it had only been seconds. The Witch's Eye was rolling around on the floor next to the pink orb. As Warrington reappeared in the library, he knocked over the pillars, and the orbs fell to the floor, rolling to all corners of the room. Ias' desk was a mess, and Ias and Eldridge were going to be mad. He had almost forgotten about the White Queen and the White Castle. His discussion with Marchavious made him wonder if his conversation with the hat hadn't actually happened.

Warrington walked into the reading room and lay down on the bearskin rug. His thoughts were churning as he drifted off to sleep. As his eyes shut, he drifted off into a world of green hats, castles and their queens, and curiously enough … rabbit holes.

# *Chapter 6*

### '1'

Warrington woke to the unmistakable sound of the reading room door opening and shutting. There was a rustle of feet scuffing across the floor and into the study. Warrington could see Eldridge jump onto Ias' desk. The other figure he could not see, but he assumed it was Ias, writing on his parchment. They ignored the mess that Warrington had created the night before. Ias scribbled furiously as Eldridge sat there watching the quill go back and forth.

"Is that wise, Master Ias?" Warrington heard Eld say while Ias' hand went up and down with each stroke of the quill.

"Yes, someone must be left in charge. I see no other options right now."

Warrington walked into the study. He could see that a new ball occupied one of the pillars, but the other orbs were still lying about: under the desk, over in the corner, stuck in a hole, and in various other places around the desk. This new orb was black as midnight and swirled with red fire, instead of white clouds like the Witch's Eye.

Warrington noticed that Ias was hunched over the desk, wincing in pain as he scrawled. Warrington jumped to the desk just as Ias was putting his quill down.

"Warrington," Ias said as he noticed the presence of a second cat on the desk. He scanned the room, distracted by its contents, which were a wreck from the great mouse chase. "My goodness, young cat ... you have been quite busy! I am quite curious to know what happened, but—" Ias' voice trailed off as he was interrupted.

"Well, Master Ias, the mouse escaped into the reading room. I gave chase, but he got the best of me. The next thing I knew, I was drifting off, and that rodent was waving to me as I floated into darkness," Warrington said, without realizing he had started speaking quite fluently.

"My goodness, Warrington! What has happened?" Ias was frantic. Eld's eyes were wide and his mouth was agape as far as a cat's mouth could open.

Eld overcame his shock first. "Seems like our old friend, the Witch's Eye, has been up to his usual tricks."

"Quick, Warrington! Tell me what you saw," Ias said insistently.

Warrington reviewed the story of the hat, the two men—Theo and Marchavious—and the White Queen. While Warrington had not actually seen the White Queen, Ias was most interested in this portion.

"Was there anything else, Warrington? Anything at all?" Ias said, shaking his hands and running them through his hair.

Warrington recounted the conversation with the hat and that the hat told Warrington his time in the library was coming to an end. Ias looked very concerned about this.

"Warrington, no matter what happens—you *must not* leave the library."

Warrington nodded and Ias scratched him behind the ears. He noticed something strange as he did this. Ias picked up Warrington and held him to the light.

"Most peculiar … Curious indeed, my young friend. It appears as though you are growing fur," Ias said, smiling and petting the few short hairs on Warrington's head. Eld looked curiously at Warrington and then back at Ias.

"Master Ias, we have much work to finish. I suggest we hurry," Eld said, sitting on the edge of the desk and watching Ias inspect Warrington by the light of the fire.

'2'

Eld and Ias had been up all night, while Warrington slept on the rug in front of the fire. He could hear their murmurings about the black ball and their adventure into the world where motorized coaches zipped through the streets. Ias spent all night writing the accounts of his adventure on the parchment he'd written on so many times before.

The night was quite old and dawn was just creeping into the courtyard when Warrington got up and stretched on the bearskin rug. He walked into the study, where Ias was still recounting his tale.

Eld looked at Ias and whispered as Warrington approached the room. Warrington jumped onto the desk, his claws digging into the side of the wood. Ias' face was frozen in an expression of shock, his eyes open wide as Warrington moved back and forth across the desk. Ias burst into a loud fit of laughter, and then coughed as if the laugh had caused him pain. Eld was also laughing quite hard.

"What is so funny, Master Ias and Master Eld? Do I have something on me? What is going on?" Warrington said, pacing up and down the desktop.

"Have you not seen for yourself?" Ias said, lifting up Warrington's front paws and inspecting his underbelly. He ran a hand down Warrington's back. "My word, his coat is like silk, Eldridge. This is a most curious side effect indeed."

Warrington looked down at his paws to see dark lavender fur with pink stripes circling his legs. Warrington jumped off the desk, ran into the reading room and jumped onto a small chest of drawers in the corner. A mirror hung above the chest of drawers, and Warrington stood there, staring into it.

His reflection showed the shape of a furry stranger, someone he had never seen before. He turned around in circles, looking at the accursed fur that covered his entire body. He felt a tingle of coldness come over him and he shivered. The stranger in the mirror seemed to shimmer as the cold crawled up his spine. At one point, he thought he saw a transparent wave rolling through his fur, but it was only a split second—if he had blinked, he would have missed it. He was so distracted by the lavender and pink fur that he thought very little of this glimpse of translucence and jumped to the floor to escape the looking glass.

"Master Ias!" Warrington yelled, running into the study. "What has happened to me? Why do I have this hideous fur? Why is it such a ridiculous color?" Warrington was panting as he sprinted through the study and onto the desktop. Eld was still chuckling at Warrington and his dance in front of the mirror.

"I honestly do not know what has happened, Master Warrington. It appears that you may have been transported to another world, another place, and another time by the Witch's Eye, or any one of the other Palantirs that, before being knocked over, inhabited the pillars. They have minds of their own: some see the future, some tell us our destiny, and some may even lie to us. Some have the power to grant life, while others can take it away. When these artifacts of the ancient days came into existence, they were very powerful. Some corrupted those who used them. This one here used to belong to a white wizard of the third age," Ias said, pointing to the black orb encircled with fire.

"Not much is known about where it went after the wizard fell into darkness and was killed by his own servant. It was believed to have passed to the king of that time for safekeeping, but honestly, it passed out of thought and lay dormant for a long time, until it was found many thousands of years later. Apparently, it took this man to another world, much like the Witch's Eye probably did to you when the mouse knocked you off the desk. I can't be sure, though, since all of the orbs were knocked over. You could have hit any number of them. The resulting side effects are most perplexing," Ias said, stroking Warrington's peculiar fur back and forth.

"Well, my friends, I must go lie down—my strength is gone and I need sleep. The dawn approaches and there is still much I must accomplish tomorrow," Ias said, standing slowly, his body almost giving out on him. He leaned over and grabbed his staff, which was sitting off to his right. The head of the staff had a broken crystal in the head of it. Ias was showing his age as he slowly crept toward the bed in the corner of the reading room. Warrington and Eld sat side by side watching him.

'3.1'

Ias was passing through the archway of the reading room when there was a strange noise that neither Eld nor Warrington had ever heard within the confines of the library. Ias paused and waved his hand at Eld and Warrington.

"Come, Warrington, we must hide," Eld said, motioning his head to a hidden side cupboard. They slipped through the door into a dark passageway with stairs leading upward. Warrington hadn't known any of this existed.

Eld and Warrington heard a trumpet and then voices as they climbed the stairway toward a balcony that overlooked the reading room. Warrington was most curious to know whom these voices belonged to, as he had never seen anyone inside the library other than Ias and Eld. After several minutes of climbing, they reached the top of the stairs. The door creaked open for them, as all the doors in the library did. Cobwebs covering the door tore in half as the opening door stretched them to the breaking point.

As they walked through the door, Warrington noticed that they were directly behind a painting hanging on the reading room wall that had been obscured by the dark when Warrington had first entered the reading room many months ago. The hidden balcony sat behind the painting, and Eld and Warrington could see everything through the thin material.

Down below, ten cloaked figures stood, five on either side of the room. A small, child-sized human with the face of a man stood in the middle; he held a trumpet in one hand and a parchment in the other.

While Eld and Warrington could see everything, they could not hear. While the material had been painted lightly enough to allow sight to anyone standing behind it, it still muffled the sound.

Ias shook his head and waved his hand back and forth. The small man-child yelled back, his anger at the boiling point. The man pointed at Ias as if to say, *You have left me no choice*. The small man-child made a *come hither* gesture toward one of the ten cloaked figures. The figure threw back his cloak and produced a dark cobalt ball that looked as though it belonged on one of the pillars beside the orbs that had now been returned to their rightful places.

The man took the ball from the creature and held it high in the air. A large plume of dark blue smoke swirled about the room. Warrington's eyes widened; the scene reflected in his golden orbs.

The smoke started taking shape in the middle of the room: hands, feet, body and then head. A tall woman now stood in the center of the room as the smoke began to dissipate into a fine mist. Warrington's eyes were fixated on the woman who had entered the room in a most spectacular fashion.

Ias stood at the center of the room, while the woman paced around in circles, talking to her heart's content. The ten figures that stood at attention around the corners of the room backed away from the tall, black-haired woman as she passed by, almost as if they were afraid they would disappear into black smoke if she touched them.

She kept a long gold scepter at her side, tucked under her left armpit, the end in her hand. She pointed past Ias at the study. One of the cloaked figures started walking and then hesitated just long enough to think about what it was doing. Warrington could no longer see it as it passed beyond the archway into the study. There was a bright flash and then nothing. Warrington expected the creature to return, but it did not.

Nine creatures now stood around Ias, four to the left and five to the right. The woman pointed her scepter at another of the cloaked figures and then at the study. The cloaked figure shook its head back and forth. Warrington imagined that he was pleading with the woman, afraid he'd suffer the same fate as the previous creature. The woman patted the creature on the head and turned to pace around Ias again. Turning sharply, she pointed her scepter at the figure. Bright blue smoke streaked out of the cobalt ball embedded in the top of her scepter and hit the figure in the chest. Warrington could not see where the figure went as it was being thrown through the air, but he guessed the fireplace had enjoyed its first meal—perhaps not its last.

Warrington's heart was racing as he turned toward Eld, but there was no black cat to be seen. Warrington looked around frantically, but he was alone. The door was still closed and had not reopened since he and Eld had passed beyond its threshold. Warrington's eyes darted furtively around the room and then moved to the ceiling. Warrington caught a glimpse of something moving along the top ledge, fifteen feet above the floor.

Eld clutched the ledge tightly as he slunk along, trying to get a better look and to hear what was going on. Due to the lack of windows, the reading room was normally pitch black, although it was early in the day. The fireplace was the only source of light for the reading room, while the orbs lit the study, and Ias often used candles if he needed more luminosity.

Warrington could do nothing but watch Eld, as any noise would surely give away their position.

The woman stood directly in front of Ias, paying no heed to his personal space. She looked down into his eyes, her arm motioning to the study from where the first figure had still not returned, her voice muttering at an ever-hastening speed. Ias turned and walked toward the study. He returned with several of the pieces of parchment that Warrington had seen him writing on. He handed them over to the woman, who had tucked her scepter underneath her arm once more. She unrolled the parchment and leaned her head back. Warrington's ears flattened as the woman let out a piercing scream. She pointed the scepter at Ias' head.

Warrington caught sight of a small creature flying through the air. The creature that had been successful so many times before was now dangling in midair, suspended just inches away from the woman's scepter. Eld struggled to free himself, but there was no leeway in the invisible grip holding him.

The woman motioned to one of the figures to come forth. The figure did so quickly, as he had seen what the woman did to those who disobeyed her. He pulled a small cage from the ground and held it open. The black-haired sorceress looked back at Ias and pointed the scepter at him once more. Ias held out his staff in defense as she fired the blue smoke, shattering his staff. Ias fell to his knees in pain. The woman lifted Ias to his feet with her scepter, holding him in its grasp as blue smoke swirled around him. She threw her head back in laughter while pointing at the cage, which now contained Eld. Eld was yelling from what Warrington could make out.

Without so much as a glance, the woman made a slight gesture to the right with the scepter, and Ias flew against the wall. The woman shook her head back and forth. The small man took the scepter from the woman and waved the dark cobalt ball in the air. The blue smoke swirled around the room, and the woman, the small man-child, the eight remaining creatures, and Eld were gone. Warrington ran out the door and down the steps to Ias' side.

### '3.2'

Several cloaked figures entered the room as the door opened without the resistance it previously had. They quickly moved around Ias, their faces snarling and gnashing under their hoods. Ias recognized the rotten stench of Dyhedral before he even saw their faces. These were the same Dyhedral he had encountered many times before. In fact, he recognized the one that was limping from their encounter at the pile of rubble beneath the towers. He had severed the creature's leg, but it appeared as though it had already started to grow back.

When all ten had entered the room, a small man of about three feet—or ninety-one centimeters—entered, holding a trumpet. Ias put his hand behind his back and motioned for Eld to take Warrington to the safe room, where they would not find him.

"By order of the Dark Witch of the Eastern Keep, you are hereby ordered to relinquish all artifacts belonging to the Dark Witch," the small man said.

Ias laughed at him and shook his head without saying a word.

The tiny man glowered at Ias. "Do you know who I am and who I represent, sir?" he yelled in the direction of Ias' face.

"No, I do not, nor do I care," Ias said in a low, demeaning tone.

"I am Doorman Strauss, steward of the Eastern Keep. You'd best remember my name, sir," Strauss said, standing on his tip-toes in order to get closer to where Ias' face was.

Ias held up his hand and made a shooing gesture, brushing the little man away from him.

"Ooooh, you are in trouble, sir librarian. The witch will not like you disrespecting her steward in this manner. She will be here any minute. In fact, I will summon her now."

Strauss motioned to one of the Dyhedral, who was tightly grasping a small velvet bag under his cloak. Strauss violently grabbed the bag from the Dyhedral's hand. The Dyhedral snarled in disapproval and then retreated as Doorman Strauss glared at him from the corners of his black eyes.

Doorman Strauss reached deep inside the bag, retrieving a shiny, dark cobalt orb. He held the orb aloft, and black clouds swirled around the dark blue sky contained within this world. Smoke permeated the glass barrier of the orb and filled every inch of the reading room. The dark smoke thickened and then, as quickly as it was there, it was gone—the only reminder of its presence was a blue mist in the air.

Through the mist Ias saw a tall, beautiful woman standing before him, hair dark as the raven and skin white as freshly fallen snow, with bright aquamarine eyes that reminded Ias of the oceans of the world on a clear day. She wore a dark blue gown—the hem adorned with silver sequins that glittered as the flames' glow radiated off of them—that fell from her shoulders to the floor. A silver choker with a charm the shape of an upside-down black heart adorned her neck. A long golden scepter had appeared under the cobalt orb Doorman was holding, but now resided under her left arm. She walked toward Ias, her hair flowing like black silk. She walked up to Ias and looked down at him.

"So, you are Ias Kindle, librarian of the Library of Universal Fiction?" she said, circling him slowly.

Ias did not reply and stood still, not turning as she walked behind him.

"I have come for that which will allow me to crush the lands of Terra-Mirac. You will offer no resistance."

Ias looked up at the woman, who had now completed a full circle of him but continued circling the room's perimeter. "I am sorry, my lady, but I cannot give any of the items in the library to you. Anything that is checked in must be checked out. This place is protected, if you had not figured that out before now. I am afraid the master of the library is not here, and so I do not have permission to check out any objects here in the library," Ias said with a small grin on his face.

The woman turned sharply to face Ias. "You mean to tell me I cannot take anything here without the librarian checking it out? This is nonsense, you old fool. I am not one to ask for things, I simply take them," she said as she pointed to one of the cloaked figures. "You—go get me the black glass ball from the other, and be quick about it."

The cloaked figure walked into the study, passing by the desk. The lizard's scaly hand reached out to grasp the black orb as it glowed on the pillar, casting no light. The Dyhedral gripped the ball and lifted it into the air. The other nine, seeing this act, cackled. The creature started walking back but was stopped abruptly as the red carpet he walked upon ended. The creature snarled as his foot began to feel warm. Without further hesitation, the creature continued, and just as he crossed off the carpet, his body flashed bright with a crimson light and was gone. The ball dropped to the ground with a hollow glass clunk and rolled backward. Grey ash coated the air around the study and settled to the floor in a pile.

The room was as still as a cemetery until the woman spoke, finishing her thought. "So you won't give them and you won't check them out. There is always a way around these types of magical influences. You!" She pointed the scepter at another one of the Dyhedral. "The ball is on the floor and no longer a danger to anyone. Go and fetch it for me."

The creature came forward shaking his head. "Please, your highness. This place is cursed—I beg you not to send me to get the object of your desire," the creature said, pleading for his life, as his predecessor had not suffered a favorable fate.

"Well, if you don't want a reward, that is fine," she said, patting the creature on the top of his head, the point of his hood bouncing up and down with each pat. Hissing, the creature returned to his place in line. The woman walked forward then spun on her heals, scepter thrust outward. Blue smoke flew from the round head of the scepter, hitting the creature in the chest and sending him flying backward into the fireplace. The fireplace roared with delight as it consumed its first meal of flesh. Although fireplaces are not alive, they may—from time to time—enjoy the meals consumed inside of them.

*Eight left*, Ias thought to himself.

The witch, now quite enraged, walked straight up to Ias and stopped an inch from his nose. "You *will* get me those balls, or I will make your last few minutes in this library as torturous as possible. Do this with the utmost haste, as my patience has run out. Give me the artifacts that you have, and I will spare your life. You have no vested interest in who controls Terra-Mirac, so why resist? Now I will ask once more—politely … Please give me the items that I seek."

Her eyes were full of fire, but Ias knew that it was just the reflection of the now brightly burning carcass of the Dyhedral.

"One moment, my lady. I will be right back," Ias said calmly.

He walked into the study and pulled out seven pieces of parchment that bore his signature at the bottom and one that had two names on it: his and Warrington J. Cat's. Returning to the reading room, Ias handed seven of the pieces of parchment over to the Dark Witch. She looked quite pleased, but as she touched them, the writing on the parchment disappeared.

"What is this trickery? Are you making a fool of me?" the woman demanded. Ias held out the eighth parchment.

"Warrington J. Cat," she read aloud, "is hereby transferred to Head Librarian of the Library of Universal Fiction. All items leaving the library must do so under his authority. Upon his death, all items will be transferred to an undisclosed location under the authority of the Universal Library Master Librarian." She quit reading and scowled at Ias. "Who is this Warrington J. Cat and where can I find him?"

Ias stood silent refusing to answer, but cringed as the woman threw her head back and screamed loudly. "I have had enough of your games, you old fool." She took her scepter from under her arm and pointed it directly at Ias' forehead. "Tell me what I want to know, or I will dispatch you from this world."

Ias remained silent.

The Dark Witch made a sudden gesture to her right, and Ias waited for the scepter to come back down upon his head, ending his life, but it did not. He looked up and saw the scepter holding a small creature in midair. He recognized Eld immediately and shook his head back and forth. The Witch motioned to one of the Dyhedral to come to her side.

"Apparently, Warrington J. Cat is actually … a … cat?"

The furry black cat struggled to escape the invisible grip that had seized him in mid-leap. The Witch held out her hand over the Dyhedral's cloak, and a small cage formed from its thread.

"Open the door!" the Witch commanded.

Lowering her scepter—cat held just inches from the tip—she placed Eld in the cage and the Dyhedral closed the door.

"Now that we have the librarian, the library is ours. I am sure he will see to it that we have our pick of anything within the library walls."

"I'll never help you, witch," Eld said, scratching at the tailored bars.

"Oh my," the woman said, leaning over and peering in the cage. "How peculiar… a talking cat. Oh, you will do what I wish, Mr. Cat. We have ways of persuading one to do our bidding. In time, you will do what we want, and maybe even enjoy your new home. In the meantime, we have safe storage for our new possessions until they are needed. Take this cat back to the keep, where he will either help us—or suffer first, and then help us."

The creature fell back in line, cage in hand. Ias stood speechless; he could not say that they had the wrong cat, for that would surely bring a quick end to Eld's life. He hoped that there would be time to rescue him before the witch found out that Eld was not Warrington J. Cat, but just Lord Eldridge.

The witch stood up straight, cracking her neck bones from side to side. "Well, now that this incident has been sorted out, we'll be on our way." The witch turned to leave and then slowly turned around. "Oh yes … your payment for your services."

The witch held out her scepter and pointed it at Ias. Ias held out his staff in defense. A blue flame shot out of the scepter, shattering the staff into a million pieces. Ias fell to his knees in pain. Blue smoke swirled out of the scepter and wrapped tightly around Ias, lifting him into an upright stance.

The small man-child moved in front of the witch. He opened the parchment the witch handed to him and read aloud. "FOR SERVICES RENDERED TO THE DARK QUEEN OF THE EASTERN KEEP, YOUR PAYMENT IS THIRTY PIECES OF SILVER, PAYABLE ON DEATH!"

"Master Ias! Do something!" Eld cried out.

Ias felt the grip of the witch's scepter tightening around him. His eyes grew wide as the sensation of being lifted in the air consumed him. With a flick of her wrist, the witch moved the scepter upward into the air. Ias was lifted backward into the stone wall of the reading room with a loud crack. His body fell to the floor. Screaming in anguish, Eld tore at his cage. The small man-child walked over to Ias and threw thirty pieces of silver on top of his lifeless body. The witch then handed the scepter to the small man. He held the scepter with the cobalt orb high in the air—which from his height only came up to the witch's chest—and blue smoke filled the room once more. And just as suddenly as they were there, they were not.

## '4'

Warrington came rushing down the steps and through the secret door into the study. He ran past the black orb in the middle of the carpet and the pile of ash that had been the Dyhedral, ash swirling into the air in his wake.

"Master Ias!" Warrington yelled, coming upon his body in the reading room. There was no movement at first, but then Warrington noticed a faint twitch in his arm as he struggled to move.

"Warrington …" a weakened voice came from the near-lifeless body. "Warrington, come closer, there is not much time." Ias was struggling for each breath. "Do not worry for me, Warrington. This day came sooner than I thought, but not by much. I was already dying, Warrington. That is neither here nor there. What is important is that you listen to me. You are no longer the protector of the library, but the keeper. You are the librarian who is master over all. You now preside over this realm and must guard it with your life. The magic here is strong and will hold against anyone or anything that tries to remove books or any other objects from the library. The parchments that I wrote on after each trip into another world bound each of the objects I brought back with me to the library, and they are protected by its magic …"

Ias was choking as he struggled to get these last words out. Warrington sat still as Ias reached out and stroked his lavender and pink fur.

"Warrington …" Ias muttered, "Warrington, I will always be here with you …"

Warrington felt Ias' hand slide off his fur and to the stone floor. Warrington's eyes watered and a single tear fell to the ground.

A bright blue light suddenly surrounded them and a transparent figure appeared. "For the term served to the Universal Library, Ias Kindle, the Great Writer has granted you passage to the other side."

The figure reached out and grasped Ias' hand. Blue flames erupted around Ias, and Warrington jumped backward, shielding his eyes from the amazing blue glow. The flames grew larger and then quickly vanished. Warrington walked over to where Ias had been. Only a brown cloak remained.

Warrington lay down in the middle of the cloak—still fresh with Ias' scent—curled up, and went to sleep.

## Chapter 7

'1'

The next few mornings Warrington woke overwhelmed by grief. The cloak that lay at the back of the reading room was now covered in lavender hairs. Warrington got up and stretched. *Is this grief so great that it should take hold of my life?* he wondered over and over again. He was, after all, the keeper now. Warrington sauntered over to the fire that, even though no one was tending it, was still as much ablaze as it had been three nights ago.

"Well, I should go and get my mind off these terrible events and see if there is any work to do," he said aloud.

The door opened as it always had and the library was dark and silent as a library should be. The smell of damp, moist air engulfed his nostrils. The library seemed emptier than normal.

Warrington strutted down the corridors, looking for any signs of mice destroying that which he was now solely responsible for. Warrington ran down one corridor and up the next until he reached the back wall. He turned and saw the tapestry that was the doorway to the hall he had first entered with Ias, so long ago. The picture on it was the same, yet seemed somehow different. Warrington was staring at the weavings of the tapestry when he spied in the corner, near the throne of the queen, a small black cat. Warrington paused and thought, *Eld! How could I have forgotten about Eld?* Ias might be gone, but the Dark Witch had taken Eld with her. Warrington headed back toward the reading room.

"How am I going to save him? After all, I am just a cat. I have no way of getting anywhere." Warrington suddenly remembered the hat. "Is this what the hat was telling me? That I would leave the library in search of the White Castle and the queen that resides there? Where do I begin, though?" Warrington asked himself out loud.

"I could go back and ask the two men I met previously for help, but I doubt they'd want to help. One man said the queen doesn't exist ... But if the Dark Witch exists, then the White Queen must as well. I guess there is only one way to find out," Warrington said, heading for the study.

He walked across the archway, where the pile of dust was still sitting, waiting for someone to clean it up. Warrington jumped to the top of the desk, looking at the Witch's Eye. *So many witches*, Warrington thought. Warrington took a step back and crouched in the jumping position.

"Here goes nothing," Warrington said, taking off across the desk and jumping through the air.

Warrington crashed into the emerald ball and then fell to the floor. The pillar wobbled back and forth and then tilted towards him. The pillar tipped over and Warrington jumped out of the way, still trying to shake off the initial impact of his fall to the ground. The green orb landed on the desk and rolled off the front and across the floor, coming to rest in the pile of ashes, creating a barrier between the study and the reading room. Warrington looked at the Witch's Eye, frustrated.

"Stupid ball, why won't you work?"

Warrington walked over and paced around it. He was so focused on the ball while he was pacing that he started getting dizzy. The room started to spin and Warrington stumbled a bit. He looked down and shook his head. When he looked up, he was in the middle of a small cottage. The fireplace was empty, but the large purple chair with the high back was still where he remembered it. The teapot was sitting off to the left of a small wash bucket.

Warrington was back in the house of Theophilus, as his friend Marchavious had called him, but the sun was high in the sky and no one was home.

Warrington looked around the small shack—cottage was being generous—and saw a small round cap on a shelf.

"The hat shop," Warrington mumbled. "It is daytime—I am sure he is at the hat shop. Now I just need to find my way out of this dungeon."

'2'

Warrington walked through the small cottage in hopes of finding a window left ajar, but none were. He walked over to the fireplace and looked up at the dark stones covered in soot.

"This is going to be quite difficult to scale," he thought out loud. Then he thought better of it.

Warrington jumped to the back of the purple chair and glanced around the small, dark room. The sun was shining in through the window over the sink and onto the broom he had knocked over on his previous visit.

Warrington shifted on his back legs and jumped down to the floor with a thud. He ran full speed at the wash bucket. The bucket smashed into the broom, sending it spiraling upward and into the sink. The broom landed handle-first in the sink and was now leaning against the window. Warrington was disappointed that his plan—the broom shattering the glass—had not worked. His eyes widened as the broom slowly moved the window outward and open. Warrington realized he had not thought to check if the windows were unlocked but took no time to chastise himself as he jumped onto the ledge and down into the grass.

Free at last, Warrington hustled down the alleyway and onto the main street, which was crowded with revelers celebrating with ale and cheers. Warrington had no clue what was happening and did not care much, anyway. He weaved in and out of people's legs as he closed in on the hat shop. Warrington dodged quickly as people's feet moved back and forth; he kept his tail closely guarded to avoid it being stepped on and his presence becoming known. He was purple and pink and did not need the attention.

Warrington reached the edge of the excited crowd and broke free. This portion of the street was quite empty, and he could see the small hat shop at the corner of town, just on his side of the small bridge he had crossed over twice before.

Warrington looked inside the hat shop yet again. The window was still dirty, which made it hard to see, but he could hear raised voices coming from inside the small shop. He could barely make out four shapes inside: three at the back of the store moving about and one moving quickly toward the door. A man opened the door wide and strutted out and down the road toward the crowd of people that were still gathered in a mob-like fashion. As the man exited, the door had gotten stuck on a small rock and was consequently closing very slowly now, dragging the rock along with it. Warrington easily slipped inside and proceeded past the clothing to the register area, where the three men were arguing.

The tall man, whose head was all Warrington could see, was talking to Theo. "Theo, I just cannot give you another extension on your original loan. While you have paid me in good faith each month, I am afraid your shop needs to be shut down. Marchavious agrees with me. This shop is not making a profit, and I am sorry to say you have been short on your payment for the last time."

The handlebar mustache on his face moved back and forth with each word. He took his hand and twirled the end of it as he finished his sentence. Marchavious was standing off to the side not saying a word, just nodding in agreement.

"I'll tell you what, Theo ... You can continue your business here until I find another tenant. That way you can make some money before having to leave."

The man picked up a brown burlap sack off the front counter and handed a small bit of parchment to Theo before he left. He started to leave but turned to face Theo and Marchavious as he reached the door.

"Remember, Theo, once I find a tenant, you need to pack up and leave. If you are not out by then, the constable can come and help you move."

With that final word, the man opened the door, kicking the rock that was now in the store, and exited.

Marchavious put a hand on Theo's shoulder and muttered some words that Warrington could not hear. Warrington leapt onto the counter next to an old brass register that had a small "NO SALE" flag sticking up. Neither man noticed him sitting there.

"Excuse me," Warrington uttered, trying to get their attention.

The two men looked around, but saw nothing.

"Am I hearing things, Marchavious?" Theophilus asked with a panicked look on his face.

"Down here next to the big box on the counter," Warrington said impatiently.

The men looked around once again and saw nothing. Warrington grew impatient at their stupidity—how could they not see a bright lavender and pink striped cat on the counter? However, Warrington looked down and to his surprise ... he was not there. Well, his legs were not there, he thought to himself. The thought of not being there in the shop was most peculiar. Warrington turned to look at his tail, which he could see outlined in the sun, but like his legs, it also was not really there.

"Theophilus, I see an outline of something. It is quite vague, but it looks like a tail," Marchavious said, slowly reaching a hand out toward Warrington. Marchavious grasped at the air and was startled when Warrington yelled out.

"Hey! That's my tail!"

With that, Warrington appeared, sitting on the counter, lavender and pink stripes in all their glory.

"Another talking cat, Marchavious? Apparently, the first one was not enough. This one is much easier on the eyes, though. Purple and pink fur is much less scary than a hairless cat, I suppose."

Theophilus was bending down, peering at the cat that had appeared out of thin air.

"Another one," Warrington scoffed. "I am the same one. I grew this fur after our last meeting."

"Oh no, you do not, Sir Cat. That meeting never took place. Marchavious and I never saw a talking cat. That was just a hallucination brought on by a withdrawal I was having. In fact, it was so strong that Marchavious saw it too. Right, Marchavious?" Theo said, standing fully erect and facing Marchavious.

"No, Theo, I do believe that night happened. At the time I did not want to believe it, but here he is again. Are we dreaming now?" Marchavious said, putting his hand out slowly to touch the curiously colored cat.

"I am in shock, Marchavious, at losing my store, and I am seeing and hearing talking cats. Cats do not talk. They never have and I reckon they never will. Good day, Sir Cat, I have work to do."

Theo turned away from both the cat and Marchavious and walked into the back room. Marchavious reached out and scratched Warrington behind the ears, marveling at the magnificent cat in front of him.

"Please do not mind Theophilus; he has much on his mind. You must be here for a reason—am I right?"

Warrington nodded and told the story of the White Queen, the Dark Witch, and the library. Marchavious could not believe what he was hearing.

"My condolences, Master Warrington. It is hard to lose a loved one. I have lost many pets over the years and quite recently, my rabbit passed on. However, the story of the White Queen is quite old. I doubt she would still be around. I have never heard of this Dark Witch before. I doubt either of them would amount to pleasant company if the stories of the White Queen are true and the Dark Witch did as you said."

Warrington looked up at Marchavious. "You knew the story, though. It told how to get to her castle, right?"

"Yes, but we are not in a fictional land called Terra-Mirac. We are in England," Marchavious said, putting his elbows on the counter and propping up his head with his hands.

"Well, there must be a way there," Warrington said. "If the witch lives there and could get into the library, there may be a doorway in the great hallway that would lead us there."

"Hallway?" Marchavious asked.

Warrington did not reply, as he was suddenly deep in thought. He remembered seeing many doors; one of them must lead to this land. That is, unless the library itself was in Terra-Mirac and the Dark Witch and her minions had just walked through the front door. However, he doubted a library with such importance as the Library of Universal Fiction would reside in such a volatile land as this Terra-Mirac.

"Warrington? Are you in there, Sir Cat?" Marchavious said, tapping him on his back.

Warrington's mind returned to the present. "We must return to my library, Master Marchavious. There is a hallway with many doors and each opens to a different place. I am sure we can find one that allows us access to Terra-Mirac."

"Let me go and talk with Theo about this. He may think it in the realm of madness, but he might try to come with us. We can always use the extra help." Marchavious walked to the back of the store.

"Absolutely not!" said a loud voice from the back. "That is not a cat, and he is probably trying to trick us into selling our souls to him." Theo sounded irritated and flustered.

"Come now, Theo, what else have you got to do? Your store is being closed, and there is a good chance that the constable is going to be looking for you," Marchavious said, playing to Theo's paranoia.

"What do you mean 'looking for me', Marchavious? I've done nothing wrong."

"What about the other night at the tavern with his daughter? I'm pretty sure he's heard about that incident. You did, after all, get on the table and start singing to her after he'd told you specifically to stay away from her."

Marchavious was embellishing the story a little; Theo wouldn't notice, since he'd been quite drunk on ale at the time. He had slipped back into drinking since seeing a talking cat. Now the thought of losing his store and being arrested made him want a drink even more.

"Well, Theo, come on. We will come back if there is nothing to this story. We have nothing to lose and could possibly gain some gold if the stories of the White Queen are true," Marchavious lied, trying to get him to agree to the adventure.

"Okay, Marchavious, but I will only stand for being gone so long before I need to return. After all, the hats don't sell themselves, right? Well, they are quite marvelous and they do really sell themselves," Theo commented, walking out of the storeroom into the front of the store, Marchavious trailing behind.

"All right, Warrington, we'll help. Lead the way," Marchavious said, opening his arms up to the store as if to say 'look at me'.

## '3'

Warrington hopped down from the counter and proceeded to the front door. Marchavious and Theo were following him when Theo halted by the mirror and looked at the ratty nest of hair on his head.

"I need a hat if we are to go out. After all, they do indeed sell themselves."

Theo grabbed a tan hat with a black band. Tucked inside the band was a card that read, "In this style 10/6." The hat matched his hideous tan waistcoat and plaid pants. A tan bow tie made the outfit a bit more ridiculous than it needed to be.

Marchavious looked at this spectacle. "Take the price tag off. You look ridiculous."

"I need to leave it on so people know that it is indeed for sale. You never know when a customer is ready to buy," Theo said, ushering Marchavious and Warrington out the front door. Theo turned and twisted the key in the lock. He then tucked the key into the inside pocket of his waistcoat and turned to follow Warrington. The street was manageable, as the crowd of revelers from the earlier festivities had dispersed.

Warrington's pace quickened as they headed back to the small cottage, but Warrington had no clue how the three of them would get from there to the library. He had only traveled by ball once before, and then he was alone. The orb had a mind of its own and had transported him back to the library whenever it pleased. He wasn't even sure how *he* was going to get back, let alone the two men.

"Theophilus! Theophilus Hatmaker. Hold up, sir," a voice cried from behind the trio. Theo and Marchavious turned to see the constable running toward them, waving his billy club over his head. The constable's belly jiggled up and down as he ran toward the three companions.

"Theophilus, Mr. Grey told me you were late again on the rent. This does not bode well for you, sir. I have a good mind to take you in and make you serve time for your debt."

"Well, Mr. Constable, sir, Theophilus and I were just on our way to get Mr. Grey his money," Marchavious blurted out, cutting off Theo as he opened his mouth to speak.

"Oh good, Mr. Harbinger. I shall accompany you and collect the money myself so I can give it to Mr. Grey right away and clear this matter up. I would not want anything to stop you from getting the money to him tonight."

The constable was looking at Theo, inspecting his now sweaty face. The constable followed closely behind Marchavious and Theo but did not see the cat traveling ahead of them.

'4'

Theo stopped in front of his door and reached into his pocket. The dull brass house key clanked against the store key in his pocket as he fumbled nervously, eventually pulling both keys out at the same time.

Shadows were beginning to become quite long as the sun dipped low behind a building. "Hurry up, please, I haven't got all day. I need to get back. Martha hates it when I am late for supper," the constable said, obviously worried.

"You are going to pay Mr. Grey, right?" Marchavious questioned the constable as Theo finally inserted the key into the door and unlocked it. The door creaked open into the dark house. Warrington slipped in unnoticed and jumped to the counter near the window he had opened by mistake. His eyes glowed yellow in the dark. The constable walked in behind Marchavious and Theo.

"All right, I'll wait here while you get the money," the constable said, taking a seat at the kitchen table.

The room was growing darker by the minute. Marchavious lit a few candles as he followed Theo into the back. They returned in a moment with a small bag.

"Here it is, Constable. We only have shillings. Hope that's okay with you. It's quite a heavy sack," Marchavious said, plopping the drawstring bag on the table with a metallic clank as the change spread out in the bag to match the flat surface of the table.

"Oh, that'll do fine," the constable said, reaching over for the bag. His hand was around the top and pulling the bag toward him as his eyes caught two yellow marbles in the darkness to his left. The constable quickly stood up, billy club at his side. "No one move! You have a wild animal in your kitchen."

The eyes closed slightly, looking directly at the portly man, who was now paralyzed in fear. "I am not a wild animal, Constable," Warrington said to him.

The constable dropped the bag of change. The metal slugs Marchavious and Theo had put in the bag spilled onto the floor. Theo had been involved in a counterfeiting operation a year prior in order to keep his hat shop open. These slugs were given to the blacksmith in town to plate into pounds and then redistributed in his hat shop. The blacksmith would take a half cut of Theo's profits. Eventually, the blacksmith got greedy and wanted more, so Theo quit. The blacksmith was eventually killed for passing these fake coins to the wrong people. Theophilus had never been suspected and had remained in the clear. That was, until right now.

'5'

The constable, wary of the creature talking with him, kept his eyes focused on the yellow eyes as he bent down and picked up one of the slugs. His eyes shifted to the round object as he held it up. Not a single marking could be seen as the constable inspected it in the flickering candlelight.

"What is the meaning of this? What game are you two trying to play on me? You are both under arrest for passing illegal currency and keeping a non-domesticated animal without a permit," the constable said, making up the last rule, which he thought was quite clever.

"Now would be a great time for us to leave, Warrington," Marchavious said, looking over at the yellow eyes.

"Who are you talking to? Who else is in here? Out the door, both of you!" The constable took out his club and waved it at them. Theo started walking toward the door.

Warrington jumped to the table where the constable was just starting to follow Theo and Marchavious out the door. "Sorry—Constable, is it? I must insist, these two fellows are coming with me."

The constable stopped dead in his tracks. "Who said that? Show yourself!"

Warrington moved into the candlelight. "I am right here, you pompous windbag," Warrington said, looking to scare the constable into leaving.

The constable looked between Theo and Marchavious at the cat now sitting in the light, grinning from ear to ear.

"Peculiar," the constable slowly said aloud.

Warrington started to shimmer as the wind blew the candle, causing the flame to flicker back and forth and nearly go out.

"What are you looking at, Constable? Have you never seen the devil cat come to claim your soul?" Warrington said, moving closer to the constable, eyes now wide.

Warrington was laughing hysterically on the inside as he remembered how afraid Theophilus had been when he put his paws on Theo's hands and yelled. The constable backed up slowly and started for the door.

"Oh, it is time, and you have a long list of debts to pay yourself, Constable," Warrington muttered, jumping to the floor.

The constable's heavy boots clapped the floor as he backed away, heel, toe, heel, toe. Warrington let out a loud hiss and the constable backed into the door, fumbling to try and get it open. Marchavious rubbed his eyes as he watched Warrington start to fade out of sight. Marchavious grabbed Theo and darted toward the constable.

"No, you won't get my soul!" the constable yelled and pulled out his club, swinging it through the air. The club swung harmlessly through the air as Marchavious reached out and grabbed Warrington. Warrington felt the familiar tug at his belly and the sensation of being lifted backward into blackness. Marchavious grabbed Theo and just as the constable took another swing, all three—Marchavious, Theo and Warrington—were propelled backward into the dark abyss of time and space.

## Chapter 8

'1'

Theophilus had never liked traveling along the road by carriage, train, or foot. The hatmaker enjoyed the comfort of familiar surroundings. While this had been true most of his life, he was, unfortunately for him, also a pushover, making him very susceptible to the will of others. He was not a criminal mastermind, as his past would lead anyone to believe. Indeed, he made more trouble for himself by giving into the whims of others. Theophilus Hatmaker was just reflecting on his life from childhood to present as he crashed through the pane of glass and into the study. Theophilus hit the desk and went sprawling across the floor face-first into the pile of ashes, scattering them on the floor around him and completely covering his face. His hat rolled on its brim across the floor and then around in a circle—finally coming to rest, hole side down, as it ran into a chair leg.

Marchavious was still holding Warrington as he crashed through the barrier and hit the desk, which stopped him abruptly. He got up slowly looking around at the study, which looked nothing like the small cottage they'd just left.

"Do you mind?" Warrington said to Marchavious.

Marchavious had not yet realized that he was still holding the cat that had brought them into this new place. Marchavious released Warrington onto the top of the desk. Theophilus coughed as he stood up, face and shirt covered in grey powder. He brushed off his shirt and jacket as he looked around

"Where are we, Marchavious? This is most interesting indeed. I do not believe we are in the cottage anymore."

Marchavious was rubbing his back, as he was in a tremendous amount of pain from their entry into this new world. "I believe we are in a castle—at least, that is what I can guess from the stone walls and tapestries around this room."

"No, you are in my library," Warrington said, now acclimated to his surroundings.

He smiled as he saw Theo's face covered in the ash of the Dyhedral. Theo walked into the reading room, bent over to retrieve his top hat from the floor, brushed the dirt from the rim, and placed it back on top of his head. Marchavious walked around inspecting the room. He had reached the thirteen pillars when Warrington piped up from behind him.

"I would not get too close to those if I were you. They do no good and they seem to have a mind of their own."

Marchavious turned around and looked at Warrington. "Well, judging by your curiosity, or lack thereof, you know this place very well."

"This is home," Warrington said, tears nearly coming to his eyes.

While cats are not known to cry, somehow the Witch's Eye granted near-human qualities to the animal it chose: emotion, thought, feeling, and sense all became part of the animal. For Warrington, it was not really home without Ias and Eld, and he sat and thought about simpler times, when his scuffles with the rodents of unusual size were the only adventures he had.

"Well, what do we do now, Warrington? You have gotten us to this library of yours, and I must say it is quite small for holding books." Marchavious was being a bit sarcastic, as he could tell they'd only seen the study and reading room thus far.

"Now we find a way to get to wherever it is we need to go," Warrington said, jumping down off the desk and making his way into the reading room, where Theophilus had taken a spot on the couch near the fire after picking up his hat, which was now a strange green color.

Marchavious picked up a quill from the desk and stroked its feathers with two fingers. Warrington turned and glanced at him with a look of irritability that made him put it back immediately.

"I suppose we need to go to the tapestry at the back of the library. There is a doorway there that will lead us to a hallway where we should be able to get to Terra-Mirac—if it exists," Warrington said, jumping to the back of the couch where Theo sat, eyes closed. Warrington walked along the back of the couch toward Theo's head and sat near him, looking at Marchavious, who was standing in the doorway.

"The tapestry?" Marchavious inquired.

"Yes!" Warrington said, startling Theo, who jumped and then almost fell off the couch. "The tapestry is the doorway to the great hall where the doors are kept. If I understand correctly, there should be a doorway to Terra-Mirac."

Warrington was smiling at Theo, who was leaning forward, his head between his legs to calm his heart rate.

"Sir Cat, I would ask that you refrain from scaring me anymore. I don't think I have it in me to be scared. I am quite easily frightened," Theo remarked, watching Warrington hop off the couch and head toward the small door embedded in the larger door leading out of the reading room.

"Sorry, I just could not pass up the opportunity. I have found that playing around with people gives me great joy for some reason. I'm sorry, and I won't do it again."

Marchavious finally crossed the threshold from the study and entered the reading room. A smattering of dust covered a small apothecary table to the right where Theo had brushed the ash off his face and hair. Warrington was sitting near the small door, anxiously awaiting his companions. Marchavious walked over to Warrington and grabbed the large door's brass handle, its cold giving him a tingling sensation down his spine. He pulled on the handle, but it did not budge. Marchavious looked confused and pulled once more, but the large wooden door made no movement.

Warrington approached the small door, which opened for him, and he passed through. The door shut slowly and Warrington was alone. He could hear the muffled sounds of Marchavious on the other side, trying to open the door, but it did not give an inch.

"Warrington, the door is stuck. Is there a lock or latch that we need to undo before it will open?" Marchavious was panting between tugs at the door.

"I don't think so. I never use the big door; the small door has always opened for me."

Warrington walked up to the small door and it swung open. Theo stuck his head through the opening, knocking his hat off once more, and looked at Warrington, who was grinning on one side at the sight of Theo, poking through the doorway without his hat.

"Silly it is to see a man who needs a doorway that is quite a bit bigger," he said as Theo tried in vain to squeeze any other part of himself through this hole. Warrington backed up and the door closed on Theo's head with a *thunk*, forcibly pushing him back into the reading room.

*Ias had no trouble getting in and out of this door so why can these men not use it?* Warrington wondered. Warrington walked back toward the small door and it opened again. He walked through to see Theo rubbing his head where the door had hit him and Marchavious standing exactly where he'd been before—this time just looking at the door.

Warrington walked through the reading room to the study. Marchavious followed close behind. Walking over to the desk, Warrington leapt to the top. The desk had nothing on it except Ias' belongings. *Well, my belongings now*, Warrington thought, again feeling a tinge of grief.

"Marchavious, can you open these drawers and see if there is a parchment in one of them? I would do it, but I lack the required digit on my paw. I guess I *could* scoop my paw under and …" Warrington was rambling on and then continued, "but this will be faster. I have a feeling I know what's going on."

Marchavious rummaged through the desk: starting at the top left and continuing to pull drawers open until he finally got to the bottom right drawer, which contained the ink well and a small stack of tan parchment. Marchavious flipped through them and set them on the desk, frustrated.

"They are all blank, Warrington. This is getting us nowhere."

Warrington walked over and placed a paw on the corner of the parchment. Marchavious' eyes widened in amazement as ink filled in the words etched on the paper. The top parchment read, "Warrington J. Cat: Authorized Librarian," and then continued down with a list of regulations and rights. The one that caught the eye of Marchavious was article V.19.6, which read:

***Article 19.6:*** *No unauthorized personnel may enter or exit any part of the library without the express verbal or written permission of the librarian. All access is granted to the librarian herein. Access may not be granted upon duress of the librarian.*

Warrington looked up at Marchavious with his paw pointing to the top document—to the very line Marchavious was reading at that exact moment.

"Well, Sir Cat, it would appear we need your permission to leave the library. As absurd as that sounds, I am pretty sure only you can give permission to open the door."

Marchavious shook his head, thinking, *Our lives are in the hands of a cat? Ridiculous!* "Well, then shall we be on our way, Sir Librarian?" he said with mock respect for the title.

Warrington nodded his head. "Can you please return the parchment to the drawer? I would not want those documents getting into the wrong hands."

Marchavious grabbed the small stack and tucked them into the bottom drawer of the desk. He closed the drawer and followed Warrington to the door leading out of the reading room, hoping it would indeed open for him now.

Warrington wasn't sure what to say as he reached the door.

"Did you get this resolved?" Theo asked, now sitting on the couch again, his top hat tilted off to one side of his head.

"We did, Theo; now stand up and let's get moving. We are sitting here wasting time when there is adventure to be had."

Marchavious seemed to have a renewed gusto for this trip. Theo had the opposite feeling, as though he might never see his hat shop again.

'2'

"I give permission to Marchavious Harbinger of the town of Chester to leave the reading room and the library," Warrington said out loud, looking at the door and wondering if anything special would happen.

Marchavious reached for the handle and pulled, expecting resistance, but the door opened as though it had never given him a problem. Theo got up off the couch and followed Marchavious and Warrington as they exited. Theo did not want to be stuck once more, and Warrington had not given him permission to leave the reading room. Exiting the reading room, Warrington spied the lantern Ias used for guiding himself through the library.

"Grab the lantern there and twist the knob to the right, Theo."

Grabbing the lantern, Theo turned the knob and a small light arose from the center. Theo was amazed at this invention and wondered how it worked. "I could sell these—'Flameless Lanterns', I suppose I could call them. Safe to use and won't burn your cottage down."

Theo was talking out loud and had not noticed that Warrington and Marchavious were following the lit candles along the bookcases. Theophilus trotted down the aisle, hurrying to catch up. Theo turned the corner after Warrington and Marchavious and then made another right.

"Warrington, Marchavious—where are you two?" Theo said, looking down one aisle and then another.

A soft *Shhhh* replied from the next aisle. He walked to the aisle the sound had come from, held up his lantern, and saw two glowing eyes.

"Ah, Warrington, where did Marchavious go?" The glowing eyes in the lantern light gave only one reply—*Shhhhhhh.*

Theo began to wonder if he was being too loud when he heard the voice again. This time it sounded more like *hiiiiisssss* than *shhhhhh*. He walked forward and saw two more green glowing eyes appear behind the first two. Theo moved closer to inspect this strange occurrence. He thought maybe he was starting to see things. He was getting older, and his family did have a history of ocular degeneration. The eyes got bigger and, as if he were seeing things, another set of green eyes appeared in the faint lantern glow.

Theo began to shake a little, and the lantern hook made a rattling sound as he held the lantern out into the darkness. Theo could see this sound was irritating the eyes, as they went from curious round green globes to thin green and yellow slits. The six eyes began to approach Theo cautiously. Theo began to take steps backward, moving away from the six objects advancing toward him. Theo could hear the click-clack of nails as they scratched along the marble surface of the library floor. The faster he backed away, the faster the sound came—click-clack, click-clack. Four sounds were clicking and clacking in unison.

Theo backed up until he hit the back of a bookcase. The lantern showed bookcases on all four sides of him. There was nowhere to go except forward, and three pairs of eyes and the eerie click-clacking blocked that exit. The eyes stopped in unison with the clicking-clacking sound. His lantern rattled quicker as Theo trembled in fear. He held the lantern up to his face and the eyes could see his fear. Theo could now see something else in the dark that worried him just a bit more. Three sets of white jagged lines—one row on top and one below—shining in the light of the lantern. The click-clacking was replaced by a louder clacking sound as the two rows of jagged white lines became one solid line and then separated again.

Theo shut his eyes and cringed as the hissing sound came again. When he opened his eyes, there were only two sets of eyes. The jagged lines were now gone and the eyes were disappearing. The click-clack sound returned and was much faster, but the sound was getting fainter until finally the sound was but a whisper in the distance. Theo started walking forward, and a pair of yellow eyes appeared out of the darkness.

"Theo, you should try and keep up," the voice said out of the darkness.

Theo came forward and the light revealed a lavender and pink cat. Relieved, Theo removed a handkerchief from his jacket pocket and wiped his forehead, the damp moisture changing the white handkerchief to a greyish color. He put it back into his pocket and followed Warrington along the bookcases until they came upon a dark figure standing at the back of the library. The corner of this area was lit by the natural light coming from the very end of the hall from the open door that led to the courtyard.

Marchavious was looking behind the tapestry when Warrington and Theo arrived.

"I found him. He took a wrong turn and the rodents were having their fun with him," Warrington said, grinning widely and taking much pleasure in these events.

"Those were rodents? Just ordinary rodents, you say? I would have thought they were small bears or dogs. They were going to eat me." Theo was being dramatic, swinging his arms and the small lantern around in big circles.

"They would not have eaten you. They have a taste for paper, and while you are scrawny and pale, you do not have any other characteristics that would make them think you were a tasty book. They were probably wondering what intruder was interrupting their dinner. At best they would have taken a few nibbles and left." Warrington grinned at the thought of this as he said it. "They won't be back for a while, though, as one of them met a most unfortunate fate, and his friends were not going to stick around to share it."

Marchavious flung the tapestry from over him and put his hands on his hips.

"Well, it looks like we are stuck unless you know of a weird-shaped key that can open this. That is, assuming that the hole in the wall is indeed a keyhole," Marchavious said, looking around the tapestry for any sign of a seam in the rock that would indicate a doorway.

"Actually, I do believe there is a key. If anything, it would be in the reading room," Warrington said, thinking that if there was a key, it would be in Ias' cloak. "I'll go and fetch it," he said and took off down the corridor toward the reading room.

Theo and Marchavious continued inspecting the rock wall for any other signs of a doorway.

'3'

Warrington entered the reading room, where the cloak lay in the corner. He walked over and felt around for the key. His paw hit something hard in one of the pockets. He tucked his head under the cloak and opened it.

He dug his paw inside the pocket and pulled out the shape that was wrapped in a small piece of cloth. Warrington put it between his teeth and hurried out the door, down the corridor and back to the tapestry.

When Warrington arrived back at the tapestry, Marchavious and Theophilus were nowhere to be found. Warrington placed the key on the floor and pawed at the cloth. The cloth unfolded, revealing a small key with a small belt attached to it.

The key shone in the thin strip of light that lay across the marble floor. Warrington moved the key and noticed the small piece of cloth had writing on the inside of it. He patted the cloth with his paws and opened the cloth further to reveal a note that read:

*Dearest Warrington,*

> *If you have found this key, I am no longer with you and you are no doubt*
>
> *leaving the library. This key opens the door to the great hallway. Do not*
>
> *lose it, as there is only one. Whatever your task may be, remember your first*

*duty is the safety of the library and of each other. I may not have said it, but you and Eld were my family. Take care of each other at all costs.*

*Always,*

*Ias Kindle*

Warrington looked down at the key, placed his head against it, and began to sob. In this moment he knew he must rescue Eld and make the wrongs that had been committed right once more.

'4'

Marchavious and Theo walked in from the courtyard to see Warrington waiting by the tapestry. The small key was fastened to the belt around his neck. They noticed this brass key had a golden aura around it.

"All right, Warrington, are we ready to go?" Theo said, mesmerized by this glowing key not much bigger than a hatpin.

"I most certainly am," Warrington said, walking up to the rock wall.

He put his two paws against the wall as far up as he could. The key tugged at his neck as though a magnet was pulling it. The key slid into the hole, clicked, and then fell back at Warrington's neck.

Marchavious and Theo stepped backward as a bright yellow glow raced around the outside of the tapestry, forming one large rectangle. Theo covered his ears as the door ground open with the piercing sound of rock sliding against rock. The tapestry split in two down the middle, following the edge of both doors as they opened.

Marchavious' eyes widened as the walls opened into a hall unlike any he had ever seen or even read about. He squinted as the doors opened fully, the light in the hall bright from the glow of the chandelier. It had been a long time since Warrington had seen the hallway: almost five years had passed. The hallway was the same as it had always been: different doors separated by lit candles, chandelier still burning with an unnatural light.

Warrington, Marchavious, and Theo stepped through the open hole in the wall. The large wooden doors with the gold handles slammed shut behind them, echoing twice and falling from their ears. The hallway was quiet, and Marchavious marveled that he could not see either end.

Marchavious knelt down and peered into his reflection in the floor. He felt like he'd only been in the library for an hour, but the reflection in the marble floor of the hallway showed a beard on his face that would have taken a year or so to grow. "My goodness, my face looks like it's been a year since we left home, but it could only have been hours," Marchavious commented.

Theo glanced at Marchavious with a look of concern. "You have no hair on your face, Marchavious. You look as though you visited the barber yesterday."

Marchavious reached up and felt his face. It was smooth to the touch, but when he looked down he could still see the reflection of a much older man. "I must be seeing things; when I look down at my reflection in the floor, I can see my beard long and bushy. Look at yours, Theo."

Theo looked down and frowned at the sight of his reflection. "My goodness, no wonder I haven't sold any hats. I am hideous looking. Is my head really this big? It looks like someone filled it with air!" Theo said, looking up at Marchavious.

"You fool. Your head is fine; your reflection makes it look big," Marchavious said.

"Well, gentlemen, we should be getting on. I don't know how far this hallway goes or where the doorway is exactly. I just know it is here somewhere. Let's head right, and if that doesn't work, we'll come back and go to the left," Warrington said, motioning down the hallway with his paw.

The first door they came to contained no writing on its placard so they continued on. Each door looked different, but all appeared to be doorways to nowhere. Theo tried one of the doors, but it would not budge. The twentieth door they came to had *The Salesman* engraved on the placard, but the door (like many of the others) was locked when they tried opening it.

Theo noticed the wall starting to get darker and changing to a wood pattern. Doors began to get less frequent and there were no longer candles between each door. The floor began to look like a checker or chessboard, Theo thought.

The room grew dark, and all they could see was a small candle up ahead in the distance.

"Maybe we should turn back? We are obviously out of doors, and I cannot see anything in front of my face," Theo said, giving up hope of finding any end to this long hike down the hallway.

"Wait, I see another doorway," Warrington said, starting to run through the darkness.

Marchavious and Theo followed Warrington. Just as the hallway became pitch black, it was illuminated again at its end. It was not actually pitch black; the walls themselves were black. Theo turned and saw nothing but blackness filling the hallway behind them. Were they still in the hall, or had they walked through another magical doorway?

Warrington stopped at the small door that was just barely big enough for a normal-sized cat. A small golden placard on the front of this door read, "*Terra-Mirac Travelers.*"

"Well, I guess they were expecting us," Marchavious said with a hand on his chin.

"Or someone a bit smaller," Warrington added.

The three companions looked at this tiny door, wondering how they would ever get through. Warrington knew he could fit through without issue, but Marchavious and Theo would have a difficult time. Theo looked at the small door in wonder. The gold on the placard seemed to glisten, glowing in the darkness of the room.

"Well, this does not help us any. The door is much too small for me; I doubt Marchavious could fit through, and he is half my size," Theo said, walking over and bending at the waist to inspect the door a bit closer.

"Well, Warrington, maybe you should go through and see if there is another way in," Marchavious said hopefully. "I would hate for this to be where we part ways. I was so looking forward to adventure."

Warrington walked over to the door and arranged his neck in order to get the key into the hole. The key snapped in as it had for the previous door. This made Warrington happy since cats do not have thumbs, and so handling small objects with precision is almost impossible. The key went in and turned slowly, clicking as it did. Warrington crouched down to go through the door but was surprised at how large the doorway had gotten. He thought he was imagining that the door had grown to accommodate his size. He turned toward Marchavious, who had sat down at a small glass table off in the corner.

"Marchavious, I think the door has grown a little bit since it opened," Warrington said, looking back into the hallway that had just opened. It was dark and only a small pinpoint of light shone through at the other end.

Marchavious stood up and walked over to the doorway. He knelt down and looked at the opening. "Looks the same to me," he said. He began to stand to return to his table, but he noticed the doorway was moving with him. "I must be going crazy. I am imagining that the doorway is moving with me as I stand up."

Warrington, who had noticed this as well, was bobbing his head up and down as Marchavious stooped again … then stood again. Marchavious backed away from the doorway and it shrank back down to Warrington's height.

"Well, I guess if a cat can talk, a door can grow, right?" Marchavious said, sitting back down in the chair at the glass table. Theo was sitting there with his eyes closed and head back. His hat somehow stayed glued to his head.

## Chapter 9

'1'

Theo was rudely woken by a sharp pain in his side. His eyes opened and a blurry outline that looked like Marchavious was poking him in the left side of his rib cage.

"Get up, lazybones. We are leaving," Marchavious said, leaning over in Theo's face.

"Where are we going? Did Warrington find another way in? I feel like it's only been a few minutes," Theo said, yawning and stretching his arms.

"It has been only a few minutes. The door is a magical doorway, Theo," Marchavious said, standing back up.

"Oh, a magical doorway, you say? Well, I must be a talking cat then," Theo said sarcastically, closing his eyes once again. "Wake me up when you have found a way through that is not a magical doorway to nowhere."

Marchavious pushed Theo in the shoulder, spilling him backward out of the small rod-iron chair. Theo hit the ground with a thud, his hat now rolling around in a circle and landing on its brim. Theo stood up awkwardly and grabbed his hat from the floor. He looked it over and inspected its condition. Although it had no dust or dirt on it, Theo still brushed the brim in case there might have been something he could not see … anything that would make the hat less valuable.

"So how do you suppose we fit through the tiny magical doorway?" Theo said grumpily, putting his hat back on top of his head.

"Watch," said Marchavious, walking toward the doorway. He approached the door, and the small black opening climbed up the wall and adjusted to his height. Theo opened his mouth, so dumbfounded that no words came out. Talking cats aside, he was still trying to get used to the idea of a growing doorway. Theo walked over to where Marchavious was standing and the doorway grew to 185 centimeters.

"Some magical doorway—it forgot to make room for my hat, as I am not taking it off," Theo said to the doorway. The door instantly grew another 20 centimeters to compensate. "Well, that's more like it," Theo said, walking through the door and tipping his hat to it.

Theo stopped and turned around to see Warrington and Marchavious still standing in the hallway. "You two are coming, right? I am tired of being inside and would not mind a breath of fresh air. There *is* air in this place we are going to?"

Theo started to walk back toward the hallway. Marchavious walked forward and pushed him down the tunnel toward the distant light.

"Well, we cannot worry about that now. We'll breathe whatever they have when we get there. There are people there, and they have noses, I assume, so it would be safe to say there may be a bit of air or at least something breathable that will not harm us."

Marchavious continued pushing Theo down the hallway, not to keep him from turning back, but more because he could not see anything in front of him. Warrington was following the two shapes in the darkness as best he could. The light at the end of the tunnel was growing bigger and wider as they continued for what seemed like an hour into the darkness.

"I need a rest," Theo said, stopping abruptly. Marchavious bumped into his back, almost knocking them both over. "We have been walking forever, and it seems like the end of the tunnel is no closer than when we first started. The door from the hallway is only slightly farther away from us than when we first went through it. Maybe we're going the wrong way." Theo sat down and leaned against the darkness.

"Well, Theo, what do you want to happen?" Marchavious said, looking down at him.

"I want to get out of this hallway. I am getting claustrophobic being in here," Theo sighed. His companions looked at him blankly, without any alternatives to offer. Theo relented, realizing the only way out must be the way forward; he stood up and turned to continue toward their exit only to see that it had completely disappeared. The only light showing through the darkness now came from the doorway they had entered.

"Well, this is just great. You complained and our only way out has magically disappeared. Now we have to go back and see if there is another way," Marchavious said, annoyed at Theo's lack of backbone.

"We'll be okay. Let's just go back to the door and maybe the doorway has some other interesting ideas as to where we can go." Warrington turned and started walking toward the door with the two men behind him.

As the cat and two men approached the entrance, they could see what appeared to be sunlight coming through the doorway, the walls beginning to carve themselves into clear view out of the darkness. The closer they got, the wider it became, until it was a large tunnel entrance.

"This is not the way we came in," Theo whispered under his breath.

Marchavious put his hand up to the stone and then pulled it back. Theo and Warrington had stopped just up ahead. "Most peculiar that the walls are both cold and damp." He held his hand up and rubbed the wetness between his fingers. The moisture glistened off his hand as the light reflected off his skin.

Theo began to feel his feet turn cold from the water that had sprung seemingly from nowhere. He felt a sharp pain as Warrington scurried up his leg and onto his shoulder. Warrington's claws ripped into Theo's tan jacket, making small paw prints up its back. Theo shook as he jumped in a circle on one leg from the pain. Warrington held on tightly for the ride. Theo could feel small trickles of blood coming from the several tiny needle-sized holes in his leg.

"Dreadfully sorry, Master Theo—the water startled me," Warrington said, retracting his claws as Theo calmed down.

Marchavious was sloshing past them toward the opening. He stood and stared at the gaping mouth of the tunnel that had formed around them. The stone archway looked like the teeth of some enormous rock golem he had seen in a picture book once. His mother rarely let him look at such books, since they were considered nonsense.

"You will never grow a brain looking at those pictures, Marci," she would call after him. Marci was his nickname as a child, and he absolutely loathed the sound of his mother calling it. His friends mocked him and called him a ninny girl. They would dance around singing…

*Marci Hare, Marci Hare,*

*Give the boys a whirl.*

*Your mother used to have a boy*

*But made you a ninny girl.*

This continuous mocking followed him through his childhood until he got out of primary school. Once he started college, he never let any of his instructors shorten his name for fear that it would come back to haunt him. One day, during a study session, a friend had seen him walking across the quad.

"Marchavious!" he yelled, but Marchavious did not hear him. His friend sprinted across the quad, coming alongside him. "Hey Marci, did you not hear me calling you?"

Marchavious turned and punched him in the jaw knocking him to the ground. "My name is Marchavious!" he blurted out in anger, his fist cocked back and his eyes glowing like fire.

"Sorry, I didn't mean anything by it."

From that day the rumor spread that Marchavious Harbinger was as mad as a March Hare. Marchavious had heard the rumors quite a few times, but chose to ignore them.

'2'

"Marchavious, you okay?" Theo grabbed his shoulder and shook him slightly.

Marchavious turned to Theo. "Yeah, I'm all right, Theo." Marchavious looked up and saw that above the teeth of this monstrous tunnel mouth was a placard that read:

*Terra Mirac*

*(Wonderland)*

*Est. 42*

"Wonderland, huh? I guess if you think about the Latin, it is indeed a land of wonder," Marchavious marveled.

Marchavious could hear the water rushing off the edge of the tunnel but could not hear where it was going. Curiously, he walked to the edge of the tunnel and looked out.

Theo, seeing Marchavious stop, walked up beside him, wondering why they would not be leaving the tunnel sooner rather than later.

Marchavious had an expression of fear and wonder on his face as he looked toward the horizon at the expanse of sand ahead of him. There was sand as far as the eye could see, with no sign of vegetation in sight.

Theo peered over the edge of the tunnel down to where the water was going and clutched onto Marchavious immediately. Warrington clung onto Theo's shoulder to keep from falling off into the water.

"What are you doing, Theo?" Marchavious exclaimed, confused; his eyes had only been on the horizon. "Let me go, you nut!"

Theo pointed downward and then backed farther into the tunnel.

"Well, if that is not a sight to see. We must be a few hundred feet up," Marchavious said, leaning over and looking at what appeared from this height to be a small body of water below them. "Theo, come and have a look at this. I have never seen anything like this before. There's a massive ship floating down in the water beneath us."

Theo crawled on his hands and knees, disregarding the water soaking his extremities. He leaned over the side, his hands gripping the edge as tightly as he could.

"Well, I could almost reach the crow's nest if it floated just a bit more to the right. It's directly beneath us," Marchavious said, getting on his knees and looking over the edge as well. Warrington had climbed onto Theo's back, since his shoulders were slumped over the edge of the tunnel.

"Well, we have to get down somehow," Warrington interjected. "If it does come in this direction, it may be our only way down."

Theo laughed nervously at this thought. "You're joking, right? Even if we get down there, how would we get back up here?"

"Why would we want to get back up here?" Warrington said from Theo's back. "I do not think we should be coming back this way. There is probably a much better way home once we find a town or something, I would say."

Without a word of warning, Warrington was gone.

"Where did Warrington go? He was *just* here. I felt pressure on my left shoulder blade … and then—nothing. Oh golly, Marchavious—he jumped … and left us out here to die." Theo was panicking and rambling on nervously.

The water started to rise and rush faster by their legs. Marchavious stood up and looked around for Warrington.

"Well, would you look at that, Theo?" Marchavious said, pointing down a bit to where the water was falling over the edge.

Warrington was sitting on top of the ship's main mast, which was rocking left and right with the sway of the water below. Warrington was not a happy cat, as he was now considerably wet. "Alright, you two—your turn to jump. It's the only way down," Warrington said, holding on as the ship continued to rock.

Marchavious looked at the timing of the mast as it swung out from underneath the tunnel. He bent his knee in a running position, bracing himself for a good start. "You are not seriously thinking about jumping down there, are you?" Theo said, standing up. The water was now rushing around his calves.

"Only way down, dear boy. Come on, we can do it," Marchavious said cheerfully. "The adventure part has to begin somewhere. I cannot think of a better way to start ours than by jumping from a tunnel to the mast of a ship." Marchavious spit into his hand thinking it might help him avoid splinters if he slid down the mast.

"You know I am afraid of heights, Marchavious. I don't think I can do it," Theo said, backing away from the edge. The water seemed to be rising and rushing at a swifter pace.

"Alright, stay here then, Theo. Enjoy your swim back to the hallway if you can find it," Marchavious said, and with that he jumped.

Everything slowed as he left the lip of the tunnel. The ship's mast swayed back toward the tunnel and away from Marchavious. Changing directions again, the mast swayed back toward Marchavious as he fell. Warrington, now in the crow's nest, watched Marchavious fly through the air.

Gripping his hands around the mast, Marchavious suddenly felt as if he'd been hit with a cricket bat as the rest of his body collided midair into the ship's mast. Holding on tightly, he slid downward, splinters stabbing him in the legs. He came to a gradual stop inches from the floor of the crow's nest. Marchavious let go and dropped to the floor, his hands and legs stinging from the small wooden daggers embedded in his skin. As Marchavious began to pick these tiny jagged pieces of wood out of his hands, he heard Theo calling from above.

"Marchavious, did you make it?"

"Yes!"

Theo had lost sight of the ship as it drifted back under the tunnel. Theo was now struggling to keep his balance, as the rushing water was up to his knees and pushing him toward the edge. Theo continued to resist jumping and fought his way backwards against the current. He could feel the water continuing to rise and realized he would soon have no choice but to jump or swim out of the tunnel. Theo inched closer to the edge and looked over. He could see the lip of the crow's nest peeking through the cascading water. Marchavious and Warrington were yelling at Theo, but the rushing water was too loud and drowned out any sound from below.

The water seemed determined to push him out of the tunnel, and he struggled to keep his footing, as the floor became slippery and provided little traction for his boots to grab onto.

Theo paused to reflect on where the water was coming from. They had seen no rivers, streams, waterfalls or anything else that water could possibly come out of as they'd walked down the hallway.

Cold water reaching his groin area quickly snapped Theo's attention back to the present. He realized he probably did not have much time left to jump off the edge before the water swept him over, but jumping seemed suicidal to him.

He, of course, had had suicidal thoughts in the past—on mornings following nights of heavy drinking. *A drink right now would be a huge help in getting me to jump.* Theo looked out through the tunnel and braced himself. *I can do this. I am an eagle. I can fly higher than one,* he repeated in his head. But before Theo could move, the water swept him over the edge. Theo felt the massive stream of water pushing him downward towards what he believed to be certain death. Despite the fear of death, he waved his arms, trying to swim upward, sideways, or any way, but downward he went. He fell for what seemed an eternity, then plunged into the lake below.

Theo tried furiously to swim to the surface, but was continually pushed downward by the unseen force of the water above. The water was dark and murky, and Theo could make out nothing in the darkness. He gave one last push before he gave up and succumbed to the water's grip.

"Man overboard!" a voice rang out through the now darkened sky.

The ship's bell clang and rang furiously. Theo, having given up just seconds before, felt something hit him in the side, and he grabbed on for dear life. He could see nothing but dark water beneath him and grey sky above. Rain whipped at his face as massive waves smashed against the side of the vessel. Two large hands gripped him under his arms and hoisted him to the deck. He fell against the smooth wooden surface coughing violently. Theo heaved and vomited the water that had filled his lungs just moments before. The wooden deck was slick with a mixture of water and bile thanks to Theo, but he was just glad to be alive. Theo looked left and then right and felt his face collide with the wood where he then closed his eyes and drifted off to a restful slumber.

## '3'

Warrington and Marchavious sat in the crow's nest as the ship rocked back and forth, the water splashing into the wooden bowl as it drifted under the waterfall. Warrington was trying his hardest to not get hit by any of the liquid but was hugely unsuccessful in his attempt.

Water started coming down faster and in a thicker stream—indeed, more and more water was rushing off the edge of the tunnel.

"Theo, you need to jump now! There is too much water!" Marchavious' words fell on deaf ears, as the water had already overtaken Theo.

Marchavious stood and reached out a hand to catch him, but Theo was swept away in the massive surge of water that poured over the edge. Marchavious leaned over the side and saw Theo disappear into the blue mass below.

Marchavious jumped out of the crow's nest and onto the shroud below. Water from the tunnel was being blown horizontally by the wind. Marchavious felt like he was in a typhoon as he climbed the shroud to the ratline.

Jumping down several feet to the deck, he began shouting, "Man overboard!"

The deck bell started ringing furiously and several sailors came rushing onto the deck in an orderly fashion. One of the men yelled something, but it was lost in the wind and rain pelting Marchavious in the face. Warrington was sitting on the Lubber's Hole looking down at the frantic but organized movement of the men below.

A large man at the railing was pointing and yelling; he grabbed a life preserver from the side and heaved it over the railing. Six of the large sailors in striped shirts started tugging on the rope, heaving and hoeing their catch toward the ship. A man in a blue jacket ran over and pointed toward the water, yelling at the black-striped-shirted man to help the one in the red striped shirt. They leaned over the rail, muscles flexing, and hoisted up a motionless but breathing figure. The man pointed to something else in the water and then to another red-shirted man. This man moved swiftly to the edge and dipped the gaff hook into the water and pulled out a top hat—its price tag still attached to the band.

They dragged Theo over to the center of the deck. Marchavious was wondering if he was still alive when he saw him arch his back and vomit a concoction onto the deck.

Warrington and Marchavious ran over and leaned down next to Theo, but he was already face down on the deck, unconscious.

'4'

Just as suddenly as the storm had started when they had gotten on the ship, it stopped. The sky that had gone from blue to grey was once again a perfect shade of azure. Two of the red-striped shirt sailors with log-sized arms picked up Theo and carried him through a large door and below deck. The man in the blue coat and captain's chapeaux stomped his boots against the wooden planks of the deck as he moved toward them, coat dripping heavily from the hard rain. His face was old and grizzled, with many scars. Marchavious looked up to see a brown leather belt with a scabbard hanging off the left side of it.

"What do ya think ye be doin' stowin away on me vessel?" he demanded in a raspy voice, looking at Marchavious.

"We were not stowing away on your ship, sir. We actually just arrived from the tunnel above your ship," Warrington said, sitting down next to Marchavious and looking up at the man with white hair covering his face.

"The tunnel above me vessel? There be nothing but blue skies smiling at me. Wait a minute … did ye talk, ya furry feline?" The captain looked at Warrington, bewildered.

"Yes sir, I did. Warrington J. Cat, head of the Library—" Warrington started to say but was interrupted by the captain.

"Talking cats! This is a special day indeed, for I saw another pass by me ship just a while ago. Ye wouldn't be related per chance?" The captain reached up and scratched his beard.

"You saw another talking cat? How long ago?" Warrington's eyes grew large with intrigue at this news.

"Oh, right before ye both showed up stowin' away on me vessel. Twas' a royal ship with a black upside down heart with crimson sails be travellin' the ocean out here. Looked a dark evil so we tried to stay a distance. They came alongside and one cloaked hand asked for directions to the northern shores of Heartwick. I reckon they headed at that bearing, but they be long gone by now." The captain removed his hat and ran his fingers through what little hair he had.

"Long gone?" Marchavious inquired. "You said they passed by just before we got here."

"Yar, they did. Twas' not more than a year ago now, I recall." The captain looked toward a small figure coming towards him. A small boy wearing a blue striped shirt handed the item fished out of the water with the gaff hook to the captain.

"Yar, this be a fine spectacle of a top piece. Your friend's, I suppose?" The captain stuck his face inside and breathed in deeply.

"Well, no sir … Well, I mean … I guess it is … I am not sure. A hat for sale has no owner. That is what Theophilus said," Warrington rambled. "He is a hatmaker and that is his last hat. He is trying to sell it, but has not been successful."

"Well, I would give him a bottle cap and three sand dollars for it," the captain said, patting his pockets as though he had money.

"I do not think that he would much care for things of those sort, Captain … um … Captain …" Marchavious trailed off. "I am sorry, Captain, how rude of me. I am Marchavious Harbinger. Our friend whom you have down below is Theophilus Hatmaker, as his profession states."

"Well, I am Captain Santiago Manolin. That which you stand upon is *The Hemingway*—my one true love. The sea and her sway are a close second." The captain took his hat off and placed it upon his chest.

"Well, Captain Santiago, we really should get Theophilus and be on our way since our friend passed by over a year ago," Marchavious said as he began walking toward the doors that led beneath the deck.

"Yar. Wait a sec, ye scallywag. We still have not discussed the crime that hath been committed here. Stowin' away on me vessel is not something I take lightly," the captain said, pointing to the two sailors standing by the door. "Let's go down below deck and talk about your indiscretions and see if we cannot come to an understandin' about this."

The guards grabbed Marchavious by the arms, and he went along willingly. Warrington followed close behind and down the stairs.

## '5'

Theo was looking around as he lay on the small bunk that was afforded to him after he fell into the water. He wondered where he was and how he had gotten there. His memory was quite foggy. Theo sat up on the edge of the bed and felt nauseous.

The door to the room burst open, almost hitting Theo, and a hulking sailor grabbed him by the arm and lifted him to his feet.

"What are you doing? I demand you take your hands off me. Where am I?" Theo pleaded as the sailor dragged him down the interior of the ship toward the galley, but the sailor said nothing.

Yanking the door open, the sailor thrust Theo through it without a word and then slammed the door in his face as Theo turned and banged on the inside of the door. He tried to pull and turn the handle, but it did not move.

"Theo," Marchavious whispered. Theo turned around slowly to see Marchavious sitting at the table with Warrington in the seat next to him. Captain Santiago had taken the seat at the far end, where he normally dined alone.

"Theo, come and take your seat and quit acting like a fool," Marchavious scolded him in a low whisper.

Theo walked toward the empty chair, pulled it out and sat down.

The galley was a simple room with an eight-foot long table at the center, adorned with all manner of exotic-looking food. A candelabra sat in the center, marking the halfway point of the table. Theo adjusted himself to the table and took his napkin off the plate in front of him that shone with a golden glitter. Theo tucked the red napkin into the top of his shirt. He was still a bit damp from his excursion into the water, but he ignored it in favor of the feast before him.

"Well, now that we are all here, Mr. Theo, can you please tell me how you three came to be on my ship?" the captain said, reaching for what Marchavious thought looked like a four-legged turkey. Theo reached out his hand for a piece of what appeared to be pork when a hand slapped his.

"Ye shall not eat unless de captain gives de order," the sailor hiding in the darkness said. Theo rubbed his hand as it began to glow bright red. "You will answer de captain's question, stowaway, or ye see our cat of nine tails," the sailor added with a grin that Theo thought looked similar to the one Warrington often wore.

"You have a cat with nine tails? How coincidental, our cat talks! We get these two together and we can put on a carnival," Theo said, looking around the room, but no one said anything. "Well, Captain, to tell you the truth, I do not quite remember how I got here. I am not even sure where here is. I thought maybe I had dreamed the talking cat up in my mind, but here he sits across the table. Honestly, the last thing I remember is a tunnel."

"Well, that is a point for your friends' story. However, a tunnel in the sky above my vessel makes about as much sense as a talking feline, yet I have seen two. The cat on the other ship was in a cage swinging from the yardarm. I asked why they be having a cat in a cage, but the cloaked deckhand just hissed at me and waved the ship's navigator in the direction I sent them. The feline was asking for water, but we had none. We only get fresh water when we hit dry land, which is not very often, so the water we have needs to be rationed." Captain Santiago took a large bite of his leg of animal.

"Captain, there is land all around us," Theo interjected as the Captain was chewing.

"What? We've run aground? Why did ye scurvy swine not tell me sooner?" The captain spit as he stood up in a panic.

The large sailor appeared out of the darkness. "I assure you, Captain Santiago, we have not run aground. See for yourself."

The captain looked out the window behind him and saw the water surrounding the bottom of the ship. He let out a big sigh and frowned at Theo. "My friend, you must have swallowed more water than I thought. Your brain is playing tricks on you. There is water all around me vessel."

Captain Santiago sat back down in his chair and picked up his meat once again. Theo looked at Warrington and then Marchavious. Marchavious shrugged his shoulders and whispered something that was inaudible to anyone at the table besides Theo.

The captain looked over at the two men, who were speaking closely. "Secrets? Secrets! Ye would tell secrets at me table on me ship? Ye two be setting yourselves up for walking da plank. I digress, though. Back to the current charges of ye three bein' stowed away on me ship. From the sounds of yer story, ye did indeed fall from a tunnel into me ship, but then the tunnel disappeared if I understand ye correctly."

Theo nodded his head in unison with Marchavious at this. Warrington was busy looking at the cooked meat on the large silver platter in front of him. He licked his chops and drooled at the wondrous sight of it. It had been a few days since he had eaten anything of substance.

"Excuse me, Captain Santiago. I do not mean to interrupt the conversation, but might I partake of some of the food on the table? I have not eaten for a few days now."

The captain put down his meat and stuck out his hand. He made two gestures to the right and picked his meat up again. The sailor from the shadows came over and picked up a piece of meat from the captain's side of the table and put it on Warrington's plate.

"Thank you, Captain Santiago," Warrington said and began to eat.

Theo was starving and seeing this as an invitation, stuck out his hand toward the plate in front of him. The hand that had slapped his before came down once again. Theo did not even see the man who had been standing behind Warrington move. His hand throbbed as he pulled it back.

The sailor repeated himself, "Ye shall not eat unless de captain gives de order."

"Well, Captain, may I have some of the food in front of me? I am starving, as well," Theo said, looking down at the table.

"Ye may, Theo. That is, if ye can get some." The captain let out a hearty laugh.

Theo saw no humor in this, as he was hungry. He reached out and grabbed for a piece of the meat. His hand passed through the meat and came out the other side. Theo noticed a large chunk was missing from the other side where it had not been missing before. Marchavious was looking at Theo as though he had just seen a ghost.

"Captain, why can I not grab the food? I see the food, but it eludes my grasp."

"Maybe the food deems ye not worthy of its touch or does not wish to be eatin' by the likes of ye." The captain laughed again, tearing off a piece of meat from his side of the table.

Theo noticed that the meat in front of him was missing another piece. Warrington noticed very little of these events, as he was enjoying the meat on his plate. Theo put out his hand and brushed it over all the food in his reach, but disturbed none of it.

"Now Master Theo and Master Marchavious, since ye be stowin away on me vessel now, I find you both guilty of these charges regardless of the mysterious tunnel ye be comin' out of. The plank ye shall be walkin' this day." The captain stood up and pointed to Theo and Marchavious. Four sailors appeared from the darkness around the room and grabbed them by their arms. "Take them topside and prepare them for a watery grave," the captain ordered.

"What about Warrington?" Marchavious said, struggling with the two sailors dragging him backward.

"Thee talking cat be me good luck charm now. He can stay aboard and enjoy his days as long as he likes."

Warrington did not like the sound of this. "Sir, I am on a quest to save my friend. I really cannot stay."

"Oh, ye will stay, as there be no land for you to run to."

The captain laughed as he pushed in his chair and walked toward the door. Warrington quickly followed him up the stairs to the top of the deck, where the sailors had Theo and Marchavious. One of the sailors with a black-striped shirt kicked his foot against the starboard railing. The wooden plank fell with a vibrato.

Santiago opened the door and stood on the port side of the poop deck overlooking the ship. "Now, any last requests before ye be fish food?" he yelled loudly. The crew on deck laughed out loud, as if they knew no request would be granted.

Theo raised his hand and said, "Captain, I have a request. I brought a hat with me, and it appears that I have not gotten it back. I would very much appreciate it if the hat was returned to me."

"Ye wants yer hat back?" the captain yelled to the crew. The crew cheered and then laughed.

"It is not my hat. It belongs to no one, but I must take it with me. You never know when someone wants to buy a hat such as that," Theo said matter-of-factly.

"Well, gentlemen, give this man what he wants."

The small deck boy ran through the crowd, pushing and shoving his way to the front. "Here is your hat, sir."

The boy of no more than twelve lifted the hat up. Before Theo could take it, one of the sailors grabbed it and held it aloft.

"I almost forgot, I bought this hat for the price of one saved life," Santiago said, laughing and gesturing to the sailor to move the prisoners into position.

The sailor moved Theo and Marchavious out onto the plank. The sailor with Theo's hat put it at the end of the gaff hook and waved it out over the edge of the boat, taunting Theo.

The captain yelled out over the ship, "For the crime of stowing away on me vessel, I hereby order ye to walk the plank!"

Theo, seeing his hat close enough to grab, jumped off the side, reaching out. His hand almost closed around the brim, but he felt the soft material slide through his fingers as gravity carried him toward the water. Marchavious watched the sailor lift the hat just in time to make Theo miss. There was a large splash down below, and Theo was gone.

Marchavious quickly leapt into the water after him, and the crew let out a loud cheer.

"Set sail for the mainland," the captain ordered, and the men dispersed to their positions. The sailor stuck the gaff hook in a small hole on the railing with the hat still fixed in the top.

## Chapter 10

'1'

Warrington sat on the railing, watching the water for any signs of Theo and Marchavious down below, when the ship started to pivot to the port side. Warrington ran to the poop deck to see if Marchavious and Theo were still in the murky water. His eyes widened as he spied two figures climbing onto the beach not more than fifty yards from the ship. Warrington looked to see where Captain Santiago had gone but could not see him anywhere.

Warrington jumped to the deck toward where the hat was still perched on the gaff hook. He walked along the railing and looked up at the hat that tilted and swayed in the wind that was now catching the sail and turning them back to the starboard side. Warrington reached up and tried to knock the hat off with his paw but was unsuccessful.

"You! Cat! Get away from there," a voice bellowed in the crowd of chaos that was the crew preparing the ship for departure. Warrington looked to his left to see a large sailor with a black shirt coming toward him. Warrington, knowing he had to act quickly, jumped upward, knocking the hat into the air. The grey top hat floated upward as the wind took hold of it. Warrington felt as though he were floating alongside it. The sailor reached out to grab Warrington, but the cat disappeared right before his eyes. The sailor shook his head back and forth, as though he were seeing things. There was no sign of any splash in the water, but the cat was gone and he had no explanation as to why. Warrington clutched the side of the railing and wondered why the sailor had given up pursuit.

The sailor turned as he heard the captain shouting.

"What happened to me cat, you scurvy infested dog?"

The sailor shrugged his shoulders and pointed to the water. The captain pointed to a red-striped sailor and brought his finger across his neck in a throat-slitting gesture. This sailor reached down into the empty sheath at his side and pulled out what appeared to be ... a handful of nothing. He held his hand out as though he had a sword within his grasp, walked to within a few feet of the black-striped sailor, and thrust out his arm. The sailor doubled over as though the invisible blade had run him through. The sailor's shirt began to smoke and formed the tip of the sword the other sailor had just used on him. He slowly disappeared into fumes, and the shape of the blade appeared in the red-striped sailor's hand. The sword disappeared once again from the sailor's hand and his red stripes turned black, as though he had just absorbed the other man.

Warrington sat on the railing and noticed at that moment that all of the sailors appeared to be the same man wearing different-colored striped shirts. Each one bore a striking resemblance to the captain himself, only at various ages of life.

Warrington sat on the railing, wondering how he could possibly get to Theophilus and Marchavious without getting wet. Since he was no longer being chased by sailors, and the ship was going nowhere—it just rocked back and forth regardless of the sails being full and the wind blowing—he knew he could take his time. However, he worried that the sailors would eventually notice him sitting on the railing and take him to a more secure facility.

Warrington could see the hat still floating in the wind and drifting over what the captain called an ocean. The hat would dip close to the water and then be propelled upward by a gust of wind that appeared to be having a good time playing with the hat.

Warrington followed the hat with his eyes until he was looking straight down. He noticed that he was actually not there; he had turned invisible while floating in midair with the hat. He wondered how long he would stay invisible, as it seemed to happen at random intervals.

Warrington looked out across the water to the shore, where Marchavious and Theo were standing. They were moving their hands in wide gestures, and it appeared that they were, without a doubt, devising a way to rescue him. Warrington, thinking he would be there a while if those two were coming up with a rescue plot, started looking for a way off the ship.

Two of the sailors were stowing a yard of rope when Warrington saw the captain go through the door that led below deck. Seizing the opportunity but not knowing for sure if it would work, Warrington yelled out to the sailors in his best captain's voice.

"You! And you! Ready the dinghy. Do not ask why; just do it, and then go below deck and polish the brass." Warrington sounded amazingly like Captain Santiago.

The sailors stood up immediately and without question readied the dinghy to be lowered into the water. Warrington ran toward the dinghy and jumped inside. The sailors looked at it strangely as it swayed back and forth from Warrington's jump, but continued working.

After pushing the dinghy out over the edge, the sailors began lowering it to the water below. Warrington, still invisible, waved good-bye to the two sailors and the ship as his head lowered past the railing and down the side of the ship.

"What in Davy Jones' locker are you two doing with my dinghy?" the captain yelled, and the two men dropped what they were doing and stood at attention.

The ropes sped hastily through the rigging as the dinghy and Warrington fell through the air and crashed into the water below with a splash. Warrington stumbled as the force of the blow knocked him over. He stood up and shook his head back and forth, dizzy from the fall.

"My dinghy!" the captain yelled, looking over the side of the boat. "And my cat!" Captain Santiago was now pointing toward Warrington and yelling at the sailors. "Pull up the dinghy now or I will run ye through with yer own cutlasses."

Warrington could feel the sailors tugging on the rope at the top as he began to stumble from the jerking of the ropes. He looked down and noticed he was very much visible and began to think of a plan that did not require going back to the ship.

Moving quickly, Warrington clawed at the rope attached to the bow of the dinghy. His claws cut quickly through the soft fiber, but the sailors with the large muscles were pulling with much haste. Warrington's claws cut the final strand and the rope snapped, sending one of the sailors to the deck of the ship.

The bow of the dinghy dropped sharply and unexpectedly, and Warrington was suddenly floating in the air and then falling downward with the boat. Warrington reached out and grabbed onto the bow, which was now pointing to the ocean's surface.

Warrington swung back and forth with the small vessel and then climbed up the dinghy to the stern. Standing on the stern of the boat, he clawed furiously at the remaining rope. Halfway up, Warrington could hear the sounds of the strands cracking under the strain. Another quarter of the way up there was but a thread left, and Warrington could feel freedom just seconds away.

The thread snapped and Warrington waved once again at Captain Santiago as he plummeted downward, free from the ship. Warrington felt the wind in his fur as he rode the dinghy down. Warrington started to worry as the dinghy slowly rotated in the opposite direction. The feeling of wind in his fur soon changed to wetness as he and the dinghy plunged into the murky water. The dinghy sunk into the water and then bounced back up, tossing him into the air as it surfaced.

Warrington came back down into the water once more—something he'd been trying to avoid altogether by having the sailors lower the dinghy. Knowing he was out of luck, as the dinghy was now floating upside down next to the ship, Warrington began to swim in the direction of Theo and Marchavious, who were still standing on the beach discussing their rescue mission.

"Forget him, he'll be shark food by the time he makes landfall at that pace. You two have a date with me saber," the captain said.

Behind him, Warrington could hear the captain yelling, followed by sailors screaming. Warrington did not care, though, since he was almost to the beach and no sharks were going to eat him in these waters.

When Warrington washed up on the shore of the beach that faced the starboard side of the ship, Theo and Marchavious were arguing about who was the strongest swimmer. Theo had been on the swim team during their years in college, but his confidence—or lack thereof—told him Marchavious should be the one to go and rescue Warrington from Captain Santiago and his table of food that was not really there.

Marchavious, however, did not agree. "Just swim out there and grab Warrington and bring him back. It is that simple. I doubt anyone would even notice you were there," Marchavious said, not noticing the soaking wet cat that had just walked up behind them.

"I would notice," Warrington said, giving Theo a fright.

"Oh good, now neither of us needs to go. I was just about to go and rescue you," Marchavious said to Warrington.

"You mean I was!" Theo said, thumb pointing at his chest and trying not to laugh at the sight of the sopping wet cat.

"Well, the important thing is that you are safe and we are off that ship and on dry land," Marchavious said, looking over at Warrington.

The three companions looked out at the ship and watched storm clouds begin to form over the topmast. Heavy rains started pouring down over the top of the ship as the captain began to bark orders at the crew. Marchavious looked up and noticed the faint outline of a small tunnel just over the main mast.

'2'

"Well, we should start heading north to Heartwick. It was north, right? Or was it east? The Dark Witch lives to the east, so why would she head north?" Marchavious was thinking out loud while they began walking down the beach. Small waves lapped at Theo and Marchavious' heels, while Warrington walked farther up the beach, away from the water, to avoid getting wetter than he already was.

"Well, the captain said the northern shores of Heartwick. Maybe that is the easternmost landing," Marchavious said, talking to himself.

Theo just looked at him, baffled, since he was not privy to the conversation they had had while he was unconscious.

"Heartwick?" Theo said. "Sounds like a splendid place to spend a night and get some sleep. I feel like I have been awake for days. So which way is north?" Theo was looking around him for any sign he might see.

"Well, the captain pointed toward the way we are going, so I assume we should keep heading in this direction," Marchavious said, pointing down the beach.

"And what happens when we cannot see the beach anymore?" Warrington said, looking over the first dune at the expanse of endless desert.

"Good point, Warrington. Well, I do have a trick or two up my sleeve that might help us. I saw an old trail guide use this method. Theo, give me the lid to your tin," Marchavious said with his hand out toward Theo.

Theo pulled out a small tin he used to keep various items like tobacco in. He took the lid off and handed it over to Marchavious.

"Now give me one of the pins you keep on you for attaching the tags to your hat."

Theo looked at Marchavious. "Speaking of hats, do you know where the one I was wearing went to? I have not seen it since we were on the boat." Theo was looking over at the boat once again.

"The captain took a liking to your hat. He probably still has it," Marchavious said, turning and cupping a hand over his eye to see if he could spot the captain and any hat he might be wearing.

"Well, he owes me six shillings, then," Theo said, walking a little way into the water.

"Oh, *now* you will go to the ship and confront the captain over a hat, but if I am stuck on the ship, you would rather argue than rescue me?" Warrington said, offended.

"Well, it's the principle of the matter," Theo said, walking back to the sand.

"No matter," Warrington said. "What's done is done. Besides, I knocked your hat into the water during my escape. It's probably at the bottom of the small pond by now. I guess we are even."

Theo stood with his mouth open, unable to say anything.

"Theo, a pin if you will," Marchavious said, breaking the tension.

"Oh yes," Theo said, reaching into his pocket and pulling out a small case with several small pins. He opened the lid and took one out, handing it to Marchavious. The pin gleamed in the sunlight as it exchanged hands. Marchavious walked closer to the water and bent over, scooping some water into the tin lid. Marchavious dropped the small pin in the middle of the lid now full of seawater. Floating on the surface, the pin spun in circles counter-clockwise, slowed down, and then stopped, pointing in a single direction.

"There we go—that is our heading, if I am not mistaken. I would get into the science, but I would rather not," Marchavious said, moving down the beach once more. Theo and Warrington followed close behind.

The end of the beach was quickly closing in upon them when Marchavious spotted an oddly shaped object floating in and out of the shoreline.

"Theo, is that your hat on the shoreline there?" Marchavious said, pointing to the grey object that had just come to rest on the beach, barely out of reach of the receding tidal waters.

"I do believe it is," Theo said with gusto and smirking at Warrington.

Theo walked down the beach toward his hat while Marchavious and Warrington stood waiting to continue toward their destination. Theo saw the hat sitting on the beach, dry and oddly, in the same condition in which he had left it. Bending over to pick it up, Theo noticed it was weighted down. He let go and the hat began to move slowly up the beachhead. Theo took two steps toward the hat and reached out for it. The hat pulled away from him as he struggled to pick it up. The hat continued up the beachhead to the top of the first dune, where it stopped. Theo looked in perplexity at his hat, which was bewitched by some invisible creature.

"What seems to be the problem?" Marchavious yelled from his position down the beach.

"It won't budge!" Theo yelled back. "And it seems to be moving."

Theo moved closer to the hat and grabbed on tightly. He yanked the hat upward and fell backward down the dune. At the top he saw a large hermit crab looking at him awkwardly. The hermit crab looked displeased and started walking toward him, pincers opening and closing with a cracking sound. Theo scooted back as the crab progressed toward him quickly. He tried to get up, but tripped, as he was holding the hat in one hand. The crab snapped at his ankle, missing narrowly. Theo stood up as the crab pursued him and the hat that the hermit crab had made his new home. As he clumsily ran down the beach toward Marchavious and Warrington, Theo waved his prize above his head. Seeing its new home shrink in the distance, the crab gave up pursuit and turned to look for new quarters elsewhere along the beach.

Theo breathed heavily as he reached Warrington and Marchavious; he bent over with his hands on his knees, panting. "Well ... I got it ..." Theo said between heavy breaths.

"We can see that," Warrington said, grinning. "Did the creature that was chasing you want to buy it?" Warrington grinned wider.

Theo glared at Warrington, not amused by his levity.

"Well, now that we are a whole group once more, let's get moving before we are stranded in the desert at nightfall and that crab thing comes looking for his home," Marchavious said, pointing toward the hat on Theo's head. Theo looked nervously back at the beach and started up the dune.

## '3'

They had been walking for what felt like three hours when Theo pointed toward a small pond with a few trees around it in the distance. While this *was* a desert, it was not hot or dry, but the three companions were still thirsty from their endless walk. None of them had thought to bring any water with them, and they could use a rest. The sun was now coming down behind them, even though the needle on Marchavious' homemade compass still pointed straight ahead. The small oasis grew bigger and bigger as they approached. The trees were larger than they had looked in the distance, reaching almost fifty feet into the air, with wide branches providing shade.

The edge of the oasis was covered in grass and would provide a soft bed for an hour or so of rest. Passing the two trees that formed the entrance, they walked over to the water's edge. Warrington knelt down and lapped the water.

"Seems to taste fine. Does not taste the least bit salty. It actually tastes a bit sweet," Warrington said, continuing to lap at the surface. Small ripples spread across the surface.

Theo and Marchavious knelt beside Warrington and cupped their hands, scooping water into their mouths.

Marchavious leaned back at the water's edge and looked up into the trees. The cool breeze blew over him, giving him a sensation of relaxation. Theo sat against one of the large trees.

"I bet you could see for miles if you climbed to the top of that tree there. Maybe we are close. Warrington, you are the most agile—why not climb up the tree and give us a look?" Marchavious said, still staring at the branches that seemed to block out the light from the sun.

Warrington did not object to this idea, as it was not a bad one. He sprinted at the tree and up its bark to the first branch. Marchavious could see the needles of the tree rustle and fall as Warrington bounced higher and higher into the canopy. Warrington could feel the tree swaying in the wind as he reached the highest branch that would support his weight.

He looked in the direction they were heading and could see nothing but sandy dunes off in the distance. He looked left and it was more of the same: miles of beach with no water. Looking to his right, Warrington could see a small speck off in the distance. It looked like a town or a village, but it was hard to make out with the other tree in the way. Warrington hurried down the branches to the very bottom perch.

"It looks like there is a town or village to the northeast of us, if I am not mistaken. It was far off in the distance and hard to see, but I am sure something was out there. We could make it by nightfall if we left now." Warrington jumped down to the grass.

"Well then, we should probably get going if that is the case," Marchavious said, standing up and stretching. "We have rested enough, and I would rather sleep in a bed tonight if they have an inn."

Theo was sitting against the tree with his eyes closed. Marchavious walked over and kicked his boot. Theo looked up, annoyed.

"I was having the most wonderful dream, Marchavious. We were sitting here and there were three women singing to us."

Marchavious laughed and recalled the Sirens from *The Odyssey* he'd read in school. "You have been bewitched by the Sirens' song, Theo. We should go now before they strip the flesh from your bones." Marchavious looked down at Warrington and winked. Theo got to his feet in a hurry.

"All right, ready to go," Theo said, tugging at his jacket and straightening his hat.

Marchavious and Warrington followed Theo out of the trees in the direction Warrington had pointed. Theo thought he could still hear the music from his dream but tried to shut it out for fear of being a meal for some mythological creatures. Marchavious stopped as they reached the edge of the oasis.

"I hear music, Theo. Do you hear it as well?"

Theo slowly nodded his head up and then down.

"It sounds absolutely lovely. I think I'll go back and listen a bit," Marchavious said, starting to turn.

Theo grabbed his arm. "We should keep going, Marchavious. Like you said, Sirens."

"I was only kidding. There is no such thing as Sirens or flesh-eating creatures that sing."

Marchavious was walking back into the clearing. Warrington did not hear anything and wondered what Theo and Marchavious were talking about. Theo followed Marchavious to the edge of the water once again.

"Marchavious, Theo, we really need to get moving …" Warrington started to say, but was interrupted by Marchavious putting his finger to his lips and shushing him.

"Listen—it's coming from the water," Marchavious said, looking at Theo.

Theo looked over at the center of the water, where the sound was coming from. The water began to get dark and murky.

"Marchavious, I think we should get going," Theo said as the water started to displace a little, rippling across the surface.

"I think you may be right. Let's go," Marchavious said, waking from his trance.

Theo and Marchavious hurried out of the oasis and back to the sandy beaches of the desert. As soon as they were no longer in the oasis, the music stopped. The silence was broken by a splash of water, and then it was silent once more. Curious, Marchavious turned around slowly, but Theo tugged at his arm.

"Come on, Marchavious. No use sticking around here and finding out what that was," Theo said, pulling him along.

Warrington was already at the top of the sand dune. Theo and Marchavious could see the small village at the top of the dune. Marchavious thought it could not be more than a couple hours away now.

They walked for another hour through the sand, until they reached the wreckage of a small ship partially buried in the sand; the remains of the sails blew in the breeze. The silence around the ship was eerily still. Wood creaked as the wind shifted the boat's skeleton back and forth.

"This is most curious. There must have been water here at one point in time. Ships do not exactly travel on sand, do they? At least, none that I have ever seen," Marchavious said, inspecting the ruins.

"Well, it would make sense that there was once water here, as we have come across two small bodies of water since coming here. The water from the tunnel probably keeps that small body of water from drying up," Theo said, as though he had been pondering the ship's existence in this desert for days.

Warrington jumped up on the side of the ship and crawled out on the mast that was jutting out of the desert. He could now see the small village up ahead, no more than fifteen minutes away if they ran. *But why would we need to run?* he thought.

Marchavious sat on the side of the ship.

"I can see the village. There is a ship sitting in the sand at what looks like a dock or pier," Warrington said.

Marchavious could hear his voice as it drifted off in the wind. Marchavious thought he heard the music again as he sat there.

"What is it, Marchavious? It's the music again, is it not? I can hear it as well. We need to leave before we go mad from this melodious trap." Theo walked around to the front of the ship.

"Warrington, come on, we are leaving. The music we heard at the oasis is …" Theo trailed off as a large black fin rose out of the sand.

"Warrington!" Theo barely got out his name before the large black object moved upward out of the sand toward Warrington. The creature's jaws came down on the mast, snapping it in half and sending Warrington to the sand below. The creature dove back under and was gone. Warrington landed on his feet, dazed by what had just happened. Theo stood there, gesturing frantically with his hands, motioning Marchavious to come quickly.

"Marchavious!" Theo yelled from the other side of the ship. Marchavious came running around the side of the ship and stopped suddenly at the sight of the large piece of mast laying on the ground.

"What is it, Theo?"

Theo was shaking and visibly frightened. "Sh … sh … sh … shark." Theo muttered.

"Shark?" Marchavious questioned. "Don't be silly. There is no water around here. No water. No sharks," Marchavious said, relieved that Theo had only been hallucinating, but concerned that he was seeing things.

"Warrington, tell him there was a shark," Theo said, looking around, but Warrington was nowhere to be found. Theo looked up and saw Warrington standing on the side of the ship, looking wide-eyed into the distance. Theo started to hear the music in his mind again. Theo followed Warrington's gaze and could see a black fin rising out of the sand and moving quickly toward them, the music getting louder as it approached. Theo tried to tell Marchavious, but he was preoccupied with the sound of the music.

"Do you hear that, Theo? Do you hear the wonderful music? It makes me want to go back to the oasis."

Theo ran around and climbed up to where Warrington was sitting. He grabbed onto Marchavious' shirt and pulled at him furiously.

"What are you doing? Are you mad?" Marchavious said, smacking Theo's hand. "Get off me this instant."

Theo pointed out into the open sand as the black fin closed in on them. The music was growing louder, and Marchavious was cupping his ears in order to block some of it out. He looked at Theo, who was still pointing.

Marchavious turned and saw the back fin racing toward them at full speed. The music was deafening at this range, but Marchavious uncupped his hands and began to run in the opposite direction.

The fin dipped under the skeleton of the ship and reemerged on the other side in pursuit of Marchavious.

"Marchavious, come back!" Theo yelled.

Marchavious turned and could see the fin almost on top of him. He turned and ran toward it. The fin sank into the sand and resurfaced, heading in the opposite direction. Marchavious ran toward Theo and Warrington. Theo's hand was motioning as though it were helping Marchavious run faster. The black fin moved swiftly straight toward Marchavious.

Marchavious leapt to the side of the ship and reached out his hand. Theo grabbed it and pulled him to the upper level. The fin grew as the creature leapt from the sand and onto the side of the ship, jaws smashing through the side as pieces of wood flew around them. The music halted as the creature rose out of the sand. The large sand shark, as they would call it when they retold the story later, sank down into the sand beneath the ship. The music started up again and then got softer.

"We should hurry and get to the village. If we run, it is only fifteen minutes," Warrington said, watching Theo and Marchavious pant with exhaustion.

"Are you crazy? That thing is waiting out there for us to get down. Once we start walking, it's going to spring up out of the sand and eat us. *You'll* probably be fine 'cause you're bite-size, but it would take quite a few bites to get us down," Theo exclaimed as Warrington rolled his eyes.

"No, Theo, Warrington is right. If we stay here, that thing is going to eat us either way. It smashed through the wood as if it was nothing. This place will be in ruins in a matter of minutes if we don't make a run for it," Marchavious said.

"Okay," Theo said reluctantly. "I should be okay. I don't have to outrun that musical abomination. I just have to outrun you," Theo joked and then frowned.

"Very funny," Marchavious remarked.

## '4'

Theo, Marchavious and Warrington stood at the edge of the ship, getting ready to jump. Marchavious listened for any hint of musical notes, but heard only the wind.

"I think it might have left—maybe for easier prey?" Theo said. "Marchavious, you jump down and see if it comes. If it doesn't come, we'll start running for the village."

"Why does it have to be me?" Marchavious said, appalled. "You're faster than I. You said you could outrun it."

"I said no such thing! I said I just had to outrun you."

"Well, then, you should go first," Marchavious said, pointing to the sand below, "so that I have a chance."

"He does have a point, Theo," Warrington said, looking over the edge. "I cannot hear the music for some strange reason, so I would not be useful as bait."

"Bait!" Theo said. "I will not be bait!"

"Just get down there," Marchavious hissed.

"Fine, but if I get eaten, I will haunt you both in this world and the other," Theo said, kneeling down and jumping to the sand below. "Well, no music so far. Come on, let's go."

Warrington and Marchavious jumped down.

"All right, let's make haste. It is almost tea time!" Theo exclaimed.

Warrington was out in front by a good ten feet, with Marchavious and Theo trailing slightly. They had been keeping a slow but steady jogger's pace in order to keep some reserve in the tank if they needed to sprint away from some unseen sharks. Theo looked over and noticed Marchavious had slightly picked up his pace.

"What are you doing?" Theo said, also picking up his pace.

"Nothing, just keep running," Marchavious whispered.

Then Theo heard it—the faint sound of a harp playing in the distance. Theo lengthened his stride and increased his pace even more, Marchavious in stride right alongside him. The familiar music was getting louder, and they turned to see the black fin off in the distance, heading in their direction. Theo faltered and Marchavious grabbed his arm in order to keep him from falling.

"Marchavious, I hear the harp, but now I hear the sound of a piano as well," Theo panted, out of breath.

Marchavious slowed for a second and then picked his pace back up again.

"Indeed that is a piano, but I don't see what that has to do with it. Music is music, right?"

Both Marchavious and Theo were gaining on Warrington. Warrington turned his head to see Theo and Marchavious at a full sprint, a set of fins kicking sand into the air as they traveled toward the group of runners.

"Did you know there are two fins back there?" Warrington said, out of breath, but still running at full speed.

"What? Two fins!" Theo exclaimed, trying to run harder at this new development.

"Guess I just have to outrun you and Warrington, huh, Theo?" Marchavious joked.

The village was in full view and no more than a half-mile ahead of them. The music was still getting louder, no matter how fast they ran. Theo looked behind him and almost tripped again.

"I thought that was what I heard," Theo said, lunging ahead and leaving Marchavious behind by a few feet.

Marchavious looked back to see that a third fin had joined the chase. It was hard to tell what the instrument was, but it could have very well been a guitar. The instruments blended nicely to create a very soothing musical ensemble.

"Violin!" Marchavious shouted.

They quickly reached the pier at the edge of town. Warrington jumped onto the first large wooden pillar on the right side of the pier and climbed up to the dock. Turning, he could see the three black fins no more than fifty yards away. Marchavious and Theo ran past the first pillar, looking frantically for a way up, but could not find one.

"The ship has a rope ladder on its side!" Warrington yelled. The fins were now thirty yards out and closing fast. Marchavious ran around the side and grabbed hold of the ladder. He climbed furiously, but the ladder was slippery against the side of the ship. Theo was standing on the bottom rung trying to climb up, but was impeded by Marchavious' boots.

"Climb, Marchavious!" Theo pleaded.

Marchavious grabbed on and hoisted himself up halfway. Theo climbed higher, but was still close to the ground. The sharks were now just ten yards out. Theo pushed his legs against the side in order to get some height. One of the sharks leapt for Theo, its fin cutting into the back of his leg. His leg buckled as he felt the gash open. Marchavious grabbed his arm and pulled him up as another fin materialized into a large black blur with jagged teeth. The second shark, considerably smaller than the first, grabbed onto the back of Theo's boot and pulled downward.

"Do not let go, Marchavious!" Theo pleaded, wincing in pain.

Without warning, Warrington jumped, claws out, from the railing of the ship onto the back of the shark that dangled from Theo's boot. The shark let go and fell to the sand with a hard thud. The small shark thrashed back and forth with large crescendos and the sound of breaking strings. Warrington held on, remembering his first large mouse encounter in the library.

The third shark had circled and came back, leaping out of the sand toward Warrington and the smaller shark. Warrington, remembering his training, leapt off the shark and up to Theo's leg, climbing up to the deck of the ship. Theo let out a loud scream from the small claws as they ran up his back. The third shark grabbed the smaller shark and dragged it down into the sand, unaware of what it had done.

Marchavious finished hoisting Theo over the railing and onto the deck of the ship, where Warrington waited, licking his paw. Marchavious climbed over the railing and looked down to see only one fin circling below. The music then drifted off: the harp and piano, but no violin.

Warrington sat on the deck, tending to his wound from the rough skin of the small black musical shark. Marchavious tore the sleeves off his shirt and wrapped them around Theo's leg, which was bleeding profusely.

Looking around, Warrington saw a small cage—just big enough to hold a cat.

"This is the ship. The cage the captain spoke of is over there. We are in Heartwick and one step closer to finding Eld." Warrington forgot about his wounds and walked over to the dock. "Let's go find somewhere to spend the night."

## Chapter 11

'1'

Marchavious walked down the gangplank and onto the dock. The large wooden structure swayed back and forth in the wind. Large plumes of dust were coming off the vast ocean of desert that the three companions had just trekked across.

"Well, if I never have to set foot on sand again, it will not be too soon," Marchavious said, moving down the dock.

Theo and Warrington had already begun their stroll past the large wooden barrels and ropes that littered the dock.

"I guess I should not have doubted the captain when he said I was going to be shark food," Warrington commented, stepping off the wooden surface of the dock and onto the bright red surface of the street that led to the center of town.

The town was not as large as they had imagined, but it was big enough. Theo looked around and was reminded of Chester and his hat shop. Wooden buildings rose up all around them, leaving a wide path down the middle of the street. At the center of town was a large stone fountain with a woman in its center, holding a heart-shaped rock in the crook of her right arm. The statue was as grey as any other statue, but the heart was the same color as the road. This perplexed Marchavious and Theo, as they had never seen a mineral of this color before. Theo bent over and investigated the surface of the road with his hand. The surface was smoother than any other surface he had felt.

"This is the strangest road I have ever felt. There are no cracks or seams in its surface, and it is smoother than the felt of a hat's material, although I dare say I would not wear it on my head."

Warrington had noticed the intricacy of the road as well, but did not show the same signs of curiosity, which is strange for any cat.

"Look," Theo said, pointing to a strange figure crossing the street. "What is that?"

The creature walked out into the middle of the street, pecking at the surface with its beak. The pecks easily made small divots in the surface, and it appeared as though the creature was eating the road.

"Stop that!" A man came running by with a large burlap sack. The creature, which resembled a large chicken with two legs and fur like a small horse, poked its head back and forth, unaware of the man or the crowd of spectators that had stopped to watch the mysterious animal. Holding the burlap sack over his head, the man jumped. The furry chicken dodged this easily, moving off to one side as the man slid past the creature and onto the other side of the road.

Warrington laughed as he jumped up to the lip of the fountain for a better view. Marchavious and Theo sat down next to him in order to observe this event.

Getting to his feet, the man brushed himself off, attempting to remove any dirt that might have gotten on his clothes, but the spectators saw none come off. The animal's two paws stomped the ground back and forth, taunting the man, who was standing with his bag outward as though he expected the creature to jump inside on its own. The creature turned its back on the man and continued pecking at the street. The man walked slowly toward the furry fowl, bag at the ready. The chicken seemed unprepared as the bag came down and scooped up the strange-looking bird.

Marchavious and Theo broke into hearty applause for the man as he lifted the bag onto his back and started to walk off. The noise of their hands coming together made the man turn around slowly, now aware that he was being watched.

The man had the eyes of an eagle as he peered at them through thin slits and cautiously approached the two men sitting on the fountain. He was wearing a yellow tunic and blue overalls; his white hair blew in the wind as he walked down the street against the breeze.

The sun was starting to dim its light in the south, and three large moons were rising in the north. The man stopped ten feet from the two men and the one cat that he had just noticed sitting between them.

"I nevah seen you round these parts before. What have ya?" the old man said, straightening up.

"We just came in from the desert, where we had a run in with a Captain Santiago. We are tired and seek a place to stay for the night," Marchavious said, standing up. "We have had a very tiresome journey and would appreciate you pointing us in the direction of the Heartwick Inn."

The man laughed and pointed down the street. "Well, it's down that way, but I doubt ya find anyone who will put ya up for the night."

"Why is that?" Theo said inquisitively.

"Well, that would be because this is Heartwick, population one. I do most of the upkeep round here since the great exodus, but I can't do everything, ya know?" The man looked down the street and pointed to a building that was falling apart and looked badly neglected. "Tell ya what, you help me get a couple more of these here furry chickens, and I'll let ya stay with me up in my house. I can tell ya all about the Dark Witch and the great exodus from Heartwick over tea."

This sounded especially delightful to Marchavious and Theo, as they had not had tea for quite some time now.

"So they are furry chickens?" Warrington said, licking his chops, remembering the taste of the juicy meat from the ship.

"Ay, that they are ... wait a minute. Did you just say something?" the man said, pointing at the cat with wide eyes.

"Yes sir, I am Warrington J. Cat. Pleased to meet you," Warrington said, bowing his head downward. ∎

The man scratched his head and wiped his brow with a handkerchief he had pulled from his right front pocket.

"It's been a small bit since I heard a talking cat. Not since the Dark Witch strolled through here with her troop of lizard men, I call 'um. One of 'um was carrying a cage with a small cat in it. I was hiding as they passed through in their carriages. The cat was talking to the Dark Witch, but I couldn't make out a single darn word they were saying. I was too interested in keeping quiet to get a closer look."

"That was Eld, which is why we are here. We are following the Dark Witch on the chance we can catch up and rescue our friend," Warrington said. "Do you know how long ago it was that they passed by here?"

The old man looked up with one hand on his hip and the other still tightly grasping the burlap sack with the furry chicken in it.

"Oh, I would say not more than a couple of weeks now. Could have been sooner, but time here does not keep well. He is a fickle fella and can play tricks on your mind. Never know how long a day is or whether the night will come some days." The old man looked up at the three moons, which were almost directly overhead now. The sun, however, had not moved an inch since the moons began to rise. "Either way, we can discuss this all up at the house over tea, like I said before. I appreciate any help. The chickens tear up the road, and I just don't have the strength to stop them all."

"Okay," Warrington said. "That sounds like a fair trade. By the way, what do we call you, sir? Everyone must have a name, you know."

"Well, my name is Wiglaf. My friends—before they left—took ta' calling me Willem Glaf. Wiglaf will do, though as that was what I was called in my old life," Wiglaf said, smiling. Warrington returned the kind gesture.

"These two without manners are Marchavious Harbinger and Theophilus Hatmaker," Warrington said, looking up at each.

Theo tipped his hat but remained relatively silent, except for a small, "Nice to make your acquaintance."

'2'

After spending several hours chasing the furry chickens, Marchavious and Theophilus were exhausted. Warrington still had lots of energy and would have preferred chasing more of them, as they were much easier to catch than the rodents he was used to. He did have to learn to be more careful, though, as he found they were not as durable as the rodents. Theo was slightly scared of the chickens and spent most of the time running away from them. Somehow the chickens seemed to catch on that he was afraid and would ambush him just as Theo was about to catch one of them.

"I have never seen anyone so adept at catching chickens, Warrington," Wiglaf said as they were walking up the hill to the front of the mansion he had called a simple house.

"Thank you, Wiglaf. Back home it was my job to catch the mice that would try and destroy the books in our library. I became very efficient at disposing of them."

"Library, huh? Musta been some unusually sized mice if you can catch chickens that well," Wiglaf said, looking down and raising an eyebrow.

"Oh, I must say they were quite large, Mister Wiglaf. A group almost ate me as we were leaving," Theo piped in.

"Nonsense, Theo, they were only gonna take a nibble here or there. The chickens, however, are a different story," Warrington said, laughing along with Marchavious and Wiglaf.

Theo frowned and quickened his pace.

"Come now, Theo, Warrington is only joking. No need to get your knickers in a bunch," Marchavious said as the group reached the top of the hill.

The gate to the mansion was made of brushed steel bars that climbed ten feet into the air. Only half of the gate remained standing; the other half rested in the grass some twenty-five yards away. The stone pillar on the right side looked as though the gate had been ripped off its hinge by a man of incredible strength.

"I've been meaning to fix that, but it is lower on my to-do list than keeping the road from being food for those accursed birds," Wiglaf said, disregarding the gate and continuing through the entryway into the front yard of the enormous house.

"What happened to the gate?" Theo said, looking at the pillar and inspecting the large claw that had broken off in the stone.

"Oh, that's a story for tea, as well. All part of the exodus, I am afraid. I'll tell you more about it inside." Wiglaf continued walking up the long road to the doorstep. The three companions followed close behind, not mentioning the portion of the gate they were now passing.

The sky was beginning to grow dark as the sun finally sank down in the desert ocean. The three moons looked as though they had almost caught up with the sun, but it dipped down before they had the chance. Darkness slowly crept over the town of Heartwick in an eerie silence. Wiglaf climbed the marble steps of the three-story home and up to two large doors that stood guard over the house. To the right of the door was a plaque with the numbers 2295.

Marchavious stood in wonder at the large structure that went on as far as he could see in either direction. One section bowed out in a circle and was covered from floor to ceiling with broken windows. The other side, a mirror image, was still intact and the windows reflected the three moons as they too were reaching the point of slipping down into the sandy ocean.

"You gonna stand out there all night, or are ya coming in for tea?" Wiglaf said, yelling from the large open doors.

Theo ran up the steps, followed by his companions.

'3'

The entryway opened up into a large foyer of marble pillars and a wide staircase that went up and to the upper left and right sides of the house. The upper left side, however, was inaccessible, as the wall that allowed entry into this wing had been reduced to a pile of rubble that spilled onto the stairs.

"The butler should be down momentarily. Until then make yourself at home. Pardon the mess. Since it's just me, I haven't had any time, or will, to clean up the aftermath of the exodus."

Wiglaf turned and started walking out the door with the large bag of furry creatures, which, oddly, showed no signs of struggle in their burlap prison. Marchavious opened his mouth to ask him about the butler, but he had turned the corner before he had the chance.

"I thought he said this town was a population of one?" Marchavious said in a whisper.

"I wondered the same thing, Marchavious. Hopefully, this is not like the captain and we shall be fed as dinner to those furry wretches he has in the back now," Theo said, cringing.

"Oh, Theo, you worry too much. There is nothing to be afraid of here. I doubt an old man who spends his days catching chickens that peck at a red road could be of much trouble," Marchavious commented.

Warrington walked around, inspecting every inch of this first room. "Well, whatever happened here, I am sure we will find out over dinner," he said just before he turned a corner and disappeared around the doorway.

"Warrington is right, Theo. Let's find some place to relax and wait for dinner."

Marchavious and Theo followed Warrington into the library that was just off the foyer. Bookcases went all the way to the top of the ceiling and stopped. There were a great many books on the shelves, but the shelves were far from full; books littered the floor of the library as well. Theo walked over, took off his hat, and set it on the end table next to a light blue sofa with gold trim. He sat down and picked up one of the books off the floor. Theo scratched his head as he looked at the cover and found no title or author. He looked at the binding and noticed that there was no title there, either. Opening the book, he started thumbing through the pages, slowly at first, and then gaining momentum. Theo slammed the book shut, the noise echoing throughout the room. Marchavious jumped slightly and turned toward Theo.

"This is odd, Marchavious … The book is blank," Theo said, stretching out his hand with the book toward Marchavious.

"Well, some books just don't have covers, Theo," Marchavious said, looking at the outside.

"No, Marchavious, the entire book is blank. No words, no writing, no anything. Blank as if the story has not been told yet," Theo said, grabbing the book from Marchavious and opening it.

"Maybe it is a diary, Theo," Marchavious rebutted Theo's foolish thought.

"These are all blank," came a voice from behind a table at the other end of the room. Warrington hopped up on the desk and stared at the open book. "This one is the same as the one on the floor. Nothing but blank pages and covers. I doubt this is coincidence. I am sure Wiglaf knows what is going on. We should ask him once dinner is ready."

"Dinner is ready," came a voice from the library doorway. Wiglaf walked in through the door wearing a black smock and black trousers. His shoes shone in the candlelight that illuminated the room. "I will show you to the table. Follow me."

Theo and Marchavious walked out the door and down the hallway. Warrington jumped down from the desk and hurried after them.

"So *you* are the butler, Master Wiglaf," Marchavious said as he entered the enormous dining hall.

Candles circled the perimeter of the ceiling, giving the room sufficient light to see. The chandelier reflected the light, increasing its illumination tenfold.

"Yes, I am, although I am more of a steward you see. I left home quite some time ago in search of peace. So far this is where I have gotten to," Wiglaf said as he pulled out three chairs from around a large oak table in the middle of the room.

The walls were covered with many tapestries that looked as though they were telling a story, but Marchavious noticed that one portion of the wall was not covered—one of the tapestries had gone missing. Marchavious counted fifteen tapestries in all, with the missing one bringing the total to sixteen.

Warrington jumped up to the chair, then onto the table and sat down, looking straight ahead. This table reminded him of the captain's table on the ship, but Wiglaf sat down at their side of the table instead of at the very end where Captain Santiago had taken his seat. Marchavious sat down in the pulled-out chair next to Wiglaf. Theo was busy walking around, looking at the tapestries.

"You know one of your tapestries is missing," Theo commented, scooting between the table and the back wall. While the room was large, the table was enormous and encompassed most of the floor space.

"Yes, Theophilus, it was gone when I got here. Not much sense in worrying about something that was not mine to begin with, though."

"Theo …" came the voice from the end of the room.

"I beg your pardon?" Wiglaf turned to face him.

"You can call me Theo. Unlike my friend Marchavious, I don't mind the shortening of my name. Theo will do."

"Well then, Theo, come and have a seat. I would not want our meal to get cold," Wiglaf said, leaning over and pulling the lid off a silver platter that was set in the middle of the table.

Steam billowed from underneath the cover of the serving tray. Warrington's eyes widened as the lid rose into the air and the steam settled. His excitement subsided, though, as he saw a large squash on the tray—quite possibly the largest squash any of them had ever seen. Warrington was visibly disappointed at the apparent lack of furless chickens.

"Not what you were expecting, Warrington?" Wiglaf looked over and winked. "Sorry to disappoint, but the chickens serve a different purpose. Surprisingly, they keep the Rebobs away."

"What, pray tell, is a Rebob?" Theo said, sitting down and inching his chair closer to the table. "I cannot imagine anything more horrifying than those furry little abominations."

"Rebobs are what I refer to as flying monkeys. They appeared after the exodus. Some took up residence in the houses, but those furry abominations, as you call them, scared them off. They live just on the border where Heartwick ends and the Frost Woods begins. They keep to themselves for the most part, but every once in a while they will cause some ruckus."

"Wait, I missed the first part," Theo said, his eyes wide. "Flying monkeys?"

"Yes, sir," Wiglaf laughed as he cut a piece of squash off the platter and gave some to Marchavious. "I was surprised to see them, as well. There are probably only handfuls that still live in the woods though."

Theo looked down, disheartened at the thought that there would be more dangerous creatures along the road to the White Queen. He took his plate in hand and held it out toward Wiglaf. He may have been scared at the thought of these flying primates, but it would not deter his appetite.

"The Rebobs aren't much bigger than the chickens, though. Maybe twice their size, I suppose. Nothing to be too fearful of." Wiglaf put a piece of squash on Warrington's plate. "Eat up, Warrington. You might be surprised that it tastes nothing like it looks."

Warrington took a small bite and then another. He quickly realized that the squash did in fact taste like chicken. "It tastes like chicken," he remarked.

"Actually, it tastes like what you want it to taste like. Chicken, fish, or even squash," Wiglaf said as Theo held out his plate for more.

"Apparently, I was craving some shepherd's pie. Quite delicious, if I say so myself." Theo was tapping his handkerchief at the corner of his mouth. "Now for some rice pudding." Wiglaf laughed and put a small slice of the squash on his plate.

"Now, Wiglaf, if you will—we would love to hear about the exodus," Marchavious said, putting his fork down on his plate. Warrington looked up, interested in this piece of the conversation.

"Ah yes, of course. Where to begin?" Wiglaf looked up at the tapestries and then back down at the table.

'4'

The day was hot and sweat beaded on Wiglaf's forehead as he rode his horse out of the Frost Woods and past the borders of Heartwick. He could see an outpost just a small way up the path and rode towards it.

"Halt, sir! Who goes there? And what business do ye be having in Heartwick?" the voice boomed from out of nowhere, echoing across the field.

"My name is Wiglaf, and I am looking to settle down. I have fought many a war and foul beast. I am looking to end my days in peace."

Wiglaf got down off his horse to show he meant no harm. The sword hanging off his hip glistened in the sun, and his long golden hair flowed in the wind as it came off the plains and over the garrison. A small figure dressed in armor came out from behind a barrel.

"Well, come over and let me see ya," the figure said, looking up at Wiglaf. "Are you a Procerus? You look like one," the small armored figure added.

"What is a Procerus, my friend?" Wiglaf asked, leaning down to be more at eye level with the small man.

"Procerus are the tall ones who come in during the night and take what they want." The small man backed up a few inches.

"No, I am not here to steal or take anything. I am just looking for a place to forget the past and settle down for the future. Do you have a name, my friend?" Wiglaf's eyes were kind but courageous. The small man, obviously a soldier of some sort, trusted Wiglaf almost immediately.

"My name is Sir William Beach, Knight of the Fourth Garrison of Heartwick and protector of the city. I slew a dragon once, before it had a chance to attack the city. It came right up out of Heartwick Lake, snarling and gnashing its jaws. Must have been a small one, but a dragon nonetheless. Maybe it was a sea serpent. Either way, it was the size of a small house." Bill was gloating and standing as tall as he could.

"Well, I will sleep well knowing you are guarding the city. I was once in the service of a mighty king and together we slew a dragon, but I wish to put those days behind me. I will be put at ease knowing that Sir Bill the Dragon Slayer is watching over the city."

Bill puffed out his chest at this. "I like that much better than Little Bill. If you see any more guards, tell them I am Sir Bill the Dragon Slayer now."

"Very well, Sir Bill. I will be on my way. If you could direct me toward the magistrate's office, I would be more than grateful," Wiglaf said, climbing back on his horse.

"Oh yes, just travel into the city and look for the fountain in the middle of town. You'll see a sign that says *Office of the Magistrate*. You'll find the magistrate in there."

"Thank you, Sir Bill. You are most kind, and I will remember that. Come see me in town when I have gotten things squared away," Wiglaf said, looking down. He raised his hand and waved to Bill, shunted his heels in the side of his horse twice, and continued down the dusty road into town.

The streets of the town were bustling with life as people walked in and out of shops in the town square. Wiglaf rode his horse to the edge of town and halted in front of a man wearing green overalls that were stained red on the knees. An elderly face looked up from beneath a straw hat and he held a paving stone in one hand and what appeared to be a bloodstained cloth in the other.

"You're gonna have to tie your horse up here, sir. Animals are forbidden along the golden road." The elderly gentleman moved closer, looking up at Wiglaf.

"Golden road? Sir, this road is blood red. How is it golden?" Wiglaf said, forgetting his purpose.

"Well, a man came through here selling gold bricks. The bricks were left over from an improvement project in another county. Replaced their emerald road with a gold one, is what he said. He offered them to us at a good price since we originally had just dirt for a road. The Magistrate liked the idea, but hated the gold color. He said, 'This is not *Goldwick,* Carl' and so he ordered the gold be melted down and mixed with the roses growing on the hillside. I did not have much hope for a color change, but sure enough, the gold turned to a deep red color. I spend my day polishing divots from the furry birds that peck holes in the road. They like the taste of the roses, you see."

"I see," said Wiglaf politely, climbing down off his horse and tying the leather reins to the wooden hitching post.

"Thank you, Mister. The horseshoes would make short work of our road, you see. The road is soft and smooth, but easily damaged. They probably didn't think about such a thing in that other city when they installed them." Carl got back down on his knees, where a small hole had been placed in the road.

"My name is Wiglaf. Pleasure to meet you, Carl. Can you point me to the magistrate's office?"

Carl pointed one of his fingers to the right without looking up. His left hand was moving in a methodical circle with the paving stone and then polishing it in the same fashion with his right hand, which held the red cloth. Wiglaf moved down the street and toward the center of town.

The road glimmered, creating a reflection that danced back and forth off the surrounding buildings. Wiglaf stood and looked at the large building with the words: *Office of the Magistrate* on an old wooden sign that sat at the bottom of the red stairs. Wiglaf walked up to the top, his metal boots clanking against the concrete as his boot hit each step.

The building was made of a beautiful ivory material with two giant red pillars standing guard over the doorway. There was a large stone heart crested in the middle between the pillars with the word *HEARTWICK* written across the front. Below *HEARTWICK* was written *LIVE*, *LOVE*, and *LIFE*.

Wiglaf passed between the crimson pillars, under the stone heart and through the large wooden doors that were propped open by tiny burgundy doorstops. The floor was a large red-and-white checkered pattern, which fit the theme they seemed to be going for on the outside.

Wiglaf proceeded across the floor to the desk at the center of the room. His boots echoed throughout the large hall and garnered the attention of everyone there.

Wiglaf approached the desk and said quietly, "I am here to see the magistrate."

"Are you a knight? You appear to be a knight, and we sent for one many months ago. Of course, it could have been yesterday; time here is out of sorts. The magistrate really should not have made him mad." The voice was tiny and belonged to a black-haired lady with round glasses.

"Well, I was a knight, but I doubt I am the knight that you sent for," Wiglaf said, tapping his finger on the desk. "I am just here to see the magistrate. I would like to settle here and need boarding and possibly a job."

"Well, Sir Knight, I am sure there is a job here for you, since we have need for a knight and we do not have any knights here in town, nor do we have anyone who wants to be a knight." The voice was very squeaky and sounded nervous. "I will let the magistrate know of your arrival, Sir …"

"Wiglaf," he said, finishing her sentence.

"Sir Wiglaf, very well. Please have a seat over there, and I will get the magistrate."

Wiglaf walked over to the small bench along the wall, looking at the pictures lining the wall. Each of them with the last name Heartwick and all of them with the first name of Magistrate, it would appear. Wiglaf turned and started to sit.

"Sir Wiglaf, please follow me," the squeaky voice said as Wiglaf was bending down to sit. Wiglaf stood up and started walking behind the woman who was as tall standing as she was sitting in her chair.

Wiglaf and the concierge walked down the long, barren hallway for what seemed like an hour. Halfway down, a small child with black hair was playing with a wooden fire cart on the floor. The woman, proceeding past him as though he was not there, almost kicked the boy. Wiglaf turned to see the boy unfazed by the near collision.

Two large doors at the end of the hallway opened immediately and the woman shouted, "Sir Wiglaf of …" there was a pause and she looked over and whispered, "Where are you from?"

"I am from Geatland," Wiglaf whispered back.

"Sir Wiglaf of Geatland, your royal Magistrate."

The two stepped through the door into a large beige room that broke the red and white theme. Wiglaf looked down, but the woman was gone. He turned to see her walking backward and closing the doors they had just passed through.

"Sir Wiglaf," a large voice boomed across the room. "So, you are the savior of Heartwick?"

"Magistrate, I am not sure what was told you, but I am here to settle down and live a peaceful life for the rest of my days. I was a knight in the service of a king, but those days are behind me. While I am still young, I sincerely doubt I am the best hope you have for a savior. I would just like a job and a place to make a home." Wiglaf walked closer to the desk that provided a stopping point for the red carpet.

"Well, Sir Wiglaf, my concierge tells me you indeed need a job and we have need for a knight. At least for a month or so. Nothing long-term, and if it works out, I might have some more work for you. Something easier, perhaps chicken-chasing."

The chair spun around to reveal a slender man with a wooden crown adorned with red marbles. His robe was red and white with black spots on the fringe.

"What about Sir Bill on the outer edge of town? I thought he was a knight," Wiglaf said, pointing at the wall in the direction he imagined Bill would have been in.

"Sir Bill? Oh my! Is he still out there stopping people along the road? William used to be a squire when we had a few knights here. The Procerus attacked and made off with the three knights we had. Ever since then William has been standing guard out there. He thinks he is a knight, but he is just a squire with large hopes."

"He said he killed a dragon that came out of Lake Heartwick. That has to count for something, right?" Wiglaf said, insistent that Sir Bill was a knight.

"Well, that is true if you consider small crocodiles dragons. William is delusional at times. If you would like, I can make him your squire." The magistrate pushed back and stood up. He was much taller than any of the other people Wiglaf had encountered in town.

"Maybe you should make him the knight, and I will be his squire," Wiglaf said smiling.

"Well, that simply won't work. We need a trained knight. He has no training at all. I would not want to be responsible if someone were to get hurt." The magistrate moved around to the front of the desk and leaned against it. "You see, friend, you are the only one here who can do the job. You may recruit Bill, I mean William, but that will be up to you. I give you my blessing as the Magistrate; whatever resources you need are at your disposal."

"Well then, I would like Sir Bill and a house that would be suitable for a knight."

"You drive a hard bargain, Sir Wiglaf. You may take the house marked 3120 near the docks. It overlooks the ocean. Marvelous view, really—from the second story, you can see the ships as they dock." The magistrate walked over to Wiglaf and put his hand on his shoulder. "Go with my blessing, Sir Knight. I will send for William and have him report directly to you. He is your responsibility. The house is yours as long as you live here. Your orders will be sent after I draft them; a courier will deliver them tonight. I would stay indoors at night though; the Procerus come in large numbers and your job is not to die by their hands. You are dismissed."

The magistrate lifted his hand and waggled his fingers back and forth, shooing Wiglaf away. Wiglaf turned and the black-haired woman was standing in the middle of the open doors. Wiglaf walked toward her, the doors closing as he exited. The black-haired woman walked Wiglaf to the entrance of the magistrate's office.

"Here is your house key, Sir Wiglaf. If you require any additional resources, please come and see me."

The woman turned and retreated to her desk in the middle of the room. Wiglaf attached the key ring to his belt and headed out the door.

## '5'

Bill was eager to accept the position of First Knight under Wiglaf and even more so since he would be staying in a house instead of the outpost that was barely big enough for *him*, let alone a larger man.

Wiglaf and Bill spent the next months patrolling the town during the day and sometimes defending it against the Procerus that came in the evening. The Procerus did not like confrontation, and it seemed the stories of their frightful killing and stealing were exaggerated rumor spread by the town officials in order to keep the citizens inside after dark.

After the third month, the Procerus only came around every so often. Wiglaf and Bill had been doing a good job of keeping them from their thievery. One particular night Wiglaf and Bill were walking past Old Maid Mackenzie's fruit stand when a cloaked figure dashed from the shadows and into the alley. Wiglaf and Bill quickly ran after the figure. The alley was dark, but some light from the moon shone down. The cloaked figure stood trapped against a brick wall.

"Stay where you are, Procerus, and you will not be harmed," Wiglaf stated. Bill drew his sword, but Wiglaf held his hand over the front of Bill's chest. "We mean you no harm. We just want to talk."

The single cloaked figure dropped the fruit it had been holding and the shadowy figure became three shadowy figures standing at the back.

"Why should we trust you?" the voice came out of the darkness. "You work as a knight of the magistrate. He said you would kill us and eat the meat off our bones."

"I would do no such thing, Procerus. I am not a knight of the magistrate, but my own person, hired to do a job, which is to make sure the streets are safe." Wiglaf held his position and held Bill as well.

"You lie, Sir Knight. The magistrate told us you would say such things to lure us into your web and then kill us like the spider kills the fly." The three figures moved backward up against the wall.

"I promise you, the magistrate is the one lying. Here, I will even give you my sword." Wiglaf drew his sword and tossed it along the ground at the feet of the cloaked creature. The blade sparked as it slid across the ground. "There, I am now unarmed. Come, let us talk, and I will see if I can be of help."

The figures moved forward and picked up the sword. "Keep your distance, Knight, and we will speak. Now move back and give us room to move."

Wiglaf and Bill backed up and out of the alley. The cloaked figures moved forward as one shadow. Bill and Wiglaf stood next to the fountain, the moon illuminating the ground around them.

One of the figures broke free and set Wiglaf's sword on the edge of the fountain and backed away. The first cloaked figure walked forward and pulled its hood back, revealing a head of long golden hair. Her eyes were white in the moonlight, and her lips were crimson red.

"I am Vitok of the Procerus," the woman said, looking at Wiglaf and smiling. "My fellow Procerus here are Tanak and Visok. We dwell within the forest outside these lands, exiled by the magistrate for treason against the Dark Witch. She has control of the town and the magistrate. She seeks to use it in order to bring her war machines across the ocean. Without Heartwick, the White Queen would have an upper hand in the war. We are those who resisted. The Dyhedral used to come at nightfall in order to scare the villagers. They killed several of them to prove that the Dark Witch was not to be trifled with. The magistrate blamed their deaths on us and we were exiled. Bill here was our squire, but we had no idea who could be trusted and so we fled, leaving him to watch the garrison. For that we are sorry, Bill."

Bill walked forward and bowed. "I understand, Vitok." Bill backed up and went to the fountain to sit down.

"The Dark Witch is planning something big. We have seen a large army marching toward Heartwick. They should be here in two nights. I would suggest staying off the streets until they have loaded their boat and left." Vitok looked behind her to see that her partners had pulled their hoods on once again. "For now, I must be going. If what you say is true, then be safe, Sir Knight. If you are not with the Dark Witch, then we share a common enemy." Vitok pulled her hood back on, fled into the darkness and was gone.

"Bill, do you know anything about this?" Wiglaf said, looking down.

Bill looked back up and shook his head. "I do not know if what they say is true, but I do believe them. The magistrate told me that the Procerus had killed the villagers. I assumed he was telling me the truth. Apparently, we had best guard our backs," Bill said, grabbing Wiglaf's sword and handing it to him, hilt first.

"I agree, Sir Bill. Let's keep a low profile until we find out what is really going on."

'6'

The bright light of the torches reflected off the street as the large group of cloaked Dyhedral came through the middle of town. Wiglaf and Bill could see them marching toward the dock in unison. The Dyhedral in the middle of the large horde carried a tented structure on their shoulders. When they reached the pier, the Dyhedral set the structure on the ground and a woman stepped out from underneath the tent. She pointed in several directions, but nothing could be heard from inside the house.

The large group of Dyhedral boarded the ship docked at the edge of town. The white sails fell loosely and then stiffened as they caught wind. Five Dyhedral stood on the dock and hoisted the lines off the cleats. The ship began to move slowly as the wind picked up. The Dyhedral on the docks scurried along the pier and jumped aboard. The last one grabbed onto the side of the ship, slipped, and fell to the sand below.

The Dyhedral made a loud ruckus as the music began to play. The Dyhedral on the sand ran for the ladder as the music grew louder and black fins now appeared, shimmering in the moonlight. The Dyhedral grabbed hold of the ladder and started climbing. He grabbed the next rung, but noticed he was unable to progress upward as his body began to get heavy. He started to lose his grip on the ladder and struggled furiously and unsuccessfully. The massive black shape had his leg and pulled at the Dyhedral. Losing his grip, the Dyhedral fell backward and disappeared into the sand as the darkness took him under. Wiglaf could hear a thunderous applause from the ship as it moved farther and farther away. The symphony that had once been playing was silenced, and the ship drifted out of sight and into the darkness of the desert ocean.

Wiglaf stood looking out the great bay window that overlooked the pier. He was broken out of his trance by a knock at the door. Bill disappeared and returned with a cloaked figure.

"We must leave tonight, Wiglaf. We are gathering the village and fleeing." Vitok was standing in the doorway. "The Dark Witch is bringing something back with her. We do not know what it is, but if she needs that many Dyhedral to bring it back, then it is not something we should be around for. We are asking everyone to leave with us."

"If she is bringing back a machine of war that she plans to use against the free people of this land, then I have no greater duty than to stop it. If that means I give my life to save this land, then so be it. Bill, grab your gear and go with Vitok," Wiglaf said, picking up Bill's sword and handing it to him.

"I certainly will not. I am in your service now and will not abandon my post," Bill said, standing defiantly.

"Well, Bill, you leave me no choice. I relieve you of your duties. Please go with Vitok. The people of this village need you now. I will call for you when the danger has cleared."

"Okay, Wiglaf, not because you relieved me, but because you ordered me. I go," Bill said, taking his sword and picking up his traveler's pack.

"Wiglaf, I beg you to come. You will do more for this village alive than dead." Vitok put her hand on his shoulder.

"I must do as I have been taught, Vitok. If this is my last battle, then I will fight to the end. I will not see another village enslaved by fear and guilty conscience. If today be the day, I will join my king in Elysium." Wiglaf put a hand to his chest and bowed his head.

"Go forth with honor, Wiglaf, and may our roads cross again." Vitok turned and walked down the stairs.

"Bill, you take care of them. You are a knight of my order, and I expect you to defend the people under your care with your very last breath." Wiglaf knelt down on one knee and put his hand to his chest. "Go forth and protect those in your care."

"Thank you, Wiglaf. I know we will see each other again some day. May the Maker protect you and show you favor." Bill put his hand on his chest and bowed his head. He then turned and walked down the stairs and out of the house.

'7'

Daylight broke over the horizon of the ocean. The light shone on Wiglaf's face and woke him from his slumber. Wiglaf stood and could see the silhouette of a ship in the far distance, moving quickly. Wiglaf reached to his left and grabbed his chest plate and put it on. It rattled against the chainmail he wore underneath. Wiglaf reached for his sword and sheathed it. The sword whispered as it slipped into its home. Wiglaf turned and grabbed his bow and quiver of arrows and walked downstairs. The door was opening and closing by itself as the wind whipped it back and forth.

Wiglaf grabbed the door and held it open as he walked outside. The sun beamed down brightly on his face as he walked down to the pier. The ship was quickly approaching, and Wiglaf could see it clearly now.

As it approached, it became clear that the ship had been in a great battle. The sails of the ship were torn but still functional.

Wiglaf sat on one of the barrels at the edge of the dock until the ship began its turn to dock. The Dyhedral hissed as they saw the figure waiting for them at the edge.

"You may not dock here. This town no longer belongs to the Dark Witch. Let her come forward and reap what she has sown here." Wiglaf pulled the bow off his back and fitted it with an arrow from his quiver.

"There is no Dark Witch here, human, and we far out number you. I would suggest you make room before we dig your grave." The Dyhedral jumped off the boat and tied the line around the cleat. The dock lurched under the strain and the rope crackled as it tightened under the pressure.

Wiglaf pulled the arrow back and released it into the back of the Dyhedral that had jumped off the boat.

"I don't have enough arrows for all of you, but my sword has enough blade for the rest." Wiglaf pulled back another arrow and fired a warning shot over the heads of the Dyhedral and into the side of a large burlap tarp that was tied to the dock.

From within the tarp came a beastly roar. Wiglaf dropped his bow and covered his ears. The Dyhedral did the same as the sound of ropes tightening became the sound of ropes snapping.

Dozens of Dyhedral rushed to the large, moving tarp and grabbed onto the ropes. They tried to pull the ropes down but were slung through the air effortlessly. Two immense wings sprang from underneath the tarp, knocking countless Dyhedral overboard into the sand. The Dyhedral were scattering like mice leaving a sinking ship. Many jumped into the sand without regard for the evil that lurked beneath it. Wiglaf thought, *Whatever this is, apparently it is safer to jump into the sand where the beasts under the sand play music and take you underneath.*

Wiglaf stood paralyzed as the Dyhedral came running past him, fleeing for their lives. The creature under the tarp flapped its wings and crushed the main sail. Wiglaf, breaking free of his paralysis, dodged out of the way as the mast smashed down onto the pier. Wiglaf turned to see a giant creature emerge from beneath the tarp, its long neck reaching out and seizing a Dyhedral off the deck of the ship and swallowing it whole. The jaws of the creature bit down on another Dyhedral that his claws had snatched up from the deck of the ship.

The creature shook the remaining restraints loose and lifted high into the air. It swooped down into the street, grabbing fistfuls of Dyhedral and throwing them high into the air. The creature flew to the top of the magistrate's building and perched. Wiglaf ran back to the dock and grabbed his bow. He could see the creature perched, its long neck following the Dyhedral, watching them panic as they ran through the street.

The creature was dark as midnight, with a long neck that attached to a head with many teeth. Its neck curled down like a snake as it watched the many Dyhedral scrambling, obviously looking for its next meal.

"Well, my King, it would appear not all dragons have been vanquished during our time. I will let fate decide whether or not I join you today." Wiglaf drew his bow back and shot an arrow toward the beast, piercing its neck. The beast roared furiously, flapping its wings. The gust from the wings knocked over several Dyhedral that had been running by.

Wiglaf ran to the fountain at the center of the town, where the beast hovered above the magistrate's office. Large claw marks outlined the roof where the creature had dug in to perch. The beast looked down and saw Wiglaf standing there with another arrow at the ready. Wiglaf released the next arrow aiming for what might be the heart of the beast. The arrow pierced the skin, but only increased the anger of the creature.

The magistrate, hearing the commotion, ran out of his office. "What is going on out here?" Standing there looking at Wiglaf, the magistrate was unaware of the beast now moving quickly toward them. Wiglaf jumped into the fountain, just out of reach, as the creature's claws brushed past.

"Magistrate, come with me quickly! That thing is coming back."

Wiglaf grabbed the magistrate's arm and pulled him toward the office. The two ran through the doors quickly as the creature came down, smashing the heart between the pillars. A large chunk smashed to the ground and blocked the entrance to the door with the word "LIVE" facing inward.

"Wiglaf, you must save the village. The people here are depending on you." The magistrate was gasping for air.

"The people in the village are gone, Magistrate. I know you struck a deal with the Dark Witch. That thing outside is the fruit of your deal," Wiglaf said, holding out his sword.

"No, the Dark Witch said no harm would come to our village if we allowed her the use of our port." The magistrate was leaning over with his hands on his knees. "She never said anything about bringing the Jabberwocky back here and releasing it."

"Jabberwocky? So you knew what was going on and you did not warn us? I should kill you where you stand! However, I fear killing you won't help us get out of this," Wiglaf said, putting his sword down.

"Wiglaf, I hired you just in case this happened. Now you must go out there and slay the Jabberwocky," the magistrate pleaded with Wiglaf.

The magistrate turned toward the door as the stone covering it was ripped away, revealing a head with large eyes peering inside. The head growled and hissed as its rank breath permeated the air. The magistrate, seeing the end, turned toward Wiglaf.

"Beware the Jabberwocky, my son. Go to Relic House on the hill. There you will find a Vorpal Blade with which to slay the creature."

The magistrate started to say something else, but was whisked backward as the snake-like head grabbed hold of him and recoiled. Wiglaf ran toward the door, but no creature was to be seen.

'8'

Wiglaf ran up the hill to the gate outside the Relic House. The gate was locked with a heavy steel chain. Wiglaf drew his sword and struck the chain, but it had no effect. A shadow grew over his head, and Wiglaf turned to see the Jabberwocky standing over him. Without warning, Wiglaf was hurled backward through the gate, where he fell just on the other side; the iron gate lay twenty-five yards away in the ground. Another claw came swiping down, crushing part of the stone pillar. The creature roared in pain as one of its claws broke off in the stone.

Wiglaf scrambled to his feet, ran up the steps and threw open the large wooden doors. He ran to the left into the relic vault. The large window behind him shattered and glass rained down from above. Wiglaf ran to the back where the weapons were kept and threw open the battle-chest lid, unaware of the blood streaking down his arms from where the glass had cut him. The creature smelled blood and thirsted for a taste. The Jabberwocky threw its head into the room, but the glass dug into its neck and it retreated.

Wiglaf grabbed the Vorpal Blade from the back of the chest and turned, but the fell beast was gone once more. He walked out into the foyer, listening for any sounds that the Jabberwocky might still be around.

Wiglaf climbed the stairs and to the left. He could hear a faint cry and thought that it might be someone trapped. He rushed through the door, but the roof caved in around him. The Jabberwocky thrust its head toward him, knocking him out the back window and into the gardens below. Wiglaf was slow to get up, but knowing he had to, he willed his muscles to obey.

Wiglaf looked around, but could not see the sword anywhere. The Jabberwocky came down, grabbing Wiglaf from the garden while he was still looking for the Vorpal Blade. Wiglaf struggled as the creature's claw dug into the armor, crushing it inward. The Jabberwocky rose high into the air over the heavily wooded forest. Wiglaf, gasping for breath, pushed against the claw, to no avail. Thinking of nothing else, Wiglaf bit down on the hard skin that stretched between the claws. The creature's claw relaxed and Wiglaf pushed himself up. He climbed up the creature's back, toward its head. He could see something shiny stuck in the side of its head.

The Jabberwocky struggled to get Wiglaf off its backside. Wiglaf climbed upward toward the Vorpal Blade, which must have stuck in the creature when it knocked him off the staircase and through the window.

The creature dove into the Frost Woods and through the trees. The branches whipped Wiglaf in the face as he reached out toward the blade. Wiglaf reached, but could not grasp the blade. He stretched outward, his fingertips just barely able to touch the hilt. Wiglaf knew he could end this now if he had the blade, so he jumped out for it. His hand grabbed the hilt as a tree branch hit his armor in the chest, sending him backward toward the ground. Wiglaf fell for what seemed like eternity, spinning through tree branches. He could not tell if the breaking sound was tree branches or bone. Without warning, he hit the ground at the bottom of a Tumtum tree. His body felt broken, and he could barely move. The Vorpal Blade lay on the ground thirty meters from the tree.

The Jabberwocky, realizing it was free of the rider, turned and came to rest on the ground, looking for its meal. The shine of the Vorpal Blade caught its eye and it slunk along, looking for the wielder. The blood from the wound on its neck made the Jabberwocky's cry gurgle as it walked through the wooded area. The creature stood over the blade, smelling the air. The head snaked around to the left of the Tumtum tree and then to the right, but Wiglaf was not to be found where he had fallen.

Wiglaf had crawled around a much larger tree that would provide him more time to recoup. His leg was bleeding badly and he could not walk on it. He could hear the Jabberwocky smelling the scent of his blood trail. The creature moved, gurgling through the tulgey wood.

Wiglaf pushed himself against the tree, propping himself up. The creature moved closer to his location with each breath. Wiglaf turned to look around the corner, but the creature was gone. He breathed a sigh of relief, but the gurgling sound came from above him. Wiglaf looked up to see a large set of teeth breathing down on him.

The jaws came down and Wiglaf swung his sword upward, shattering one of its teeth. The sword fell away with the shards. Wiglaf fell to the ground before the creature. Wiglaf knew his time had come and that the creature had bested him.

He closed his eyes and prayed his final prayer. The creature's breath came warm over him. The creature opened its jaws and closed them around Wiglaf's leg, tasting the blood. The Jabberwocky lifted Wiglaf into the air, savoring the flavor of his blood.

Wiglaf shouted into the air, "If you are going to eat me, eat, you wretched beast!"

The creature snarled and Wiglaf fell back to the ground. Twisting its head back and forth, the creature roared with anger. Wiglaf saw a figure holding the Vorpal Blade, which was plunged deep into the back of the Jabberwocky. It was Bill! The Jabberwocky was writhing back and forth in pain. Bill pulled the sword from the back of the creature and tossed it to Wiglaf. Wiglaf pulled himself along the ground toward the creature. With what remained of his strength, he swung the blade across the creature's neck. The creature screamed and then was silent. The Jabberwocky fell to the earth with a loud thud.

Bill rushed over to Wiglaf and tied his tunic over the gash in Wiglaf's leg.

"Nice to see you, Sir Bill the Dragon Slayer."

"Quiet, Wiglaf, you need your strength."

Bill called his horse over and helped Wiglaf on it. He sent the horse back to Heartwick. Bill took the Vorpal Blade from the ground and cut through the creature's neck to remove the head, in order to ensure it was truly dead.

When Bill returned to Heartwick with the head of the creature, Vitok was tending to Wiglaf's wounds.

"He'll be okay, Bill. We'll take good care of him. He's lucky you came along when you did, Sir Bill the Dragon Slayer."

Bill smiled and dragged the head of the creature to the center of town.

## *Chapter 12*

'1'

Warrington looked up from his meal to see a single tear appear in Wiglaf's eye and roll down the side of his cheek. Marchavious and Theo were both staring at Wiglaf with their mouths agape. Neither one had touched their food.

"Food's gonna get cold if you don't start eating," Wiglaf said with a smile and a tremor in his voice. The excitement of that day brought back a flood of memories.

"Sir Wiglaf, since we see you are the only one here in Heartwick, what happened to the others?" Warrington inquired.

Marchavious put down his fork in anticipation of another story, but Wiglaf let out a sigh.

"Well, you see, that story happened many years ago. There is no way I could defend the town from an onslaught such as that of the Jabberwocky at my age. The people of Heartwick never returned for fear of retaliation from the Dark Witch and her army of Dyhedral. They fled to the peaks northwest of the Frost Woods in hopes the White Queen would have mercy and take them in. The Procerus went with them to offer them protection.

"Bill stayed behind and lived here for many years. We would often try to defend the town from the Dyhedral when they would try to import their weapons and supplies through Heartwick. Eventually it was too much for us, as we were both growing older. Bill was by my side until the age of 146. He would have stayed longer if I had not sent him away with the Procerus on their last visit. Let's see … that was almost five years ago." Wiglaf put his hand on his chin and scratched in deep thought. "I wasn't ready to leave this place yet, as I had come to think of it as home. I told Bill that I would see him eventually, though. Maybe that time is drawing near." Another tear started to well up in Wiglaf's eyes.

Marchavious, who was chewing on a large piece of "chicken" spoke up, "Well, Sir Wiglaf, we are heading to the White Queen to seek help in order to rescue our friend from the Dark Witch. We could use a knight of your reputation to make it through the Frost Woods and to the White Queen safely." Small pieces of food tumbled out of his mouth as he spoke.

"I appreciate the offer, but I don't know if I am truly ready to leave this place. I had hoped the people would come back and this place would be what it once was. I don't even know if Bill, the Procerus, and the people that fled are even alive."

"What is there for you here, Wiglaf?" Warrington said, having finished his food before speaking.

"I guess you are correct. There is really nothing keeping me here other than keeping the chickens from eating the road, but I guess I can only do so much. I thought my days as a knight could eventually be over if I just stayed and tried to restart the town. Always one final adventure, right?" Wiglaf picked up his napkin and wiped his mouth.

"Well then, it is settled. We will leave first thing tomorrow morning," Marchavious said, looking over at Warrington. "Now if you will point me to the sleeping quarters, I will ready myself for a good night's rest." Wiglaf stood up and showed the trio, which was soon to be a quartet, to their rooms.

'2'

The morning sun rose and then decided that it would go back to bed for an hour. When it began to rise for the second time that morning, Warrington was waking up on a blanket near the library's fireplace, in which a fire was still smoldering. Marchavious and Theo remained asleep, one on the couch near Warrington and the other sitting upright in a chair with his legs outstretched on the dirty crimson ottoman. Marchavious began to open his eyes as the sun's rays peered in through the large undraped window, stretching his arms out as he sat up.

"That was wonderful. I feel like I have not slept in months," Marchavious said, cupping a hand over his mouth as he yawned.

Marchavious stood up and grabbed his jacket from the back of the couch and put it on. He walked over to where Theo was sleeping still and kicked the ottoman out from underneath his legs. Theo stood up with a start, thinking he was under attack from the Rebobs that inhabited in the woods.

"Would it kill you to leave me be? I was having the most pleasant dreams and I would enjoy going back to them before going to work at the hat shop today," Theo said as he sat back down, closing his eyes.

"Come on, lazybones, time to rise. We gotta get going so we can get through the woods before nightfall. We would not want the Rebobs to get us while we were walking through the woods, right?" Marchavious said, playing to the fact that Theo had a certain fear of anything remotely threatening.

Theo sat up in the chair and then went directly to his feet. "When do we leave?"

Marchavious saw Warrington head out the door. He and Theo followed Warrington to the dining area, where there were three bowls of a watery soup-like substance. Warrington jumped up on the chair and smelled the aroma wafting out of the bowl. Theo sat down and began spooning the hot liquid into his mouth.

"Where is Wiglaf?" Marchavious said, sitting down at the table.

"No clue. I have been with you all morning. Maybe he decided not to go?" Theo said, thinking they could just circumvent the woods if Wiglaf decided not to go with them.

"I am sure he is around here somewhere. After all, he fixed our meal, and it is still warm," Marchavious said, stating the obvious.

After they had finished, the three companions gathered what little belongings they had and went looking for Wiglaf.

Although it had only been an hour since they had woken and eaten breakfast, the sun was quickly racing overhead as though it were noon already. They walked out the large front door of what they recognized from Wiglaf's story the previous night as the relic house.

There was a large wagon sitting at the gate with a great deal of stuff tied to the back. They could see Wiglaf pulling one of the ropes tightly across the back of a large lump covered with black fabric.

"Oh good, you three have finished eating. I have readied the wagon and we should be able to get underway when you are dressed."

Wiglaf climbed down off the side and they could see he was dressed in his full armor, ready for battle. Wiglaf's sword was at his side and his shield was slung snug across his back. The gold lion adorning his breastplate shone brightly in the sun.

"I beg your pardon, what do you mean dressed, Wiglaf? I am fully clothed," Theo said insulted, presenting himself to Wiglaf. While he knew he had not changed clothes for quite some time and they might smell a little ripe, he was still dressed nonetheless.

"My dear Theophilus, you are going to meet a queen. You cannot possibly think yourself presentable in those rags. I have taken the initiative to get you some clothes from the late magistrate's house. He won't be needing them anytime soon. Marchavious, I have picked out a nice pair of clothes from the relic keeper's old things for you as well. Now, let's get you changed so we can be on our way."

'3'

Warrington sat on the large black cloth covering the wagon, waiting for Wiglaf to reveal two very well-dressed men. Theophilus came out first in his purple magistrate's coat. His vest was patterned with black and white checkers that matched his pants. He had an oversized cream bow tie that had purple polka-dots over the outside. He tipped his top hat that he had worn since the day they left to come to Terra-Mirac. The tag, although smudged a bit, still read "In This Style, 10/6."

Marchavious stepped out into the light to reveal a very dapper long brown coat, a grey vest with a white shirt underneath, and a red necktie fastened around his neck in a double Windsor knot.

"Now this is a group that is ready to meet the White Queen," Wiglaf pronounced as he walked out behind the other two. Marchavious climbed up into the wagon and looked back at the large pile hidden by the black cloth.

"Wiglaf, I do not think we are all going to fit in the wagon." His voice sounded concerned.

"I will ride ahead on my old horse. Bill's horse will pull the wagon."

Wiglaf walked around the front and grabbed the brown leather reins. He handed them to Marchavious as Theo climbed into the shotgun position. There was an old rusty blunderbuss sitting in the holster attached to the front of the wagon.

"Now Theo, there is one shot in that old dirty blunderbuss there. Be sure you truly need it before you use it, because there is not a second shot."

"I am sure that with you I won't need to even touch it. I am not a fan of the black powder, you could say." Theophilus leaned backward with his hands, shielding himself from the rifle.

"Well, I am just saying if ya do, then use it wisely." Wiglaf put his foot into the stirrup and mounted his horse. His armor clanked as he threw his leg over the top and on to the other side. "Now just follow me and we are on our way. We should be there in two days, barring any trouble."

Wiglaf gave a small gentle nudge in the horse's side and he started forward. Marchavious pulled the reins and gave a hearty "Hee-yaw!" at the horse and she pulled forward. The wagon lurched and then gave way, the contents in the back crashing up and down.

'4'

The wagon was quite bumpy and after two hours, Theophilus started to complain of the wooden splinters piercing his bum when the wagon hit any small bump or pothole in the road. Wiglaf had pointed out the garrison where Bill had stood guard when he first arrived, although it was assuredly home to several ghosts at this point.

Three hours had passed, and Heartwick was just a small speck on the horizon behind them. Heartwick Lake glimmered as the sun was going down and the largest of three crimson moons began rising above the tree line.

By the time they reached the edge of the Frost Woods, the sun had decided to head back toward the moon, as if to chase it out of the sky and back down behind the trees. However, the moon did not budge, even though the sun almost eclipsed it. The sun was no match for the canopy of the trees, which shaded everything below it. The sun seemed to struggle to poke through, but only illuminated areas where the trees had succumbed to old age.

The wagon squeaked as it crossed the threshold that separated the open plain from the forest. Wiglaf rode on ahead, as he had said he would. Theo was sitting upright with his head leaned back. Loud growling noises rumbled from his nostrils as he breathed in and out.

The wagon moved smoothly over the soft dirt. Marchavious marveled at the fact that the road contained no blemishes, unlike the previous roads they had been on. It was as though it was being maintained constantly. The smooth road wound itself around several of the trees and even through the center of one of the largest trees in the forest. It was as though the tree had two legs and spread them wide open for travelers to pass through. Marchavious wondered if the tree enjoyed standing over the road, but then thought, *That is just silly. Trees do not have such thoughts.* Theo and Warrington saw none of these sights since they both had been asleep since they passed by the lake.

Marchavious could see the shaded ground lighten and then get very bright along the forest floor as the trees seemed to grow scarce. Just before the wagon reached the final line of trees and burst into the open, Wiglaf rode around the corner and halted them. The wagon jolted forward, waking Theo and Warrington simultaneously.

Theo, startled, began shouting. "What in the name of the queen is going on here? I was having …" he was abruptly cut off as Marchavious wrapped a hand around his mouth. Theo's eyes grew wide with anger and then grew wider as he saw why they had stopped.

In the clearing up ahead was a large house with a red door. Straw covered the rooftop of the second story. He looked out over the crude stone fence to see a short Dyhedral working in the yard.

"I believe this may be an outpost of the Dark Witch. We need to proceed with caution," Wiglaf said, pointing at Theo.

Warrington sat up, looking over at the lizard looking man. "One Dyhedral should be no match for us," Warrington commented.

"One may not be, but we don't know how many there are. That is quite a large house," Wiglaf replied.

"Maybe we can distract him as we sneak the wagon by. Warrington, you can do your disappearing cat thing and go in and see. Maybe even provide a distraction for us. Make a small ruckus," Marchavious said, patting him on the head.

Warrington purred and jumped between him and Theo. "Well then, I guess I will go and see. I will let you know when things are all clear."

Warrington jumped to the ground and padded toward the house. His fur shimmered in the sun as he bounded through the high grass toward the abode. Marchavious rubbed his eyes with the palm of his hand as he saw just a tail jumping through the grass and then there was nothing at all.

Warrington had not fully mastered the ability to disappear at will, but he was getting better at it, although it did still have a high probability of failing him.

The Dyhedral was still working in the yard and Warrington, now on top of the rock wall, could see he was raking leaves. Warrington waltzed past him, muttering, "*Missed a spot*" to the creature as he passed by. The Dyhedral looked up and around, but went back to raking when he saw no one.

Warrington jumped up and into the open triangle-shaped window that hung over a very peculiar trapezoid planter.

Every inch of the house had dark brown wooden floors. The room Warrington could see from the window looked like a sitting room. There was a small stone fireplace—much smaller than the library's—against the far wall. In front of the fireplace was a single crimson leather chair with a three-legged brown circular table next to it. On the table was a black, oddly shaped device with a long tail that did not seem to end. Warrington had never seen anything like this before and it made him curious.

Warrington jumped down to the floor with a thud and strolled across the wooden planks. Each one made a small groan as he walked slowly toward the staircase that led to the second story. He thought he could worry about his curiosity at a later time.

Warrington bounded up the staircase with gusto, looking out for any Dyhedral that might be in this area. Warrington looked left and then right as he reached the plateau of the stairs. The long hallway was windowless and provided no light. This was not concerning since he was a cat and cats are notorious for having good night vision. He was also invisible, which afforded him the ability to not be seen in the light or the dark.

Warrington could hear murmuring coming from a doorway just down the hall. At the third door, Warrington could see light coming from beneath the crack. He leaned down to see if there was anyone in the room. A small gust of air hit him in the face as a shadowy figure moved about. Warrington breathed in and out slowly as his head sunk toward the crack again. The smell of whatever was in this room was quite different from the stench of the Dyhedral—it smelled a bit more like wet hair and feathers than scales and unwashed lizard.

Warrington got up and headed back toward the staircase and proceeded downward. As Warrington reached the bottom, he heard a strange voice call to him.

"Well, did you finish what you were doing?" the lispy voice called from the crimson chair.

Warrington froze as though he had been caught. He could see the scaly hand on the arm, digging its claws into the leather. Warrington did not answer, but the voice spoke again.

"What is the matter, cat got your tongue? Speak up now, you foul wretch."

This time the head spun around and looked directly at Warrington. Warrington looked down to see he was still invisible.

The creature shook his head and muttered, "I could have sworn I heard the cursed monkey come downstairs."

Warrington could hear the footsteps of whatever it was that was upstairs coming down the hallway. Warrington moved quickly across the room and leapt onto the windowsill where he had entered.

"There you are, Wilford. Did you finish making the arrangements?" the Dyhedral said, looking at the black furry creature that had waddled down the stairs.

"Yes sir, the plans are ready. They will not know what hit them. The troops will be ready once you have received the time of the Dark Witch's arrival in Heartwick."

The dark-furred figure stepped out into the light of the room. Warrington could see the face of a monkey with wings attached to its back, the weight of which made the creature the Dyhedral called Wilford walk clumsily.

"The Dark Witch will fall and the Dyhedral will be free once more." The Dyhedral got up and moved toward Wilford. "Then the Rebob and Dyhedral races will have a new home in the eastern towers of this accursed place."

Wilford nodded in approval.

Warrington moved quickly back down the stairs and out the window to the ground. He passed through the gate and to the other side of the forest, where he could see the back of the wagon shaded under the canopy of the trees. Warrington jumped to the back of the wagon. "Well, there is only one Dyhedral," he said.

Theophilus jumped and fell off the side of the wagon and onto the dirt below. "Good gawd, Warrington, you could warn someone before you sneak up on them."

Marchavious had jumped slightly, but not to the effect that Theo had.

"Sorry, I forgot you could not see me," Warrington said, chuckling.

"Very funny, Warrington. Hilarious even." Theo stood up and dusted off his clothes.

"So, only one Dyhedral, Warrington?" Wiglaf came riding out from behind a tree.

"No, two, but I do not think they are the Dark Witch's servants," Warrington said struggling to get his body to reappear.

"What makes you say that?" Wiglaf said putting a hand to his chin.

"The one inside the house had a winged monkey with him—those Rebob things that you told us live in these woods. He told the monkey that he would free the Dyhedral and take over the Dark Witch's tower to the east," Warrington said finally getting the rest of his tail to reappear. He shook his back foot and it appeared out of thin air.

"Winged monkey? He had one of those winged Rebob monkey things? I think we need to stay away from that. No need to get involved in their plans—right, Wiglaf? Any enemy of the Dark Witch may not be friendly to us, either," Theo said as he climbed back into the wagon, his weight shifting it to one side and then back again.

"Well, we must not count them out as allies, but for now we will leave them to their own plotting. He may be a scout for the Dark Witch and may still pretend to have loyal ties regardless. For now we will press on to the castle and decide where to go from there."

Wiglaf pulled the reins of the horse and turned her to the left, heading down the path. Marchavious hiked the reins of the wagon and the horse lunged forward and followed Wiglaf.

'5'

The sun was finally going down when they reached the edge of the Frost Woods. The sign at the border read:

*PLAIN PLAINS AHEAD*

*CAUTION: WATCH OUT FOR*

The last piece of the sign had been broken off by age. Marchavious halted the wagon at the edge. Wiglaf had dismounted and was inspecting the broken piece of the sign.

"So, what are we supposed to watch out for, Wiglaf?" Marchavious spoke up.

Theo was once again asleep, oblivious to the fact they had even stopped this time.

"I don't know, Marchavious. This is the farthest north I have traveled since coming here from where I was. I am sure we will see soon enough whatever it is we are to be careful of."

Marchavious held up a finger in the air, "I only ask because we had encountered some sand sharks previously. We should keep an ear out for music if that is the case." Marchavious was a bit apprehensive about venturing into an area that could be infested with musical instruments of death. Wiglaf noted his concern and threw the small board off to the side of the path and looked out across the empty plain.

"How long before nightfall?" Marchavious said to Wiglaf, looking at the rapidly growing shadows of the trees.

"I would say a few minutes by the rate at which the sun is disappearing, but it could come back. You never know," Wiglaf said, looking around the ground beneath him.

"Maybe we should make camp here and continue on in the morning?" Warrington suggested, looking at Marchavious.

"That sounds like a good idea. We should be safe on the border here, but we'll make camp out a small way just in case anyone or anything comes from either side of us." Wiglaf moved towards the wagon motioning Marchavious to come help him move the wagon off the path.

Marchavious prompted the horse to move and the wagon jutted forward. They moved left and about fifty yards off the path to a large clearing. The sun dipped behind the horizon and then came back for another peek. The extra light gave Wiglaf time to get a fire going before the sun finally decided to go down behind the veil.

They were all sitting around the campfire with their bedrolls laid out. Warrington sat on top of the black cloth that covered their supplies.

"We'll need to take turns being on watch," Wiglaf said. "That sign did not give me a good feeling. We don't want to get eaten out here. Not when we are so close."

"Well, I nominate Theo for the first watch since he has slept this entire trip," Marchavious commented, nudging him awake with his elbow.

"Sounds good to me. Theo, wake me up when you get tired, and I'll take the next watch," Wiglaf said, laying his head down.

"Does now count?" Theo said. "I think all the sleep I got made me tired."

"Quiet, Theo, and stand watch," Marchavious said, laying his head down on his bedroll.

Theo put his back against the rubbery texture of the wagon's wheel and closed his eyes. As he felt his body drifting off to sleep again, Theo shook his head back and forth, trying to stay awake. He could see his hat shop at the end of the cobblestone road each time his eyes shut. Each time he felt his mind leaving the forest and moving back to the shop. He could smell the treatment chemicals for the felt. The smell made him yearn for home ...

Theo spent the day tending to the hat shop and sold the most hats he had ever sold. He could see it was getting to be past time for him to close up shop. *I think I will stop by the tavern on the way home.*

Theophilus turned the key in the lock and felt it click. He turned around, walked over to the bar and sat down.

"Barkeep, your finest ale, if you will. I have put in a hard day's work and I deserve a frosty ale, if I do say so myself."

The bartender turned around and Theo could see that he had the face of a monkey. "Six shillings," the monkey said, looking at him.

Theo stood up quickly and backed away from the bar ...

Theo quickly woke up, startled and shaking. Everyone was still asleep, so he must not have been dozing for long. Theo stood up so he would not fall asleep again. He looked around at the empty void that circled them in the woods. The darkness called to him. *Sleep* ... he could hear it say. Shimmering orbs started forming around him in the void, and he began to think he was going mad. The orbs appeared and disappeared at random intervals.

"Wiglaf," Theo said. "Wiglaf, time to take over."

Wiglaf stirred a bit and awoke. "What is it, Theo? Is it time for my watch?" Wiglaf rubbed his eyes.

"Yes, Wiglaf. I am tired and starting to see things in the woods," Theo said, sitting down on his bedroll. "I must be tired. It seemed like a hundred shiny orbs in the distance."

"Orbs? You mean like a single one here and there or—"

"No, more like pairs. There were always two that would turn on and then go off," Theo said looking out into the forest, but nothing was out there anymore.

Wiglaf grabbed for his sword and stood up quickly. He took a small pouch out of his bag and poured a small amount of the liquid it contained on his sword. He stuck the sword in the fire and it lit ablaze, illuminating the forest. Wiglaf held the flaming sword into the air. The orbs appeared in the light of the fire and then disappeared, as they had for Theo.

"I think we are being watched by the Rebobs, but they won't come near. I brought a special treat just in case they did show up to cause trouble," Wiglaf said, moving toward the wagon.

He picked up Warrington, who was still sleeping, and placed him on the bedroll near the fire. Warrington rolled over and stretched on his back, warming his belly in the firelight. Wiglaf pulled a small wooden box from underneath the black cloth and placed it on the ground. He put a small wooden spike on the ground and pushed it into the dirt. Then he took a piece of twine and wound it around the spike tying it into a knot. Theo watched in sincere interest as Wiglaf made a small loop at the end. Wiglaf opened the top of the box and pulled a large furry chicken out and placed the loop around its neck. Wiglaf put the chicken on the ground and it immediately started pecking at the ground and kicking up dirt. It looked up at Theo and made a clucking noise.

"There we go, should be fine now," Wiglaf said, smiling. "The Rebobs sure hate these things."

"Well, now I won't be going back to sleep with that furry terror in camp." Theo shuddered at the thought of it getting near him. The chicken scratched the ground and let out a loud squawk in Theo's direction as if to say, *I don't like you either.*

"Well, it's the Rebobs or our furry chicken friend here. Either way, we should be fine. Unless Warrington gets hungry, that is."

Wiglaf sat down next to Warrington and rubbed his head. Warrington pressed his head against Wiglaf's palm.

"You should get some sleep, Theo. The chicken won't hurt you. You'll need to rest up for our journey tomorrow. You would not want to be sleeping when we meet the queen, would you?"

Wiglaf patted Warrington's belly. Warrington seemed to appear and disappear with each pat.

"I guess not," Theo said, raising his arms in a long stretch.

The chicken went about its business scratching and pecking the ground, as all chickens do.

## Chapter 13

'1'

The next morning seemed to come quickly. Theo awoke with the sun in his face. He felt a warm sensation on his stomach, and as he thought he might be hungry, reached down to rub his belly. He felt fur and petted Warrington, who he imagined had gotten cold and come over to snuggle for warmth. As Theo stroked the back of the furry animal, he could see Warrington sitting across from him, smiling in his direction. Theo began to realize in terror that he was not petting Warrington, but something else with fur. Theo jumped up, flailing his arms over his head and brushing himself off rapidly to rid himself of any chicken germs that might have been transferred. The chicken got up and walked away, seemingly unoffended by this display.

"Good lord! Why did no one tell me that thing was attacking me?" Theo said, posturing like he was going to kill the furry bird.

Wiglaf and Warrington laughed at this sight.

"Be careful, Theo. You wouldn't want to be injured by the bird," Marchavious said, now awake and laughing along with Wiglaf and Warrington at the sight of Theo kicking the air near the chicken. The chicken moved quickly away from the incoming kick, even though it was nowhere near hitting him.

"Very funny, Marchavious, he did not try to accost you in your sleep," Theo said angrily.

Warrington laughed. "For the life of me, I cannot tell which one is the bigger chicken."

This received a laugh from Wiglaf and Marchavious.

"Well, now that we've all had a good laugh, we should get packed up and moving. We have a lot of ground to cover if we are to reach the queen today," Wiglaf said, moving to his feet.

He grabbed the box the chicken had been in and set it back on the ground. Wiglaf picked up the bird, removed the restraint and put him back in the box.

"I think we should name the chicken Carter," Marchavious said with a laugh. "That is Theo's middle name and, I think, very fitting for a chicken, if I say so myself."

Theo looked over, not amused by this suggestion. He turned without a word and packed up his bedroll.

Wiglaf finished packing the rest of the wagon while Theo sulked in the front seat, still mad that he had been the jester of the morning. When the wagon was loaded, Wiglaf untied his horse and mounted the beast.

"You finish up here while I ride ahead and scout for any signs of trouble. We should proceed with caution, as the sign says."

Marchavious nodded and stepped up onto the wagon. Theo moved as far to the right as he could, so as not to sit close to Marchavious. Warrington jumped up onto the back and curled up in the area between Marchavious and Theo.

"Well, I am certainly ready for this trip to be over," Warrington said.

'2'

The wagon's wheels sank deep into the sand as it crossed from the dry soil of the forest into the never-ending expanse of the barren plain. The only sign of life came from the buzzards circling the nothingness miles off into the distance.

"That does not look promising," Theophilus said, wiping the damp moisture that had begun beading up on his forehead.

The others ignored his statement and kept looking forward as though they had not heard him. The mountain sitting off in the distance was almost invisible to the human eye, if not for the faint outline of a castle sitting on top of the highest peak.

The wagon began to move faster as the sand turned to clay. The sand shifted in the wind to reveal the dry and cracked ground below. Wiglaf halted up ahead and signaled to the wagon to stop. Wiglaf turned his horse around and rode back toward them. "We can go no farther with the horses. The sand will eventually consume them."

"Well, that does not sound very comforting. What about us?" Theo looked over at Wiglaf, who was dismounting and heading toward the back of the wagon.

"While I have never been out this way before, I am pretty sure the sand is dense enough for us to stay on the top layer. The horses are too heavy, as is the wagon." Wiglaf took out a small pack and hoisted it onto his back. He walked to the front of the wagon and unhitched the horse.

"We'll leave the wagon here in case we come back this way at any point in time. I am sure it will remain untouched."

Marchavious climbed down off the wagon. It creaked to one side and then back to the other. Marchavious grabbed the small box with the chicken and set it on the ground. He opened the lid and set the chicken on the sandy clay.

"You are free to go, Carter. Have a safe journey back to the forest," Marchavious said, letting go of the chicken.

Carter squawked and pecked the ground but did not head in any direction. They grabbed the remaining items that were required for the rest of the journey and started off again across the sand.

Warrington had no trouble staying on the top since he was significantly lighter than the others. Wiglaf sank down to his knees under the weight of his armor, while Marchavious and Theo walked ankle deep. The wagon slowly disappeared off in the horizon. The horses had retreated back into the Frost Woods and presumably back to their home in Heartwick.

Theo stopped for a moment and looked around. The swarm of birds circling overhead was getting closer with each step, but that was not what was unsettling to him. He turned around and saw that he was being followed. Carter had decided that they were much more interesting to follow than going alone back into the forest.

"Stupid bird. Go away!" Theo shouted, making a shooing gesture with his hands, but the bird largely ignored him, moving across the sand with relative ease.

The mountain in the distance was growing quite large with each hour spent in the sand.

Warrington looked ahead and stopped moving. He crouched down low to the ground, as if he was ready to pounce on an invisible object. Marchavious nudged Wiglaf and pointed at Warrington. "He must see something we do not. I am sure it is nothing. Warrington …"

Wiglaf's voice trailed off in Warrington's mind as he focused on the object moving beneath the sand. He crept along the top of the sand, watching with huge, globe-like eyes. Even Carter had noticed this and stopped moving for fear he might be the object Warrington spotted next.

"Warrington?" Marchavious said, "Warrington, what do you see?" But his voice fell on deaf ears.

In a flash Warrington was sprinting through the sand and over a small dune. His companions chased after him, looking down the side of the dune that dipped down in the sea of sand. There was a large cloud puffing upward that hid Warrington and his target from view. The sand settled to the desert floor and Warrington emerged with his prize between his teeth.

"A fish?" Theo said, looking downward. "He caught a fish in the desert?" Theo put his head between his legs breathing heavily.

Warrington came bounding up to rejoin the group, displaying his shiny gold fish between his teeth.

"Well, it would appear that Warrington has caught us lunch," Marchavious said, looking at the fish in wonder.

"Looks more like a golden trout than just any old fish," Wiglaf said, grabbing the fish from the ground where Warrington had dropped it.

"There are a few more, but they disappeared after I grabbed the first one," Warrington said, smiling. "I was not sure what it was exactly, but I was curious."

"Well, we should stop and have the desert fish for lunch," Theo said, salivating at the thought of food and forgetting about the horrifying sharks. He could not remember the last time he had eaten fresh fish, whether it be from a lake or from a desert.

After dividing up the fish, Warrington said, thinking out loud, "If there are fish in this sandy area, do you think those large musical shark things live out here? After all, we did see them in the sand and they did display fish-like qualities."

Theo stopped chewing and began to wonder the same thing. "Maybe we should not dawdle in this area." Theo looked over at Marchavious, who seemed to not care.

"You're right; we should keep moving and if we do hear the music, we should move faster," Warrington said, finishing the small piece of fish he had.

Wiglaf stood up and stretched his arms. "I feel great! Like I am a young man again. I guess I needed a bit of protein to boost my energy, and that really hit the spot."

"I feel the same way. That was the best meal I have ever eaten," Marchavious said, licking the juice off his fingers. "Let's get moving. I am ready to see this White Queen."

## '3'

The pace of the group quickened as they moved closer to the mountain where the castle sat. However, as the hours went by, their energy slowly faded.

"I need to take a rest," Theo said, slowing to a snail's pace.

They had gone several miles in the past hour, but their pace seemed to be slowing down even more as the effects of the fish wore off.

"We're close, Theo; don't grow weary now. We can rest, but only for a few minutes," Wiglaf, kneeling down.

The sun dipping below the horizon in the east brought a sweet, flinty smell mixed with cinnamon in the air toward them. Marchavious pointed off into the distance as they reached the solid clay surface of the mountainside. Small bursts of lightning could be seen streaking across the top of the sand.

"Well, it's a good thing we did not encounter that while we crossed the sand. That might have been what the sign was trying to warn us about," Marchavious said, looking out across the vast ocean of sand they had just finished crossing.

Their eyes widened as a large worm-like creature breached the surface of the sand and struck down, sending a wave of sand in every direction. The creature was too far away to get a good look at, but from the size of it at the distance they were at, it would have easily crushed them with one leap.

Theo closed his mouth and stood looking out across the sand dunes. "You mean to tell me that we just crossed over—I mean, we could have been …" Theo muttered words, but nothing really came out. He breathed hard and put his hands on his knees, eclipsing the checkered pattern that made up the fabric of his pants.

"It will be all right, Theo. We are safe on this side and we won't have much need to go back. Besides, I am sure something like that would have no need to eat something as small as we are." Wiglaf patted Theo's shoulder and turned toward the mountain.

Warrington smiled and walked beside Wiglaf up a small path. Wiglaf and Warrington stopped just outside of a tall brass gate that appeared to welcome visitors from the outside.

The path to the castle looked like a snake encircling the mountain as it climbed its way to the perch where the castle sat. Warrington did not hesitate to start up the path. Wiglaf followed closely as Warrington climbed the path with renewed vigor. Wiglaf turned to see that Marchavious and Theo had not followed behind them.

"Warrington, wait up. It appears we have lost half of our party," Wiglaf said, cupping a hand over his mouth and yelling, as Warrington had climbed the path with considerable speed.

Warrington could sense that they were close and was quite eager to get to the queen. He felt like a great amount of time had passed since he had last seen Eld and wondered if he was safe.

Warrington could see Wiglaf struggling to climb the hill, as he was now carrying what looked to be a tall, unconscious man across his shoulders. Marchavious walked behind him with Theo's hat loosely placed atop his head.

"Seems like some people have an affinity for being a burden on the group," Marchavious said, catching up to Warrington, who was waiting patiently halfway up the path.

Wiglaf thought that it would be best to carry Theo until he woke up, which he hoped would be sooner rather than later. Marchavious dipped his new hat in Warrington's direction as though they were meeting for the first time. Warrington smiled at this ridiculous gesture.

"Don't tell me that you are going to start being afraid of everything," Warrington said, winking at Marchavious.

"Afraid?" Marchavious said, looking down. "Are you a cat? I am afraid of cats, and bats, rats, or anything else that ends with *at*."

Wiglaf looked at them both and sighed. "I carry the burden and you two make the jokes," Wiglaf said, moving past Warrington and up the path.

They had almost reached the top when they came upon three small cottages along the path. One of them looked to be a garrison, while the other two looked like living quarters.

"We may be able to get help if anyone is here," Wiglaf said. "Theo is getting quite heavy." He walked up the steps to one of the smaller structures. The wooden floor creaked under the combined weight of Wiglaf and Theo. The front of the structure was made out of interlacing small dark wooden planks. Wiglaf knocked on the door with his foot. The sound of metal on wood echoed through the mountain.

Warrington jumped up to one of the foggy windows and peered in. "Looks deserted."

Wiglaf grabbed the door handle and turned it to the right and left. The handle fell free of the gears as the rusty innards disintegrated under the pressure. With the handle gone, the door swung free and banged against the interior wall. Wiglaf walked in and sat Theo in the closest chair. His body lay in the chair, motionless except for a few small breaths and the movement of his nostrils.

"Well, I guess this place is abandoned. Hopefully someone still lives in the castle, or we have come a long way for nothing," Wiglaf said, looking around for any sign of who—or what—used to inhabit the quarters.

"I'm going to go and see if anyone is in the quarters next door," Marchavious said, walking out the door.

Wiglaf tried to protest, but Marchavious had already left the premises. The sun had grown dark as it hid behind the mountains they'd climbed.

Warrington walked to the doorway and looked around outside. The wind was still and a slight fog was starting to creep over the path just below them.

"Marchavious!" Warrington called out, but no answer came. "Wiglaf, I'm going to check on Marchavious. I'll be right back."

Warrington walked around the corner of the door and Wiglaf could see that he had disappeared from the tail down.

Wiglaf sat down in one of the chairs, awaiting Warrington and Marchavious' return from the next bunker. Fifteen minutes passed, and Wiglaf grew worried that something was going on. Theo sat in the chair, apparently still unconscious from the sight of an enormous worm moving through the sand.▄▄▄▄▄▄▄▄▄▄▄▄▄▄▄▄▄▄▄

Wiglaf silently crept outside to the next set of living quarters where Marchavious had gone. Wiglaf could hear someone inside and silently drew his sword. Wiglaf stood at the threshold of the door trying to figure out if he should burst through the door and surprise whomever it was or wait until the person came out. He knew that it could just be Marchavious and Warrington moving around but figured it would be safer for all of them if he entered quietly and assessed the situation.

As he entered, Wiglaf could see more than one cloaked figure standing over Marchavious, who had been tied to a chair. Wiglaf moved quickly, swinging his sword with purpose. The cloaked figure, feeling the slight breeze quickly turned and matched Wiglaf's blade against his. The sparks from the swords flickered in the dark room.

"The queen shall have your heads for your intrusion," the cloaked figure said.

Wiglaf swung his blade down and in a circle, confusing the swordsman. Wiglaf pinned his opponent against the wall.

"That is enough, Wiglaf," came a familiar voice. Vitok was standing against the far wall, watching the spectacle. "I see even at your age you can best my most seasoned knight."

Wiglaf released his captive and laughed. "Vitok, it has been too long, friend." Wiglaf walked over and extended his hand. Vitok stood without movement.

"Please, Wiglaf. We will have time for formalities later. We caught this spy sneaking around and must take him to the queen. He won't tell us what the Dark Witch is up to, but the White Queen has ways of making him talk." Vitok put her foot on a chair in the corner of the room.

Wiglaf laughed again. "This is no spy, my dear Vitok. He is with me and we are on our way to see the queen. We stopped here to see if anyone could lend us aid. Our friend has fallen into a deep sleep, and I could not carry him the rest of the way up the hill."

"I see, Wiglaf. Well then, we shall assist you with the rest of your journey," Vitok said. She pointed at Marchavious and the other two men in shiny crimson armor untied the restraints on his legs. Vitok lifted a small pipe to her mouth, took two puffs and then pointed to the door.

"What about our friend Theophilus next door?" Wiglaf inquired.

"We'll take care of him, Wiglaf. He is safe and will not come to any harm." Vitok gestured one of the guards to her. "Take the other one, who is asleep next door, to the castle. The queen can deal with him as she sees fit."

'4'

The group, now almost double what it was when they walked into the house, wound around the mountain and up to the top of the steps. Wiglaf had seen Warrington slip away and follow the guard who was to watch over Theo. Wiglaf had a bad feeling that something suspicious was going on but kept it to himself. Vitok led the group up to a large crimson door—the same color as the road in Heartwick. Vitok waved her arm in the air twice and then banged it against her breastplate thrice. The light in the window of the guard tower at the very top of the wall illuminated with a magnificent red glow. The sound of gears stuttering and squealing grew louder by the second. There was a loud clank that echoed through the mountain as the door split down the middle.

Vitok motioned to the guards, and they dispersed through the door and around the corner. She then proceeded to walk through the enormous doorway and into the front hold of the castle. The ground darkened beneath Marchavious and Wiglaf's feet as they crossed the threshold.

"Hurry, we must not make the queen wait or it would be most unpleasant for you." Vitok quickened her pace as she passed beyond the walls, which to Wiglaf and Marchavious seemed about 500 meters thick.

"It is more like 900 meters," Vitok said as she heard Marchavious whisper to Wiglaf.

"Ears like a rabbit she has." Marchavious was smiling. Vitok turned and glared at him even though he was sure she did not hear him whisper it under his breath.

They passed through several empty locks and multiple walls that were smaller than the initial wall before reaching crimson steps leading up to the two crimson doors of the castle. Five pearl statues appeared to be holding up the second floor of the castle.

"Extravagant and magnificent!" Marchavious commented.

"Be sure to tell the queen that when you see her. She will be most pleased. After all, we have been building it continuously for the past twenty years." Vitok grimaced at this thought.

"What do you mean, Vitok?" Wiglaf asked, perplexed. He saw no other people besides the guards.

"When we left you in search of safety from the Dark Witch, we were deemed spies of the Dark one. The queen ordered everyone to prove their worth by working in the mines and as her building crew. The people you knew in Heartwick have been slaves since the day we got here. Some are her personal servants, guards, builders, and miners. We all have jobs and if we do them, we are safe. If we do not, then she punishes with a swift hand. It has gotten worse as the Dark Witch's reign over the region grows."

Vitok had tears in her eyes as she turned. Wiglaf put a hand on her shoulder, but she shrugged it off.

"We will do what we can to help," Wiglaf said, reassuring her.

"You will only cause more trouble for us and yourselves. She sent me to bring you to her, as she heard the Dark Witch had sent spies to these lands. I must do my duty to the queen and bring you before her," Vitok said, motioning them up the stairs.

"Well, if that is how we are perceived, then we will try and explain to the queen that we are not spies. In fact, we are here to lend aid to her cause," Wiglaf said, reaching the last of the stairs and standing in front of the large crimson and pearl doors.

"For your sake, Wiglaf, I hope you can help. The White Queen is not known for her kindness and mercy." Vitok pushed open one of the doors. They looked heavy but moved quickly and with ease.

The great hallway they entered was dark except for the candles lit on the pillars. It was impossible to see any walls or a ceiling. The door closed behind them with a crash that was rather loud but did not echo through the hall.

Marchavious could see a small door up ahead in the darkness, illuminated around the edge by nine candles, four on the right, four on the left, and one in the center at the top of the curve.

"This is where I leave you, old friend. I may not enter. Even though I am the Head Knight of the Crimson Guard, I am not allowed. Go with luck and I hope that we meet again." With those final words, Vitok disappeared into the darkness.

"This is strange, Wiglaf. We don't know what is going to happen. This could be a trap, for all we know. This wasn't even our idea. Warrington was the one who wanted her help in getting the other talking cat back. We should not even be here."

Wiglaf held up a finger. "Quiet, Marchavious, you are starting to sound like Theo. Get a hold of yourself and let us meet this queen. I am sure that we are being looked after. Whatever happens is meant for a reason."

Wiglaf grabbed the handle and opened the door. The light from inside was a bright white. Marchavious shielded his eyes, as the light stung deep into his cornea. They could only see the outline of a chair and a throne with someone sitting on it.

While they were still blinded by the light, a voice beckoned from the other end of the room. "Enter, strangers from a distant land. Come forth, so I may better judge your intentions here."

'5'

Warrington had disappeared before he heard Wiglaf reply from around the corner. Warrington could hear voices coming from the next cottage, even though Marchavious was supposedly the only one in there. He peeked around the window and could not see anyone inside. The door opened and a tall figure in crimson armor walked out and looked around. Warrington scurried down from the window and into the room. The figure turned around and walked back in, closing the door behind him.

Warrington, with his keen night vision, could see four figures in the room. One of them was sitting down in a chair while the other three stood over him.

"Who are you and why have you come here?" The voice barking commands was female. The other two figures were still and said nothing.

"I am here to get help for a friend. We don't want trouble."

Warrington could hear Marchavious talking from the chair. His hands were tied behind his back. The woman leaned over Marchavious, her red lipstick glimmering in the darkened room. "If you are who you say you are, then who is this friend, and where is he?"

Marchavious was frantic and talking quickly. "They are in the cottage next to this one. One of my friends passed out at the bottom of the mountain. The others thought these living quarters were abandoned. We meant no harm," Marchavious said, squirming in the chair, the knots of the rope tightened around his wrists.

"Others, huh? What others are there?" the female voiced yelled in Marchavious' face,

Warrington moved behind the woman and up to a shelf, where he could spring into action if the situation began to get worse.

"Well, there is my friend, Theo—he is a hatmaker. Warrington is a talking cat who …" Marchavious knew how ridiculous this sounded as he spoke the words.

"What?" the female voice laughed out loud. "You expect me to believe you have a talking cat? That is by far the most ridiculous thing I have heard in almost twenty years."

"I know how it sounds, but he is a librarian and—" Marchavious tried to get the words out, but the woman interrupted him again.

"You mean to tell me that you have a cat that talks … *and* is a librarian?" The woman was being very serious.

"I know it sounds crazy, but—" Marchavious was interrupted again, this time by a small skirmish breaking out.

Wiglaf had moved quickly and had assessed the woman as the major threat. Warrington moved into position, but waited.

Warrington moved around the top shelf of the cottage as the fight escalated. The fight ended quickly, as it appeared to Warrington that this was the Procerus Vitok that Wiglaf had told them about that night at dinner.

After the two had finished talking, the two crimson guards untied Marchavious from the chair. Wiglaf was looking around the room as if he knew Warrington was somewhere, but he was unsure of just where. Warrington flashed his yellow eyes in Wiglaf's direction. Wiglaf winked and turned to leave. The two guards left the room and were joined by several more outside. One guard moved next door to check on Theo. Warrington jumped down and followed closely behind Vitok as she left the room. He moved quickly, but was reminded of why he hated doors as Vitok almost caught his tail in this one.

Vitok pointed at the guards in the front of the group and they stepped aside with their halberds at attention. Vitok marched to the front, leading Wiglaf, Marchavious and four additional guards up the pathway to the castle. The guard that Vitok had talked to was inside the other cottage looking after Theo.

Warrington could see the guard talking to himself while sitting in a brown rocking chair. His heels thrust him backward and his armor squeaked as the chair lunged back and forth. Warrington was moving behind Theo, who sat in an armchair with a hideously blue floral pattern. Warrington jumped up on the desk that sat behind Theo. The desk was smaller than the library's, but still sturdy in size.

The guard reached over and lit a candle as the room darkened from the lack of sun. The two buildings were on the left side of the path up against the mountain, while the garrison was built into the right side. This afforded the guards a fortified position if anyone were to attack, since this was the only way to reach the castle.

Theo shifted around in the chair and the guard readied himself, as though Theo would combat him upon awakening. Warrington moved slowly across the desk, closer to the candle.

"What is your name?" Warrington said in a low groan.

The guard stood up and looked around. He walked over and slapped Theo in the face a couple of times.

"Was that you? You playing possum with me?" The guard slapped him again for good measure.

"Slap him again and I will slap you," Warrington growled this time.

"Who are you? Show yourself!" The guard grabbed his sword and held it out, swinging it at any dark object, but he hit nothing.

"I am over here. The candle is my light and you will come palaver with me."

Warrington flashed his eyes for a moment and then allowed them to disappear again. The guard walked over to the candle and rubbed his eyes. He moved his sword over the candle flame to see if anything was there. Warrington, expecting this, moved away.

Warrington jumped down from the desk and hopped in the rocking chair, rocking it back and forth. The guard spun around on his heels, swinging the sword at the chair and breaking off a small wooden support bar. The wood chips splintered in the air and fell slowly to the floor. Warrington had already returned to his position on the desk behind the candle by the time the guard had turned and scarred the defenseless rocking chair.

"Now, are you done with trying to kill me? I am not here, but I am not there, either. You see, I am everywhere. Oh wait, you cannot see because you cannot see me." Warrington was laughing at the guard, who he could see was visibly frightened.

"Okay specter, what do you want?" the guard said, bending over and then sitting down in the deformed chair. The splinters dug into his buttocks as he shifted in the seat.

"When the man in the top hat sitting in the chair wakes up, you will take him to see the queen." Warrington puckered his cheeks and blew air on the open flame. The flame flickered in the small gust of air. "Do you understand, Sir Guard?"

The guard was just staring at the candle with his eyes wide open. The glare from the candle flickered in his eyes and made them appear that much more dramatic.

"Guard, respond or I will find a new guard to do my work." Warrington was growing impatient.

"Yes, Sir Ghost, I understand, but I do not have access to the queen. I can try and sneak him in the back way, though. Just as long as the queen does not see me letting you into the chamber, or she will have my head for sure." The guard stood up and walked over to the desk and leaned in close to the candle.

"I will have your head if you betray me or the sleeping man gets hurt." Warrington was back to his cheerful self as he explained this ultimatum to the man.

"Whatever you say, Sir Ghost. When will the man wake up?"

"He will wake up in a bit. Until then, please sit down and wait. Tell no one of what I have told you, or else things will not bode well for your future." With that, Warrington jumped into Theo's lap with his claws out.

"Yeeeeoow!" Theo exclaimed. This scared both Theo and the guard. Theo jumped up, looking at the guard. "What did you do that for?" said he asked, rubbing his right leg with both hands.

"I did nothing, sir. I am just here guarding you." The guard walked over toward the door.

"Guarding me? What are you guarding me from?" Theo turned to face the guard. "And where are the others I came here with?"

"They went to the castle, which is where I am to take you."

The guard opened the door all the way and proceeded to walk out. He poked his head back in and motioned for Theo to follow him.

"Maybe I do not wish to go to the castle. Maybe I am fine right where I am," Theo said as he walked out of the small cottage.

"Sorry, sir, but my orders are to take you to the queen." The guard pointed up the path.

"Oh good, God Save the Queen and all that," Theo said, remembering England and her queen. "Well, we must not keep Her Majesty waiting. Lead the way, good sir."

'6'

"You, in the stone colored vest, what is your name?" the queen said, pointing at Marchavious.

The queen was at least one hundred and some odd yards away, but her voice rang loudly throughout the hallway. The echo rang clearly in Marchavious' ears. It almost sounded like there were fifteen of her inside this chamber. Wiglaf and Marchavious began to walk toward the queen, who was sitting on a large white throne.

"Wait!" the queen's voice rang out again. She tapped the floor with her scepter and a small door opened. There was a whisper in the air as the floor began unfolding before them in a crimson color. The floor seemed to unroll before them in seconds.

"Now you may proceed," the queen said, motioning with her scepter for them to move forward.

The room was enormous and everything within the walls was made from pearl or, at least, a pearl-like substance. Marchavious could not imagine someone being able to find this much pearl in one place, let alone craft it into a gigantic throne room of some sort. The walk to the front seemed to take a lifetime, but as they moved closer, they could see that there was not one, but two women seated upon one throne.

The first woman, who sat on the right side of the throne, was quite portly and young. *Her hair was the color of Poe's raven,* Marchavious thought to himself, not knowing who Poe was or why he even had a raven—the thought just seemed to jump into his mind. Neither of these women wore a crown, but both were dressed elegantly. The queen on the right wore a dress spun from the thread of onyx and lined with ruby hearts. She crossed her legs as Marchavious gazed down at her shoes.

"When I address you, sir, you should be polite and answer. I have very little patience for rudeness." The queen with the dark hair pointed her scepter at Marchavious.

"Yes … my manners. I am Marchavious Harbinger, Your Majesty," Marchavious said, bowing from the waist and extending a hand forward, as to present himself.

Wiglaf moved forward and began to say, "I am Wiglaf—" but was interrupted.

"Quiet, you! Do not speak unless spoken to." The queen's raven hair flipped back and forth as she pointed her instructions at Wiglaf and then turned back to Marchavious. "You are not from around here, are you? Please intrigue me with a tale of where you are from. I love hearing of other lands where I am not the queen."

"Well, yes, Your Majesty. I am from a small town just outside of London called Chester," Marchavious began but was interrupted by the dark-haired queen's counterpart.

"Most interesting. Marchavious, is it?"

"Yes, Your Majesty," Marchavious said to the queen sitting on the left. This lady appeared to be the opposite of the queen sitting on the right. She was thin and her hair fell to the floor in long golden strands. Her gown was white lace and had red diamonds embroidered on it.

"Well, what brings you to Wonderland, Marchavious?" The queen looked over and batted her eyelashes.

"Well, I actually just came along for the adventure and to help a friend, Your Majesty," Marchavious said, speaking to the queen on the left.

"How noble, Marchavious. Is this your friend that you are here with now?" The queen leaned back and placed the scepter that was in her left hand in a hole etched into the floor.

"No, Your Majesty. My friend did not arrive when we did. I am actually unsure of his whereabouts as of this moment. He was with us, but he stayed behind to look after one of our other friends who had lost consciousness. I am sure he is all right now, though," Marchavious seemed to ramble, but was stopped abruptly.

"You mean there are two of you not here? This is unacceptable, to have strangers wandering around my castle." The queen on the right stood up and clapped her hands. There was a small noise from behind the throne and a child came scurrying out. "You, squire, go and fetch the two strangers that are wandering about my castle. Be quick about it. I would hate for anything bad to happen if you were too slow."

The small child scurried out behind the throne and disappeared.

"Now, Marchavious, since there is not a door or passageway to Terra-Mirac, or Wonderland, or whatever you want to call it—can you enlighten me and my sister on how you arrived in our kingdom?" The queen's dark hair fell over her face as she leaned forward to listen to what Marchavious was about to say.

"Hold on, Marchavious. We are not here to tell stories of how we arrived here. We are here in search of help, and these two have some explaining to do for why they have enslaved the people who came here seeking refuge," Wiglaf said angrily, stepping in front of Marchavious and hiding him from the sight of both queens.

The queen on the right stood up quickly and pointed at Wiglaf. "How dare you speak to me with such disrespect!"

"No! How dare you waste our time with foolish questions that do not concern you. We know this land is on the brink of war and you are about to lose your small portion of the kingdom. Now you answer *our* questions, or we will go and offer you no help." Wiglaf pointed his finger at the queen on the right and then put it on the hilt of his sword, as he expected a troop of guards to march out at any moment.

"Now, Hilda, they are correct. This is none of our concern. Even now the Dark Witch moves across the land with her army. We are no match for them and need to hear these travelers out. They may be able to lend us a hand," the queen on the left said, trying to reason with her sister.

"What help can an outsider and an old man offer us? We are as good as conquered where we stand. Our only option is to retreat to another land." Queen Hilda's eyes began to fill with tears. She turned to Wiglaf. "I am sorry, Sir Knight. You are right, we have no army, and so we can offer no aid to you or your friends."

"What if I can train you an army? I am a knight and will be one until I succumb to my death, on or off the battlefield. I know this now—if you gather all able-bodied men, I may be able to train them in time for battle. Would that be enough?" Wiglaf said, looking now at Queen Hilda, who had stopped her tears and was now sitting back on her throne.

"I am afraid not. Our army is not large. We have a hundred trained guards at best, and even some of them are too old to be of any use. We would need much more if we were to overcome an attack by the Dark Witch. Her Dyhedral army is at least ten thousand strong," Queen Hilda replied.

"This is a knight, Hilda; he may know of more soldiers that are willing to fight." The queen on the left was now sitting up straight, as though she was getting ready to stand. "Maybe he even knows of something that might turn the tide in our favor."

"Your words are wise, Ducia, but if they had such a weapon they would not be asking for help from us," Queen Hilda said, leaning back in thought.

A loud racket came from behind the throne, and the squire ran out again. He stopped so abruptly that he skidded across the floor and fell over.

"Foolish child!" Queen Hilda stood and raised her scepter and pointed it at the child. "You had better have information for me."

"I am sorry, but—" the child grimaced as the words came out of his mouth, but he was saved by a voice from behind the throne.

"Sorry, Your Majesty, your squire was so eager to get back to you that he—"

"Silence, please. Let the child speak for himself." Queen Hilda pointed at the squire who was just beginning to stand up. Theo looked over and winked at the kid.

"I am sorry, Queen Hilda, Your Majesty, but I only found one of them."

"You are dismissed, child, but do not go far. Your services may be needed soon enough." Queen Hilda shooed the squire away from her and as quickly as he entered, he exited once more.

"Now, who might you be?" Queen Hilda said, slowly looking to her left and pointing her scepter at Theo.

"Well, I am Theophilus Hatmaker," Theo said, removing his hat in a wide arc and bowing low.

"Oh! A hatmaker! How exciting." Queen Ducia was patting her hands together and looking around Hilda, as she was blocking Ducia's line of sight.

"Well, Theophilus, where is your friend?" Queen Hilda said, stepping down off the perch on which the throne sat.

"Well, I am not sure. He was here with me, but he seems to have gone somewhere. He did come in here with me. I just do not know where he went." Theo was looking around in circles.

"You and the child were the only ones who entered. I saw no one else," Queen Hilda said, looking at Theo and inspecting his clothing.

"Well, he was invisible when we walked in. He was not sure he should show himself," Theo said, leaning down and brushing the air, looking for Warrington.

"Do you mock me, sir?" The queen was now standing directly in front of Theo. "You are dressed like a politician, and I do not care much for politicians. In fact, the last one I saw did not live long in my court."

"I assure you, madam, I am not mocking you. He was indeed here when we walked in. Warrington … come on … enough games," Theo pleaded.

"Oh, all right," Warrington said as he appeared, sitting on the arm of the throne where Queen Hilda had been seated.

"Oh my! A cat!" Queen Ducia said, startled at his appearance before their very eyes. Warrington looked over and smiled. "Oh, and such a handsome cat, at that."

"You said there were four of you." Queen Hilda was starting to get red in the face, as she did not like being the butt of any joke. "This better not be a joke, or I will see your heads on a pike at the entrance."

"I assure you, Your Majesty, this is no joke. Warrington is a very special cat. In fact, he is a librarian," Theo said, speaking out of turn.

"Quiet, Theo!" Wiglaf said turning to Theo. "This is not the time for volunteering information."

"Librarian? Whatever do you mean?" Queen Hilda smiled a wicked grin, walked over and scratched Warrington underneath his chin.

"That is of no concern right now, Your Majesty." Wiglaf had moved Theo behind him and motioned for Warrington to do the same. "We need to focus on the ensuing war that is going to happen whether we have one man or one hundred men."

"Well, you may ask for volunteers, but I doubt you would find any here," Queen Hilda said, continuing to scratch Warrington under his chin.

"Wiglaf, what about the Rebobs in the forest?" Warrington had broken out of his trance and was now involved in the conversation.

"A talking cat?" Queen Ducia said, shocked. She had not noticed his initial speech since he was barely visible at the time and anyone could have said it. "How peculiar. We do not get very many animals around here, let alone any that can talk."

"Excuse me. If I may interrupt—the gentleman, Theo here, is a hatmaker, so I assume you can sew?" Hilda inquired of Theo.

"Well, I am not a seamstress, but I can sew. A hatmaker must know about the stitches of his profession," Theo said proudly.

"Well, we may have some need for you if you would be willing to help us out," Hilda said, walking toward Theo and putting her arm around him.

"Anything for Your Majesty," Theo said, smiling as though he had been offered the greatest gift in the world.

"Now Wiglaf, since you claim to be a mighty warrior, I would ask that you do indeed train the hundred or so troops that we have."

"One hundred troops?" Warrington interrupted. "That is all that you have to repel an army of thousands?"

"We have never had a need for a military presence. There has been order in Terra-Mirac for as long as I can remember. The magistrates kept the peace through a very democratic election process. We, my sister and I, have been the ruling body, and the magistrates bring to us any problems that the people have. However, many of the local magistrates have turned and betrayed us to the Dark Witch in return for a better place in the ruling party when she has control." Queen Hilda broke down and made some fake sniffling sounds.

"Wiglaf, as I started to say before, the Rebobs in the forest were plotting with a Dyhedral spy about ambushing the Dark Witch's minions. If we could get them to help, it could give this place a better chance for survival." Warrington jumped off the throne and over to where Wiglaf was standing.

"You may have a point, Warrington. If their numbers are plentiful, we may be able to prepare a proper defense. I will ride back to the forest and see if I can convince them to join us in return for their freedom."

Wiglaf knelt down and picked Warrington up. Warrington climbed up on Wiglaf's shoulder.

"Wiglaf, I almost forgot. I must return to the library before the Dark Witch. She is going to try and secure the contents of the library. When she is not able to retrieve the orbs, she will surely kill Eld."

"Orbs?" Queen Hilda's face lit up. "You said one of you is a librarian. Since Marchavious has not told me his profession, I assume it is you?"

"No, Your Majesty, I am not a librarian." Marchavious said. "I am more a jack-of-all-trades."

"Well then, which one of you is it? The cat? I highly doubt the cat, who can disappear and can talk …" Hilda started putting it together. "So Warrington, you are the librarian. Is this the very same library that holds the works of the ancient writing of all the worlds?" Queen Hilda asked and then turned and walked away without waiting for a reply.

No one said anything as she disappeared behind the large throne where the squire had come from. When she returned, she was holding a wooden box with gold trim. The box glowed bright crimson from each of the exposed seams.

"When I was a young child, long before the water turned to sand, a man came to these lands. He asked my mother and father about a crystal ball that he had tracked to our castle. My parents, who were the king and queen at that time, said they had given my sister and me each a crystal ball to commemorate us becoming women. He told my parents that they were dangerous and that they could bring great harm to those who had them." Hilda unlatched the gold hook that held the box closed. "My sister Ducia, scared of what the man said, gave her crystal ball over to him, but I said that I had lost mine and did not know where it went."

She lifted the lid and the white pearl room was illuminated with the crimson red of the ball. The walls glowed as though covered in swirling blood.

"I have called this the Queen's Heart since I got it. It has never brought me anything but good wishes since it bestows upon those who gaze into it a sense of compassion." Queen Hilda pushed her hand over the lid and it closed with a clap that echoed through the chamber. "So, Warrington, you are telling me that this man who came to see me was telling the truth. There is a library and there are more of these balls?"

"Yes, there are, but they are too powerful for anyone to wield alone," Warrington said, looking down at the box.

"They could save us without any bloodshed, Warrington. If you help me, I will help you rescue your friend from the Dark Witch." Queen Hilda was looking at Warrington, her eyes glowing a crimson red.

"Well, I do not see what helping you could hurt as long as you are helping me," Warrington said without thinking. "I will need assistance, though, as she will more than likely send several Dyhedral to the library to retrieve the items she needs."

"Very well, I will send Vitok with you," Queen Hilda said, turning and climbing back up the steps to her throne.

"I should go as well," said Wiglaf.

"Wiglaf, we need you here to train the troops. Marchavious will go to the woods and persuade the Rebobs to join our army. Theophilus, you will teach the women to sew tabards for our army." Queen Hilda put her hand in the air. "Warrington, Vitok will be outside of this chamber and will take care of each of you. Anything you need will be yours. Please go with haste, as we have little time to prepare." Queen Hilda flicked her hands and dismissed them.

"Something about this feels wrong," Marchavious said as they walked back the way they came. "I do not trust her. She is up to something. We should be on our guard."

"You're right, Marchavious," Wiglaf said, stopping just before the door. "She has split us up into four individual groups and so has divided us. We must be on the lookout for danger, wherever it may lurk. Good luck to each of you as you go on your way. Warrington, please come and see me before you leave. We must talk and discuss these new details of your return to the library instead of rescuing your friend from the Dark Witch's Keep itself."

Wiglaf reached out and pulled the handle. Marchavious turned and could see the queen waving back and forth from her seat.

## Chapter 14

'1'

Vitok stood outside of the entrance to the dark chamber they had entered, waiting with a small group of crimson-clad guards. The door was open, allowing light to shine through onto the marble floor and lead them to where Vitok waited.

"Queen Hilda tells me you will be training some of the men for service, Wiglaf."

"Yes, I offered my services since there is very little time and very few able-bodied men to recruit," Wiglaf said, walking down the steps.

"Very well, Tinok will take you to recruit the few able bodies we have. Marchavious, you will take Visok and a few of my personal guards and head to the Frost Woods. There you will persuade the Rebobs to join us in our fight if they are smart enough to understand what we are doing. If they resist, remind them that they can be part of the new regime or perish with the old one."

"What about the Dyhedral that was in the house?" Marchavious said, stepping down next to Visok.

"He may join us, but if he refuses, Visok will know what to do," Vitok said smirking a little. She had a very cruel way about her, and her orders seemed mechanical.

"Theo, since you are a hatmaker, Queen Hilda has ordered me to take you to the seamstresses. There you are to show them how to sew a proper stitch and then make tabards for the army. There should be plenty of material there and the patterns are fairly straightforward." Vitok dismissed Marchavious and Visok to go and get their horses.

"Warrington, the queen has ordered me to accompany you to the library, where we will wait for the Dark Witch. If she is indeed looking to turn the tide of the war with the secrets the library keeps, then we will be waiting for her when she arrives." Vitok knelt down.

"We *are* going to rescue Eld as well? That *is* the main purpose of our mission." Warrington asked, concerned that there might be some ulterior motive.

"Of course, Warrington, the queen specifically said that we were on a rescue mission first. If the Dark Witch is there, we are to engage her and ultimately destroy her. If we end the war before it starts, there would be no reason to fight." Vitok smiled at Warrington as she said these words.

Visok rode up on his horse and halted. Marchavious was sitting on a dark brown horse with one white spot on its forehead. There were ten guards around Marchavious as he sat waiting for Visok to return.

"Be careful, Marchavious!" Theo yelled across the courtyard, his hands cupped over his mouth. Marchavious waved back as though to signal that he would.

"Visok, be quick with your errand and return soon. Use the southern pass to bypass the sand. It will take longer, but it is safer than taking the road to the north. Remember, Visok, the queen does not accept failure." Vitok pulled her hood back as though to tell Visok that she was serious.

Visok glanced at Vitok and pulled the reins to turn his horse.

Vitok's red hair blew wildly in the breeze and then it was gone as she pulled her hood back up. The courtyard was silent except for the galloping of horses leaving and the squeal of the chains as the gates to the outlying wall were opened.

Tinok motioned to Vitok that he was ready to be on his way as well.

"Tinok, take Theophilus to the sewing room and put him to work on the queen's tabards. All guards are to have one within a week's time. The queen has made this order abundantly clear, and I would hate to be the one to disappoint her." Vitok was rambling at this point as she had other things on her mind.

"Well, we should get going then." Theo stepped forward and patted Wiglaf on the shoulder. "You've got men to recruit as well."

"You are correct, and if we are to win the war, we must have these men trained and ready to fight as soon as possible. Advanced combat techniques will require some time." Wiglaf looked over at Vitok.

"Well, then we should go. Follow me." Tinok turned and led Wiglaf and Theophilus to a small building off to the right of the main palace entrance.

"Well, Warrington, we should get moving if we are to rescue your friend. You will have to lead the way, as I do not know how to get to where we are going." Vitok moved toward Warrington and knelt down.

"Do you have anything to draw with? Charcoal would be the most satisfactory item, but anything to draw with will prove useful."

Warrington jumped up to Vitok's shoulder. Vitok was confused as to why Warrington wanted this utensil, but figured Warrington knew what he needed.

"We will go and gather the horses and a wagon to carry the supplies we need," Vitok said, standing back up.

"That won't be necessary, Vitok. It will not be a long journey. In fact, it won't be a journey at all." Warrington smiled, but Vitok could not see it.

"You are a strange creature, Warrington." Vitok started moving toward the building where Tinok had taken Wiglaf and Theo.

'2'

The horses moved quickly down the mountainside to the bottom of the path. Visok led the group down the winding path and to the great expanse of sand that lay between them and the Frost Woods.

"We need to go south, as the horses will not be able to cross in the sand." Visok turned the band of troops to the right and rode along the base of the mountain range towards what Visok called *The Ocean of Tears*.

"Why do they call it that?" Marchavious asked, the sand stinging as it flew up and pitted him in the face. He wrapped his jacket around his face to help shield him from the strong gusts of wind carrying the small pellets at him like gunshot.

"Well, they call it that because they say that the water will return when the tears of the queen fill the land." Visok laughed. "I do not believe the water is returning to this land anytime soon, though. The queen is not one for emotion."

"Queen Hilda does not show much emotion, but what about Queen Ducia?" Marchavious inquired.

"You met Queen Ducia?"

"Yes, but she said little and moved even less."

"Well, she is the younger sister and is not really mentally fit to continue as the queen. They both control separate portions of these lands, but Queen Ducia has been sick for a long time. That is why Queen Hilda has come to the Western region of Terra-Mirac." Visok was picking up his pace a bit.

"So Queen Hilda is not the White Queen?" Marchavious said, looking concerned.

"No, she is not. Queen Ducia is the White Queen, or at least was, before she went mad," Visok said with a look as though he had said too much. "We must ride faster, Marchavious, if we are to reach the Frost Woods by nightfall."

'3'

Tinok moved toward the large grey structure made from white soapstone. The building looked small from the outside, but as they approached, Wiglaf could see that it actually went underneath the ground. The door swung open violently as they approached the structure. A small portly man stood guard over the door, and his one duty was to open it when anyone came close. This, at least, was what Theo thought as they passed through the opening and down the stairway to the depths of the underground bunker.

Each floor was a myriad of colorful doorways and long hallways that seemed to go nowhere. The third floor was where Tinok led them. At the end of the long hallway was a regular-sized wooden door with a blue number nine just above a silver handle. Tinok grabbed the handle, pulled outward, and then turned it to the right. The sound of metal grinding echoed through the hallway as the door swung open.

The three men walked through the first door and into a small room, where they could see another small door that had a blue number eight over the handle. "Are there going to be many more of these doors?" Theo joked, nudging Tinok. Tinok looked over his shoulder angrily at him.

Tinok opened the door again grabbing the handle and turning it to the right. The door opened and the three men walked through into a larger room with another doorway. The door had a blue number seven over a brass handle. Theo walked over to the door without question.

"This is it," Tinok said in a low, raspy voice.

"What is it?" Theo asked, turning to see Tinok standing by ten women sitting at one long table.

"You are to teach these women how to sew better and faster, according to the queen. Once you are done with these women, you move on to the next room where there are ten more women waiting. Once you are done, move to room six and then room five." Tinok pointed to the door and made a motion for Wiglaf to follow him.

"Would it not be easier just to teach them all at the same time?" Theo said, but Tinok ignored him.

"Good luck, Theo. Sounds like you've got some work ahead of you," Wiglaf said, following Tinok. "I'll come back and check on you after I finish my recruitment. After all, *you* are an able-bodied man, so we could use you as well." Wiglaf turned back around. "If you have any problems, do not hesitate to come and get me."

Theo nodded and turned toward the women. "All right ladies, let's get to work."

'4'

Tinok led Wiglaf out of the door and back to the hallway. They turned right and headed down another flight of stairs that led deeper and deeper underground. The walls started to lose color and turned dirt-brown as the stone became packed soil. The stairs began to flatten out as Wiglaf and Tinok entered a long hallway and were no longer going down, but straight.

"There are many people down here mining and working. Not all of them are men. Take any of the men who will go with you and return to the surface." Tinok turned and started back down the hallway.

"You're not staying down here?" Wiglaf said, surprised.

"No. I have other duties. I am sure you can handle yourself if there is any trouble." With that, Tinok turned and climbed the stairs back to the surface.

Wiglaf stood looking into the darkness illuminated by small flickering torches. He grabbed the small wooden torch that was off to his left. The cave walls and ceiling glowed and sparkled with a rich red mineral. Wiglaf continued walking down the long corridor of earth and rock until he reached a small pit with a few metal poles hammered together to form a support structure. There was a rope and pulley system tied just above him, leading down into the pit.

Wiglaf set his torch in a small inlet and untied the leathery looking rope from its position as guard over the small peg it was tied to. The rope was oily and coated Wiglaf's hands as he began to pull. His muscles tightened as he heaved up whatever was attached at the other end. After several minutes of pulling, a small elevator emerged from the darkness of the abyss. The elevator locked into place with a metallic clunk as Wiglaf gave one final pull.

Sweat poured from Wiglaf's forehead as he walked onto the small platform he had just pulled up. He tried pulling the rope, but the elevator stayed in place. In the middle of the elevator was a small placard he had not noticed before. He grabbed his torch and held it up to the sign that, illuminated, was a bright yellow:

*To Descend, Pull Lever*

*To Ascend, Push Lever*

Wiglaf, without hesitation, reached down and pulled the lever toward him. The elevator made a small clinking sound and then started to slowly move downward. The elevator squeaked and clanked as it proceeded on its gravitational journey to the bottom of the pit, which he assumed was a mine.

The elevator clanked a few more times and then began to slow. The ropes in the center, guiding it safely to the ground, stretched and shifted as Wiglaf reached his destination. There was a small clank again as the elevator locked into place.

Wiglaf stepped out of the elevator and looked around. The light from the torch illuminated a small podium at the entrance to a larger cavern. When he approached, he could see a small man with silver hair, wearing an eyepiece.

"Excuse me, sir. My name is Wiglaf, and I am looking for any miners who may assist me in service to the queen," Wiglaf said approaching the man.

"I bag jour pardoon sur, dij shoe zay za queen?" the small man retorted with a very thick French accent.

"Yes sir, yes, I did," Wiglaf said, finally standing tall over the wooden podium.

The small man clapped his hands excitedly. "Za queen zends a mezzenger due moi? Ow very inter ez ting." The man reached out an open hand and swished it sideways as if to give passage down the hallway. "Watt iz zee mezzage?"

"I am here to collect any men who wish to join the queen's army," Wiglaf said abruptly not, moving past the man. The man stayed still with his hand outward.

"Well, I am zure many ove zee men would loaf to join zee queen's army," the small man said, still extending his hand outward.

Wiglaf began to speak, but was interrupted.

"What doze za queen need ze army foe?" the man piped up.

"Well, there is going to be a war against the Dark Witch to free the lands of Terra-Mirac, or Wonderland ... whatever you call it down here," Wiglaf , walking slowly forward.

The small man began to bring his arm back to his side with each of Wiglaf's steps. Wiglaf stopped moving forward and the man stopped his arm from progressing as well.

"A war wit zee Dark Weech, you say?" He held his position as though he were a machine.

"Yes sir. That is what I am saying." Wiglaf began to grow impatient.

"Wheel zur, I am from France—ave you eard of zis plaze?" the man said, moving his arm out as though to say that Wiglaf should continue.

"I have not heard of this place," Wiglaf said impatiently. "What does this have to do with anything?"

"Do you know what we French zay when we goze to za war, zir?" The man's accent was slowly easing up on the thickness, but would occasionally snap back.

Wiglaf looked at the man and put a hand to his forehead. "I don't know, I give up," Wiglaf said.

"That iz correct, how did ze know?" the man said, laughing hysterically and placing one hand on his belly.

"I do not have time for this. I can show myself around," Wiglaf said, moving past the man and into the large cavern.

The man finally put his hand back down to his side and looked down at his podium as though he had never even seen Wiglaf walk by.

The cavern opened up wide and exuded a glorious red light. Wiglaf looked across the cavern to see a stream of bright red liquid flowing through the cavern giving off the unnatural glow. He could see small structures down in the main canyon area just outside the red river.

"Hello!" Wiglaf shouted across the cavern.

A small hissing sound came from a man working just to his right, chipping away rocks from the edge.

"Excuse me, sir, but I am here to gather men who would like to be in the queen's army," Wiglaf said to the man, who continued chipping away at the cavern wall.

"The queen has no need for an army," the man said without so much as a glance at Wiglaf. "She controls the heart of the people and so we serve her. No one would dare go against her."

"I beg to disagree with you. Right now an army marches across the land ready to invade the castle," Wiglaf said, pleading with the man.

The man's hammer stopped swinging for a moment. "An army, you say? I doubt an army could march across the lands and take this place by force. There is not a soul in these lands who does not love the queen. If you find one, then they may not have met the queen yet." The man's hammer began chipping away at the rock again.

"So you will not fight for the queen you love?" Wiglaf said, moving closer to the man.

"If the queen wants us to fight, then she will come and tell us to fight for her. She would not send an outsider. I would suggest you leave without talking with anyone else. We have much work to do if we are going to build the queen her new palace," the man said, swinging his hammer with fervor now.

"A new palace? But you have just built the one above us here. Is it not good enough for her?"

"You ask too many questions. The queen asks us to do something, and we do it. We are gathering the red stones in order to build her a red palace. The one above is white, and she does not like white. She insists that her new palace be constructed entirely of red. Now you have caused me to get behind on my schedule. I am done talking, now be gone." With that the man moved to the left, away from where Wiglaf stood, and began hammering against the rock as though his master stood behind him with a whip. Wiglaf, suspicious of the strange miner's intentions, started walking away from the cavern and back toward the elevator. The queen could give him the answers to his questions, and he intended to ask her.

'5'

Marchavious, Visok, and the other guards rode hard across the sandy ocean. There was only one spot where the horses could cross, and it had taken them several days to reach it. They could smell the sweet odor of cinnamon as their horses dashed across the desert for the tree line, as though the path would crumble under the weight of the caravan. Marchavious assumed that, since he could see the strange creatures that inhabited these parts, the horses probably did as well.

Marchavious, being from a small town in a country none of these people would ever hear of, knew of no such creatures that could grow as large as the ones he saw that day. He marveled at all of the creatures he had encountered since entering these lands. The Frost Woods had been teeming with wondrous creatures when he had passed through the woods before. Some of them were quite strange, and he was sure some of them were quite dangerous.

The desert seemed to continue forever as they rode for several hours across this portion. Marchavious was not even sure of where they would be let out on the other side. He was unsure that he would even be able to find the small house in the middle of the forest.

"We should be coming on the forest any minute now!" Visok yelled over his shoulder, his eyes covered by a pair of steel-framed glasses with red-tinted glass.

"I don't see anything up ahead." Marchavious was worried that Visok was starting to suffer from hallucinations and that they were going to be wandering the desert for forty-some-odd years.

Visok began to slow his horse down and then he brought it to a walk. "This is where we must cross into the woods."

"There is nothing out here but sand and more sand, Visok. You are obviously going mad," Marchavious said, bringing his horse to a complete stop.

Visok said nothing and proceeded to move forward. With a small flash of light like a reflection off the sun, he disappeared. Marchavious rubbed his eyes in disbelief.

"Well, he has left us out here to die," Marchavious commented to the other guards, who said nothing in return. The guards trotted their horses forward and just as Visok did before, they vanished into thin air. Marchavious was bewildered by this sight and could not bring himself to move forward.

"Marchavious, are you coming?" The voice seemed to echo in the wind.

"Come where?" Marchavious responded.

"Just bring your horse forward and you will see," the voice said.

Marchavious was a bit apprehensive, but figured he had no choice. He gave his horse two small nudges and walked forward. His eyes widened as a lush green forest appeared in front of him.

"What just happened?" Marchavious said, looking back at where he had come from only to see more lush forest. The trees were too thick to see through.

"This is one of the Dark Witch's spells in order to discourage strangers from entering her land. It is more or less a giant looking glass that reflects the landscape but not those who look into it. We found it by mistake when we traveled from Heartwick many years ago."

Visok started moving forward again and Marchavious followed him closely, as to not lose him in the dense wooded area.

"I am surprised you made it to us. The spell must have worn off in some places. If you do not know where you are going, you could travel out here for many years without finding your way out." Visok was pushing branches aside as they whipped back and forth.

"We need to head north. The house where Warrington saw the Dyhedral and the Rebob was north of here. If our ride south was any indication, it will take us several days to reach the clearing," Marchavious said, looking over at Visok.

"Well, we should find a path then, should we not?" Visok said, pushing a branch aside and heading into a clearing.

There was a dusty old path growing in the middle of the woods.

"Well, I guess we should just follow it north, then," Marchavious said.

"I guess you are correct," Visok said smiling.

'6'

Theo was working away on the tabards with the other seamstresses. He had taught them a proper hook stitch and how to sew the patches that were brought to him by the small child who had found him by order of the queen. Theo had spent the night in the first room making sure that each of the women had their proper technique down for sewing each detail before he left. When he had moved on to the second room, he was confident that each of the ten ladies he left behind knew as much, if not more, about sewing as he did.

When he entered the second room, the small squire appeared again and handed him several bags of patches to sew onto the white tabards.

"Here you are, sir." The small squire looked weak, but he could carry his weight in material.

"Thank you, young squire. What might these be?" Theo asked, knowing they were the patches he was to sew onto the tabards.

"The queen asked that these spade patterns be sewn onto each number exactly as each of the ladies have been shown." The squire set them down by the table.

"Spade patterns, huh? The last ones were all diamonds. Seems like these tabards are looking like a deck of cards." Theo laughed to himself.

"I said nothing, sir," the squire said and quickly ran out of the room. Theo opened the bag and handed each of the women their numbers and the patches they were to sew onto the tabards.

"All right ladies, please listen carefully. I will instruct you now on how to sew quickly, quietly, and efficiently."

Theo was proud that he was doing his part in making sure the tabards were done and ready for when the queen's army would march on and crush whatever army the Dark Witch would bring to their doorstep.

'7'

Warrington rode on Vitok's shoulder as they went down into the building behind Tinok, Wiglaf, and Theo.

"Okay, Warrington, what are we going to need for our trip?" Vitok said, turning left to go into a supply room. "We have a ship that can take us as far as we need to go."

"Why would we need a ship or supplies?" Warrington said, trying not to slide off Vitok's leather shoulder pad. "We need a piece of charcoal in order to draw a door."

Vitok walked over to the side of the room and opened a small crate filled with little black rocks. "Will any charcoal do?" Vitok turned her head as though she could see Warrington on her shoulder but just looked into a sea of purple fur.

"Yes, any charcoal will do. I would not know how to get back to the library if we were to walk or float or whatever." Warrington jumped off Vitok's shoulder and onto an empty shelf near the crate. "This will also allow us to get back before the Dark Witch can, since she cannot get in the way we are going."

"Okay, so what do I do with the charcoal?" Vitok said eagerly.

"Draw a door with it, of course. Make sure to draw a handle as well so we can open it," Warrington said, sitting down and waiting for Vitok to finish so he could open the door.

"Also, draw the handle with the keyhole low enough for me to reach. I have to open it."

Vitok made a large rectangle on the wall near some old suits of armor and a shelf containing some medicinal herbs. She then drew a small doorknob with a keyhole near the bottom of the door as Warrington had instructed.

"All right. Is that it?" Vitok said, thinking that this was absurd and that Warrington had better not be wasting her time.

"That's it," Warrington said, jumping off the shelf to the floor. As he hit the floor, he turned invisible, as he was still not certain he could trust Vitok with the secrets that he had.

"Warrington, where did you go?" Vitok said in a panic.

"I am still here, just one moment," Warrington said as he placed the key into the small hole. The key clicked as it turned by itself. The outline of the door began to glow, and Vitok's eyes widened in amazement.

Warrington reappeared as the door began to materialize as a real door and not just a wall with a black charcoal door on it. Vitok reached out and touched the brass handle. The handle was cold to the touch and she pulled her hand back in shock, but reached out again and grabbed hold of the brass ring. She pulled the brass ring out and twisted the handle counter-clockwise. The hinge clicked as the door unlatched from the wall and opened slowly toward them. Vitok opened the door wide and peered around the corner into the bright hallway.

She squinted as she looked around in amazement at this secret room. Warrington walked through the doorway and started down the hallway. Vitok cautiously stuck one foot inside the door and then another. Her foot slipped slightly on the smooth floor. When she was all the way in, the door closed behind her and she turned to see a door with a blank wall plate. Then, as though a ghost had appeared with an invisible quill, words began scrawling across the plate.

"Warrington, we should get more guards if we are going to fight the Dark Witch." Vitok sounded nervous.

Warrington stopped some ways down the hallway and turned around. "Now that we have a doorway back to the castle, we can go back at any point. I think we should hurry, just in case they are already there. Besides, they cannot take anything without my permission. They will have nothing to gain by killing me," Warrington said, turning and moving forward down the hallway again.

"It is not you I am worried about them killing," Vitok said, following Warrington down the hallway.

The candles flickered as a slight breeze moved through the hallway silently, as though someone had left a door open.

Vitok grabbed one of the gold handles on the library door and pulled, but the door would not budge.

"How do you suppose we get in? The door is locked," Vitok said, moving away from the door. "Does your key work here as well?"

Warrington moved close to the door and held up his paw to the wood. He patted each side of the door six times and then four more on the left, as he had seen Ias do many times before. He was unsure if the same method would work for him, but just as he began to doubt, the door started to tremble and then split in two pieces. Vitok took a step back, away from the door, as it opened on its own. A stale gust of wind blew into the hallway, smelling of a room that had been vacant for some time. How long had it been since he had been back to the library? Had it been days, weeks, months, even? Time moved differently in Wonderland, and now that he was back in the library, he was feeling quite tired.

Warrington passed beyond the threshold of the doorway and it began to close. Vitok moved swiftly in order to make it between the collapsing set of doors. She had just stepped through into the library as the doorway closed all the way and locked. Warrington turned to see the tapestry had not changed, but looked an awful lot like the chamber of the White Queen. Vitok picked up a small lantern that was still burning and provided some light as they progressed down the library's corridors.

The library smelled like wet rat, and Warrington suspected that the mice had had the run of the library while he was gone. Warrington could see the library was a mess as he and Vitok moved down the aisles of books. Several of the books had been pulled off the shelves and sat in tattered ruins on the floor, never to be read again. Warrington looked around and saw no mice scurrying about, but he could smell them. They passed by the decaying bones of the rodent Warrington had killed before they had left the library in order to rescue Eld. Warrington thought that some months must have passed, as the carcass was just a few bones left on the floor.

"What is that smell, Warrington?" Vitok said, disgusted.

"That would be the mice that have taken over the library since I left. They can get quite big. Without me here to keep their population down, they have obviously felt that they could take up residence here in the endless buffet of books," Warrington said, turning left and then right down another corridor.

"Well, it is disgusting, whatever it is," Vitok said, following the shimmering purple tail that flickered in the light of the lantern.

Warrington arrived at the door to the study and the small door at the bottom swung open, as if to invite him in and welcome him home. Vitok approached the door and it opened for her, as well. She walked through and the door closed behind her, as though some magical force had opened it and then pushed it shut again.

The study was still quite a mess from when they had left. There was dust on the floor from the Dyhedral that had unsuccessfully tried to remove one of the orbs. The three orbs that Theo had knocked over upon entering the study were still scattered across the floor. The Witch's Eye sat in the corner, glowing green, while the golden one lay by one of the desk legs. The black one still lay in the corner underneath the chair with its orange fire burning in a circle around it. The fireplace was warm and still burned as brightly as it had the day he left. Truthfully, he had wondered if it would have gone out by the time he came back, but no, it remained in its original state of perpetual burning.

Vitok walked toward the orbs staring intently at them. "So these are the crystal globes that make up the Creator's Gift?" she said, picking up the pink globe and staring deep into its center. "I only see a few here. Where are the rest of them?"

"Well, I have only these. There are some that are unaccounted for. Queen Hilda has the crimson one that she calls the Queen's Heart. I can only imagine that the Dark Witch has one or two of her own. The golden one is over here on the floor. Ias mentioned he had taken it from a Dyhedral when it attacked him," Warrington said, walking over to the corner where it rested.

"And what do they all do?" Vitok asked curiously.

"Honestly, I do not know. They all seem to do something different. Some take you to faraway places while others show you the future. Some show you what you desire most. Eld and I both can speak because of the Witch's Eye. One of them even made me grow this strange violet and pink fur that lets me disappear. I must say, it was strange getting used to it, but I think I have a handle on how it works now." Warrington jumped up on top of the desk. "Could you reach down and grab the blank papers and the ink from the bottom drawer?"

Vitok reached down and pulled on a small brass knob. The drawer slid open and revealed several pieces of parchment.

"What are these for?" Vitok asked, placing them on the desk.

"I have to use them for checking items in and out of the library. I also need to give you permission to leave on your own. Once the door closes, only those with permission can exit."

Warrington dipped a claw into the ink and began to write, but Vitok could not make out what he was writing.

"There we are. All set for the Dark Witch and her minions when they come in," Warrington said putting a paw print on the last page.

No sooner had he put the pawprint as his signature on the last page, then the door to the study blew open swiftly. Several cloaked figures walked in and circled the study. Warrington jumped off the desk and ducked down behind it. Vitok walked over to the corner of the room, out of sight of the figures walking in and surrounding the first room of the study. Warrington could just barely see the outline of their faces. Their slithery tongues reaching out from behind the brown hoods, he recognized from their previous visit. He counted seven in the room and one holding open the door to the study as to not let it close and trap them inside.

Within a few seconds, a figure clad in black walked through the door, her face shadowed in the study. The firelight created several small red flashes against her dress. Red, heart-shaped reflections dotted the entire surface of the room.

"Bring in the prisoner, Lazard. We must not keep him waiting," the voice commanded.

A limping, scrawny, emaciated looking Dyhedral without a cloak skulked into the room pulling a long red leash. Attached to the end of the leash was a shiny black cat named Eld.

## Chapter 15

Marchavious and Visok had followed the path through the woods for quite a long time. The sun passed over them several times, but that was not a good indicator of how much time had gone by. Visok pulled the reigns of his horse and it came to a halt.

"Marchavious, stop! Do not proceed any further!" Visok said in an alarming tone.

"Why? What could be more important than getting to where we need to go?" Marchavious asked, turning his head and looking at Visok.

"Well, getting to where we need to go *alive,* for one," Visok said matter-of-factly. "We are being watched, nay hunted."

"By what?" Marchavious said, looking around nervously.

"Be on your guard, men," Visok commanded.

The six soldiers they had brought moved in a circle with their backs to each other—this way they could not be taken by surprise. The sun began to dip behind the trees for the fifth time that day. The forest grew dark and eerily quiet.

There was a sound like the flittering of wings high in the trees. Marchavious turned his head away from Visok and looked forward. From behind him there came the sound of wings flapping furiously. The soldiers started yelling and then there was the sound of someone rather screaming in the distance. The sound faded just as quickly as it had begun.

The sound of several wings came from behind him, this time followed by the sound of metal and breaking branches. Marchavious turned but could see nothing.

"Visok, what is happening?" Marchavious said, turning his head and whispering, but no reply came.

Marchavious heard the wings again, but this time he felt as though he were dreaming. He felt like he was being lifted into the air—in fact, he could now see the tops of the trees above the forest. Then he started to panic as he fell quickly toward the ground.

The ground started coming faster and faster. The trees, which were small, were now quite large and moving toward him at an alarming rate.

"Help!" Marchavious yelled as he passed the top of one tree and hit the branch of another.■

Each branch slowed his descent, but he was still falling very quickly, and the branches hurt as they whipped his body. He continued to fall into darkness and he no longer felt the pain from the branches. He felt warm and wonderful in this place of darkness.

"This one is still alive; we should take him to Bill." The voice was deep and had a grunting tone to it.

"Hello. Are you there?" Marchavious said, but no reply came.

Another voice came through the darkness. "Hello, are you alive?"

Flashes of light began sparking through the darkness. Marchavious began to feel like his face hurt. His eyelids fluttered and he began to see light breaking through his eyelids.

"Hello, little man. Are you in there?" The voice was accompanied by the sensation of pain across his face and another bright white light.

"Yes, yes, I heard you. I am alive, but if you keep slapping me, you might kill me," Marchavious said, waving his hands in front of him to ward off any more slaps to his cheek.

Marchavious looked around, realizing he was on the wooden floor of a cottage. His eyes shifted up to see two small yellow lizard eyes peering at him.

"You had a nasty fall, and I apologize. My friends were only supposed to take you prisoner, but accidents happen, right?" The lizard spoke slowly and methodically. "Why were you riding through the woods with the agents of the Dark Witch? You are no troglodyte like the other you traveled with."

"Agents of the Dark Witch? What do you mean? You are an agent of the Dark Witch. I was traveling with the guards from the White Castle. We rode to come and ask you to join us in the fight against the Dark Witch," Marchavious said, still trying to stop the room from spinning in circles.

"Well, you may have been from the White Castle, but the men you rode with were agents of the Dark Witch. Spies inside the White Queen's walls, if what you say is true. Troglodytes are what we call them because they are nothing but Dyhedral in human flesh. They were transformed by the Dark Witch many moons ago in order to infiltrate the humanoids in several of the cities around Terra-Mirac. They blended in well enough, but the humans could smell them out. They were all but kicked out of all the towns and cities."

The lizard took hold of Marchavious' hand and helped him to his feet. Marchavious grabbed his ribs and winced in pain.

"Come sit on my cushioned bench, and we will discuss why you were coming out here indeed."

Marchavious sat down on the sofa, rubbing his side. He lifted his vest and tunic to reveal many deep welts.

"Once again, I am very sorry for the clumsiness of my friends. My name is Bill, Bill the Lizard. I am no longer with the Dyhedral, as I have grown accustomed to a much simpler life here. There was one Dyhedral stationed here about a week ago that would have jumped at the chance to fight against the Witch, but he was called away suddenly. I was just a handyman, not really a soldier like the others." Bill sat down in a chair across from the sofa.

"Well, Bill, I was sent here by the queen in order to recruit the—Rebobs, I think they are called? The queen has almost no army and no way to fend off the Dark Witch, as she is apparently advancing across the land as we speak," Marchavious said, his breathing erratic.

"Well, that would not be my decision, but my friends have expressed a desire for freedom and to live in these lands as free creatures. I will be right back."

Bill got up from his chair and walked across the room. He opened a small red door and disappeared. Marchavious leaned his head back and closed his eyes. When he opened them again, in what felt to him like only minutes, Bill was sitting in the chair and behind him were several winged creatures resembling monkeys.

"They have agreed to help you, with the condition that the queen knows that when the war is over, they are to be free." Bill crossed one of his legs over the other.

"The queen is very agreeable, and I am sure she will have no trouble rewarding those who come to her aid."

"Good. They will fly you back across the sand to the castle of the White Queen. I will not be joining you, though. I am fine where I am and either way the war works out, I will be safe." Bill uncrossed his legs and stood up and turned to the Rebobs standing behind his chair. "Good luck, my friends. Feel free to return here anytime. You are always welcome in my home."

The largest of the Rebobs held out a hand and bowed low to Bill. They turned and walked out the front door. Marchavious stood up and walked to the door. In the clearing just outside was a group of Rebobs numbering in the hundreds, with more gathering every second.

"There are at least a thousand of them, Marchavious. At one point they were free, but a group of fearful humans chased them out of their home. They had no choice but to flee and hide here in the woods. They just want to be free once more. Goodbye, Marchavious, and good luck." Bill turned around and closed the door.

"Cannot speak most. Nikko I am called, sir. Need me just ask and relay messages I will," the largest of the Rebobs said, coming forward.

"Well, then I guess we are to fly west to the White Castle," Marchavious said to Nikko.

Nikko pointed to one of the larger monkeys and he grabbed Marchavious.

With a single flap of his wings, Nikko lifted off toward the sky. The rest of the squadron of Rebobs followed. Marchavious could see nothing but dark wings as they flew west to the castle of the White Queen.

## Chapter 16

Wiglaf walked back to the man at the podium, who was still standing there. He looked ahead as though he was waiting for someone. Wiglaf walked by him, but the man said nothing. A small dwarf-like man was running up behind Wiglaf with a wheelbarrow full of red stones. He ran past Wiglaf and onto the elevator. Wiglaf ran after him and barely made it onto the platform before the elevator lurched and started ascending upward.

"Excuse me, but where are you going?" Wiglaf asked the man as he stood silent, as if Wiglaf were not there.

"I am not going anywhere," the man said without looking in Wiglaf's direction.

"Well, where are you taking your load to?"

Wiglaf reached over to pick up one of the stones, but the man blocked Wiglaf's attempt. "You must not touch the stones. The queen would not like that. If you must know, I am taking them to be transported to the site of the Crimson Palace. The queen has asked us to gather the stones and build her a new palace."

The man turned his head and looked over at Wiglaf.

"Are you from Heartwick?" Wiglaf asked.

"No, but many of the workers down in the mine are. I am from Diamond Head in the northern area of the land. The queen asked us to come here and work for her when she declared our lands under her rule. She was so beautiful we just could not refuse." The man looked up, as if to see how much longer he had to stay and converse with the giant.

"So you are not worried about the Dark Witch?" Wiglaf asked.

"The Dark Witch? Never heard of her before," the man said. The elevator was screeching as it made its way to the top. "What is a Dark Witch?"

"Well, she is the one marching across the land in order to claim Terra-Mirac for her own. She has a large army of lizard-type creatures. Are you telling me you have never heard of her before?" Wiglaf scratched his head.

"Cannot say that I have. If there is such an army, I am sure the queen is more than able to handle it herself. She is the queen, you know."

The man turned toward the opening as his head came over the top of the ridge. The elevator came to a stop and the metal bars locked in place. The man started walking down the hall, but stopped. He turned around and looked at Wiglaf. "The queen has assured us that as long as we keep working on the Crimson Palace, she will take care of all of us. We are simply the pawns in a much bigger game."

The man placed his hands on the handles and Wiglaf followed closely behind him. The man turned right and went into a large room just at the bottom of the stairs where Tinok had left him. Wiglaf looked inside the room, but it appeared empty. The man dumped his load of rocks and turned around. He walked around Wiglaf as though he was invisible to him and disappeared down the elevator again.

Wiglaf walked into the large empty chamber. The ceiling reflected a bright red glow, and Wiglaf could see a deep canyon in the middle. The room was glowing with molten rock as it traveled through the canyon from the other room.

Several men at the bottom were continually heating boilers to keep the stone from becoming solid. The river of crimson flowed under another reservoir and then under the mountain.

Wiglaf quickly walked back to the stairs and up to the surface. He opened the door but saw no one. The courtyard was empty and silent. He walked over to the front of the palace, up the stairs and through the front door. The room was still dark, but he could see a small light at the end of the chamber. He walked quickly down the dark corridor and into the queen's chamber.

"Excuse me, Your Highness," Wiglaf's voiced echoed through the hallway.

Queen Ducia sat on the throne. "Come forward, Sir Knight," she whispered, but the echo of her voice still filled the room. Wiglaf's metal boots echoed with each step down the hallway.

"Queen Ducia, I must speak with Queen Hilda. I need to know what is going on here." Wiglaf stopped in front of the queen.

"Sir Knight, I am bound to my sister by her wishes. She controls my kingdom with her crimson ball. I do not know how she does it, but I am made to obey her. She told me you would come to see me after you found no one who would join you in helping her." Queen Ducia winced in agony, and she tried to fight the spell. "I am too weak to fight her, Wiglaf. There will be no war. She has captured the minds of the people of Wonderland and made them slaves to her will. Those who oppose her, she disposes of. Her Dyhedral are not marching across the land to go to war; they are coming to usher in the new era and celebrate her coronation as the ruler of all of Wonderland." Queen Ducia doubled over. "I fight to tell you this, Wiglaf, in hopes that you will be able to stop her and bring peace to the land, but I am afraid I cannot help you. In fact, she has ordered your death. Tinok, come out and dispatch this man." Queen Ducia stood up and fainted as she tried to flee.

Tinok walked out from behind the throne. He held a sword of crimson steel in his hand. Wiglaf drew his sword and stepped backward.

"There is no use fighting, Wiglaf. You cannot kill us all. The army of the queen will be upon you even if you make it out of here alive. The Dyhedral will hunt you down. Make it easy on yourself and succumb to me." Tinok gnashed his teeth at Wiglaf.

Tinok raised his sword and dashed toward Wiglaf. Wiglaf jumped aside and swung his sword, narrowly missing Tinok's right leg. Tinok stopped abruptly and slid across the floor to a halt.

The two men circled around, their swords at the ready. Tinok swung toward Wiglaf but was blocked by his sword. Tinok swung over his head, clashing with Wiglaf's sword. The swords ground together as Tinok used his strength to try and overpower Wiglaf. Wiglaf could see the crimson blade cutting through the steel of his blade.

"You're no match for me, old man. If you give up now, I will make your death quick."

Tinok pulled his sword back and struck down again. Wiglaf held his sword up to block him. Wiglaf's blade split in two as the crimson blade sliced through it. The blade cut through to Wiglaf's right shoulder and deflected off the gold plating of his pauldron.

"Now, Wiglaf, you will die and the Procerus will feast on your flesh."

Tinok ran toward Wiglaf, sword out. Wiglaf held up the remainder of his weapon at the ready. Wiglaf could hear the wind whistle and he could have sworn it was the sound of Tinok's blade slicing through the air, but Tinok never got close enough. He fell to the ground and slid past Wiglaf. The sound of his blade falling against the floor echoed in the chamber. Wiglaf could only see the contrast between the crimson blade and the pearl floor.

Wiglaf looked up and saw a man wearing a crown at the side of the throne, holding a bow. Wiglaf looked down at Tinok, who was face-down on the floor with a single arrow stuck in his back.

"Bill? Bill is that you?" Wiglaf said, rushing forward.

"Yes, Wiglaf, it is I indeed."

Bill walked forward to meet his old friend.

"Sir Bill the Dragon Slayer," Wiglaf said putting his arm out and embracing Bill.

"It has been too long, old friend. It is now King Bill the Dragon Slayer. Apparently, I have not lost my ability to save your life." Bill walked over to Queen Ducia. "Things have not been the same since Queen Hilda came around. I have had to be an obedient servant in order to make sure that the people are treated fairly. Her spells do not work on me, so I pretend. She has the whole kingdom bewitched with her dark magic."

"Bill, where has Queen Hilda gone?" Wiglaf knelt down, exhausted.

"She has gone to some library, where she was to retrieve some books or something. I overheard her say something about a cat." Bill was looking over Queen Ducia and stroking her hair. "Queen Ducia and I were married several years ago. I sent a message to you, but I assume it never made it since you did not come to the wedding."

"No, Bill, I would have come," Wiglaf said and rose to his feet. "Will she be okay?"

"Yes, she is just tired. We are expecting our first child soon." Bill picked her up in his arms and laid her on the throne.

"I must try to stop Queen Hilda, Bill. Do you know how I can get to her?" Wiglaf walked over to the throne.

"Unfortunately, I do not," Bill said solemnly.

"I must find Theo, then. Bill, I will do all that is within my power to stop this madness," Wiglaf said, hurrying down the hallway.

"I know you will, Wiglaf. I know you will," Bill whispered as Wiglaf disappeared out the doorway.

## Chapter 17

The flames from the fireplace cast shadows of the cloaked creatures along the walls of the study. Warrington could see Eld tied to the leash the hunched Dyhedral clutched.

"Oh, sweet irony. Who was to know that the librarian would have two cats? Two talking cats, at that," the voice said sweetly into the air.

The figure moved out of the shadow and into the light. Her hair was back in a ponytail and the gold crown sat on top of her head.

"Dearest Warrington, will you not come out so we may talk? Eld has told me everything about you."

Warrington jumped up to the stool. His eyes darted around the room as the red heart-shaped reflections danced on the walls and across the ceiling.

"We are all family here, Warrington. You can come out and see. The Dark Witch is gone and there will be no war. I have brought peace to Wonderland, Warrington. I just need the final pieces of the Wizard's Rainbow to complete my coronation."

Warrington stuck two paws on the top of the desk and peered up over the top.

"There you are. I am sorry if I frightened you. I'm not here to hurt you or your friend. I just needed to make sure that I got what was rightfully mine."

"Nothing in here is rightfully yours," Warrington spoke up.

"Not true, Warrington, simply not true." The woman with the lovely voice, still shadowed by her surroundings, moved forward into the glow of the study. "Your master stole several of the pieces from me, and I am here to get them back, with interest." She leaned into the light, her face pale.

"So, *you* are the Dark Witch?" Warrington said to her.

"Oh, I do hate that unpleasant title. Queen Hildania will do. Or just Queen Hilda. You see I am Queen, not a witch." Queen Hilda raised her scepter. She tapped it twice against the desktop. "Witches carry brooms—I carry a scepter. There is a huge difference between the two. Now, let's talk about these magnificent crystal balls taking up so much space in here. You just let me have them and I'll let your little friend here go. After all, I would never have taken him if I'd known he was not the librarian. I treated him well and I brought him back without a scratch. That must count for something?" She put her scepter up to her chin and batted her eyelashes.

"That does not excuse the murder you committed here the night you took him, now does it?" Warrington replied. "You must be held accountable for your actions."

"Justice? You dare speak to me about justice? *I* am the queen! And *I* make the laws!" Queen Hilda said angrily.

"You are not queen *here*. You are out of your jurisdiction." Warrington walked to the front of the desk.

"Warrington, my dear kitty. We are getting off on the wrong foot. Look, I will let Eld go as a gesture of good faith. Release the cat, Lazard."

Queen Hilda turned and pointed to Lazard. The skinny Dyhedral reached down and lifted the loop from around Eld's neck. Eld ran over to the desk and jumped up on it.

"Gone and had yourself quite an adventure, have you, Warrington?" Eld said, walking by and chuckling at him. "Still a bit on the purple side, as well, I see."

"Funny Eld, making jokes while I am dealing with the person responsible for Ias' death." Warrington smiled. "Good to have you back, though."

There was a loud tapping sound that brought their attention back to the front.

"Excuse me. I am glad you two are having a good reunion, but we are still talking about you giving me the crystal balls."

"I've already told you, I am not giving you a single item in this library," Warrington said, puffing out his chest.

"Well, I am sorry to hear that. Vitok, kill them and burn the library to the ground."

Queen Hilda held out her scepter and pointed to Vitok, who was still sitting in the shadows.

"My pleasure, Your Majesty," Vitok said, moving out of the shadows and toward the desk. She raised her sword.

"Wait, Vitok. Now Warrington, all you have to do is give me what I want and you can go free. I promise not to hurt you, and we can just go about business as usual. If Vitok kills you, I'll just take what I want and leave, anyway." Queen Hilda moved forward and picked up the lime green crystal ball that had been glowing in the corner.

"You're right, Queen Hilda, there is no reason for anyone else to die. I will give you your crystal balls," Warrington said, taking his paw and dipping it in the ink. He put his pawprint in the corner of the paper and the ink disappeared. He repeated this for the next several pieces of paper.

"Warrington! What are you doing? Ias worked hard to get those. You would let his death be in vain?" Eld looked at him in disgust.

"I'm sorry, Eld, but there has been enough bloodshed on account of these accursed things. There is no reason we should die as well," Warrington said in dismay.

"Yes, dear Eld, listen to Warrington." Queen Hilda looked at the Dyhedral and pointed at them. "Go collect my things and wait outside for me." Queen Hilda pointed her scepter at the Dyhedral and then at the crystal balls. "Do not forget the ones on the floor."

The Dyhedral moved forward and picked up the remaining pieces of the Wizard's Rainbow. They put each one into small boxes that they were carrying and closed them up. The Dyhedral carried the boxes to a small chest that Lazard had carried in. They placed the boxes inside the chest.

"Well, my dear cats, this has been a pleasant experience, but we must get back. There is going to be a celebration in my honor. You really must come and join in on the festivities. Oh wait, you won't be able to attend. Vitok, burn the library to the ground."

Vitok opened up the small chest and pulled the yellow orb free from its box.

"My pleasure, Your Highness." Vitok held the yellow ball high into the air.

"That will be quite far enough, Vitok," Wiglaf said, pulling the crimson sword from the limp body of the Dyhedral that had been holding the door.

"Ah, Wiglaf, well, this *is* a special occasion. I assume Tinok did not do his job," Queen Hilda said, annoyed. "No matter, if you kill Vitok, you can be the general of my army. I prefer human to Dyhedral, anyway. Vitok, finish the job, and come back to the castle. You other Dyhedral bring my chest to the door." Queen Hilda, who was still holding the Witch's Eye, stroked it and turned to Warrington. "Do not feel too bad about giving up so easily. Your master would be proud."

Queen Hilda spat on the floor of the study. Warrington hissed at her.

"Goodbye," Queen Hilda said as she disappeared into the Witch's Eye.

Vitok looked over at Wiglaf and held out the yellow orb.

"Wiglaf, watch out!" Warrington yelled. Wiglaf dodged just as the beam of fire destroyed the couch into a thousand pieces. Vitok pointed the ball blindly, channeling the fireplace's light across the room, spraying it with fire. Flames engulfed the entire room. Wiglaf jumped from behind the chair and threw his sword. It twirled through the air, striking Vitok in the leg.

"You have no weapon now, Wiglaf. You are at my mercy and now I will finish the job the fell beast should have finished back in Heartwick when we unleashed it on the town in order to destroy it," Vitok said, moving forward.

She crossed the threshold into the first room of the study and paused. She turned around and saw the yellow ball drift toward the ground. White dust particles floated down before her eyes and she fell to the ground in a pile of ash.

The other Dyhedral grabbed the poles on the box and began to run with it, but disintegrated into heaps of ash on the floor.

"What just happened, Warrington?" Eld said, looking down at the piles of ash on the floor.

"I never gave them permission to take them. I signed the paper giving all rights and control of the library over to Wiglaf," Warrington said, looking over at Wiglaf, who was scurrying to put out the flames that engulfed the furniture and rugs. The rest of the fire had smoldered out, as stone does not burn as fabric and wood.

The fire in the fireplace grew bright and a great wind swept over the room. The ashes from the Dyhedral whirled into the air. Warrington could feel the strong force pushing him toward the fireplace.

"Warrington, jump down here," Eld said, jumping off the desk and moving underneath it. Warrington followed.

When the wind had stopped, Warrington looked out from under the desk to see what had happened. Wiglaf stood in the corner of the room with half of a singed rug covered in ashes.

"Wiglaf, are you all right?" Warrington moved past the chest and into the now-empty study.

"Yes, Warrington, I am," Wiglaf said, tossing the remainder of the rug into the fireplace.

Eld came out from behind the desk and jumped on top of the chest. "Well, Wiglaf, you are now the new librarian," Eld said. "Warrington and I are at your disposal."

"Librarian? I do not know the first thing about libraries except that books go into them. Besides, we have to go and save Theo and Marchavious from the queen. They are still there."

"All in due time, Wiglaf," Warrington said, looking up at the picture that was still hanging above the fireplace. A single tear rolled down his cheek as he finally could make out the picture—it was a portrait of Ias watching over the library.

# *Epilogue*

### '1'

When the queen disappeared, she did not travel to another dimension or to an alternate universe, as Warrington imagined the Witch's Eye would take her to. Queen Hilda had been studying for a long time about what he had come to know as the Creator's Gift, Maerlin's Rainbow, the Wizard's Rainbow, or the many other incantations that they had been called over time. She frequented the libraries in order to read books and to ultimately find out where they came from and where they disappeared to after each story ended. When she used the Witch's Eye to teleport herself out of the library, she had only one intention: to return to the White Castle, where her army of Dyhedral would be waiting.

Queen Ducia and King Bill were sitting inside the white throne chamber when a plume of green smoke swirled around the center of the chamber. When the smoke cleared, Bill could see Queen Hilda standing in the middle of the room just in front of the body of what used to be Tinok.

"Poor Tinok, you were indeed worthless," Queen Hilda said, looking behind her. She faced forward and saw her sister and Bill sitting on the throne. Queen Ducia was still quite weak and unable to say much. "Ah, my dear sister and my brother in-law. You will be pleased to know that your services are no longer needed. Well, maybe yours are still needed, Bill, but my sister is free from her rule. My army is awaiting the coronation of Queen Hilda, Queen of Wonderland." Queen Hilda laughed an evil laugh.

"You will never get away with this, Witch." Bill picked up the remainder of the sword that had broken during the confrontation between Wiglaf and Tinok. He dashed forward with the blade outward.

"This is trivial and I have no time for games." Queen Hilda held up the Witch's Eye and with a puff of green smoke, Queen Ducia was gone. Bill stopped in his tracks, his mouth agape, as his wife was no longer sitting on the throne.

"What did you do with her?" Bill turned toward Queen Hilda.

"Bill … William—you are a smart man and much too old to fight with someone of my stature. Queen Ducia is safe for now, and if you would like to see her again, then you will serve me." Queen Hilda walked by Bill to the throne. She walked up the few steps that led to the large white throne and sat down.

"*What* did you do to her? I will murder you!" Bill said angrily. He was still in shock from this turn of events.

"She is safe and sound in another world, but I need a king, Bill. Please do not make me use the Queen's Heart to persuade you. I enjoy the freewill service that comes from the natural desires of the soul." Queen Hilda sat down and crossed her legs.

"Fine. I will serve you. But I will not do it willingly." Bill stood in front of the queen.

"Kneel, Bill, and take your place as my king." Queen Hilda pointed her scepter at Bill.

Bill knelt before her without a word.

"Good, now we will vacate these premises. My new palace should be ready soon. Your precious Ducia will have quarters nearby, but she will not remember you, Bill. I will allow her to be my Duchess if you would like. She can live in the forest as an old hag." Queen Hilda laughed heartily, pleased with herself. "Now, Bill, I need you to go and summon all of the city magistrates. Tell them they are required at the coronation of the new queen."

"Yes, my Queen, as you wish, my Queen," Bill said, standing up, his head lowered in defeat. Bill walked to the end of the room and opened the door.

"Oh Bill, when Vitok and her guards get back, please tell them to take my things to the Crimson Palace." Queen Hilda stood up and walked behind the throne, grabbing the Queen's Heart from a pedestal there. She gazed into it, her eyes reflecting the crimson-red glow. The white chamber glowed like Christmas as she carried the red and green orbs out to the courtyard, where her coronation would usher in the coming of a new era in Wonderland.

'2'

The sky was clouded over by large dark grey rain clouds that had moved in as a convoy for the coronation. The cloaked minions of the Dark Witch had climbed the winding pathway to the top and awaited their queen in the courtyard. Marchavious could see the large cloaked army in the courtyard as the Rebobs flew in from the east.

There was much snarling and gnashing of teeth in the ranks as the uncivilized lizards pushed and shoved each other. The Rebobs landed behind them, their numbers in the thousands. Marchavious was released from the Rebob that had been carrying him and landed on the ground, which was now slightly damp as a light mist came raining over the crowd. Marchavious worked his way past the large crowd and could see Theo standing at the front of the group.

"Theo, Theophilus, what is happening?" Marchavious shouted over the loud ruckus of lizard sounds.

"Oh, Marchavious! You are back." Theo embraced his friend. "From what I understand, the Dark Witch has given up and we are to celebrate the victory. I am saddened slightly that my tabards will not see battle. Maybe they will still be of use, though. Have you heard from Wiglaf or Warrington?" Theo said, his arm still around Marchavious.

"I have not, but I can only assume that they are the reason that the war ended without a fight. They probably vanquished the Dark Witch, and without a master, the Dyhedral gave up." Marchavious was pretty sure that this was probably what had happened.

The soft dirt was beginning to turn to mud as the rain started coming down harder. The lightning streaked across the sky, illuminating the clouds as the thunder followed with its roar of applause. The crowd grew silent as the large doors to the throne chamber opened slowly and Queen Hilda walked outside. She was wearing a crimson dress with black hearts made from onyx draped around the side. White frill crowned the top of her neck. The crowd roared as she exited the building and came into the light. The rain was coming down harder now, but just stopped short of getting Queen Hilda even the least bit wet.

"My loyal servants and my soon-to-be loyal servants, without you this day would not be possible. Today we usher in a new era where human and beast shall live in harmony. Today's coronation will mark the beginning of peace and an army that shall enforce that peace. Those who oppose our rule will be punished for their insolence." Queen Hilda held her scepter up high into the air. "Where are the magistrates of the cities? Are they here? Bill, where are they?"

Bill came forward, leading a group of six men dressed in what could only be described as colonial-era attire.

"You, Magistrates, have been loyal to a fault. Loyal to the White Queen! When I offered my services and a chance to be redeemed in the coming days of my rule, only one of you saw the coming tide." She pointed to a small gentleman wearing a vest and a pocket watch. "You may stand over there with the other humans." The small man walked over and stood next to Theo and Marchavious.

"Now, for you insubordinate fools! You have been corrupt and foul all of your days, taking from the people what is theirs and pretending to serve them when you were really out to serve yourselves. That is what I admire, and I am going to reward you accordingly. Come forward and receive your prize." The men stepped forward with their heads held high. They were proud and arrogant as they stepped forward and stood before the queen.

"Kneel and show your loyalty to your queen, Magistrates!" Queen Hilda said. The men knelt low, their heads looking down. Queen Hilda pulled the Witch's Eye from a small box one of the Dyhedral behind her was holding. She held it outward toward the men. "Now you foul creatures shall be that which you have acted like."

The men doubled over in pain and agony. Their skin began to grow feathers, each of a different variety. Their noses began to harden and grow as beaks formed on their faces. Marchavious looked over at them, horrified, as they began to change shape into birds: five distinct birds of different sizes and shapes. There was a black crow, an exotic green parrot, a white pelican, a blue eagle, and a large fat dodo.

The five birds squawked and chirped as they walked around on the ground in front of the queen. Marchavious began to speak out in protest but thought better of it.

"Cage these foul beasts and take them out of my sight. Let this be a lesson to those who are not loyal to my throne. I was merciful. From this day forward, anyone who breaks the law will lose their head. Now that we have that unpleasantness out of the way, let us move forward with the crowning of the new Queen of Wonderland."

A small procession of Dyhedral came out of the doorway behind her, carrying a small golden crown.

"Wait! I demand music while I am being crowned. Who knows a song that will be fitting for a queen's coronation?" Queen Hilda looked out across the crowd, but no one stepped forward.

"I can sing you a song, Your Majesty," a voice came from the crowd.

"Theo, what are you doing?" Marchavious said, pulling at Theo's jacket.

"I am going to sing a song for the queen. I feel it is only fitting for this special occasion," Theo said, moving forward and shaking Marchavious' hand free from his jacket.

"Well, Mr. Theophilus Hatmaker has a song for this occasion. Proceed, Mr. Hatmaker, with your musical interpretation of my coronation."

Theo stepped forward and began to sing, "Twinkle, twinkle little…" Theo stopped and looked at Marchavious, perplexed. "I have forgotten the words," Theo said, looking over at the queen.

"You had better find them or you will find yourself missing more than just a few words." Queen Hilda looked irritated, but smiled as Theo began once more.

*"Twinkle, twinkle little bat,*

*How I wonder where you're at.*

*Up above the world you fly,*

*Like a diamond in the sky.*

*Twinkle, twinkle—"*

"Stop! Stop immediately! You are terrible and that song was horrible. In fact, it was so bad it probably killed those few seconds of time. Yes indeed, that killed time and in defense of time, I have no choice but to sentence you under the new law… OFF WITH HIS HEAD!!" Queen Hilda shouted out across the courtyard. The Dyhedral let out a loud roar across the yard. Two Dyhedral walked up and grabbed Theo by the arms and dragged him across the courtyard to a small building.

Marchavious stepped forward in protest. "Queen Hilda, how could you? You asked for a song and he did his best. I beg you to let him go. He has been nothing but loyal to Your Majesty. You have no heart!"

"Heart? You speak to me of not having a heart? I am the Queen of Hearts! You simply must be mad. Mad as a March Hare, I would say. Yes, yes, that will do." She held up the Witch's Eye and pointed it at Marchavious. He jumped out of the way, and the magistrate who had been dismissed as her loyal follower fell to the ground ill. His ears began to grow and a small puffy tail grew in the back; white fur sprouted out of his skin as he rolled around in agony.

Several Dyhedral rushed forward and grabbed Marchavious. They held him as Queen Hilda took the green orb and held it out toward him again. "You shall not only share your friend's fate, but we will be eating rabbit stew tonight."

The Dyhedral roared in agreement to this. Marchavious fell over in pain as she held out the ball and laughed as he rolled on the ground. Marchavious' ears grew long and his feet large. Grey and white fur sprouted from his skin.

"Now take him away, and we'll execute them when we are finished here." Queen Hilda pointed off to the right, to the small building they'd taken Theo to. Marchavious finished his transformation as they dragged him to the small building.

"Now, place the crown on my head and receive the reward I have promised you." Queen Hilda ducked her head down as the Dyhedral placed the small crown on her head.

She looked out and pointed to Nikko, who was standing in front of the large group of Rebobs. "You, monkey… what can I do in order to obtain your loyalty?"

Nikko stepped forward to the front. "Freedom is what we ask—to no longer be under the control of the gold hat," Nikko grunted.

"Very well, you will gain the same reward as the Dyhedral have earned." Queen Hilda stood up. The rain clouds parted and the sun peeked through the opening.

The large Dyhedral stepped forward and shouted, "All hail Queen Hilda, Queen of Hearts, Queen of Wonderland!" The crowd of Dyhedral and Rebobs roared in applause.

"Now for your gift of freedom and service." Queen Hilda raised the green orb and the red orb together. The Dyhedral and Rebobs fell to the ground. They screamed in a chorus of agony as the Queen laughed. "This is your gift, you wretched creatures. You shall be human and free from your previous life. With the Queen's Heart, you shall be loyal servants to only me." Queen Hilda laughed at the crowd of thousands rolling in the mud, agonizing as their scales turned to skin, their wings were stripped from them, and their claws turned to fingernails.

"Now that I have given you the gift of being human, you will serve me, as I have kept my word. You will come over and take a tabard from the pile and wear it according to your rank in my army." Queen Hilda pointed at each of the Dyhedral to take a red diamond or heart tabard, while the Rebobs were made to take a black club or spade tabard.

"Now we shall finish our celebration at the Crimson Palace. Fetch the prisoners! Captains! Move your troops to the Crimson Palace." The queen barked orders for the troops to double-time it. The large army moved across the land to the Crimson Palace.

"You, Magistrate. Since you are a white rabbit and I have need for a messenger, you may be the Royal Messenger. Please report to King Bill." Queen Hilda moved her hand in a dismissive motion.

The queen stepped down as one of the men with a red number three in hearts on his chest hurriedly approached her. "Your Majesty, the prisoners have escaped." The soldier wearing the tabard with the three on it bowed his head as to not make eye contact with the queen.

"That is okay, my dear," she said politely. She turned to the soldier next to her, wearing a number nine in hearts. "Off with his head for telling me bad news. I will not tolerate failure."

The soldier with the number nine stamped on his chest, grabbed number three, and dragged him off. The queen smiled as she watched her orders being carried out.

Queen Hilda climbed inside her coach and pulled the cover closed. "To the Crimson Palace, and hurry."

The four soldiers with a single number on their chest—one heart, one diamond, one club and one spade—carried the queen's coach away from the White Castle and toward the Crimson Palace.

'3'

Marchavious was thrown in a crudely made jail cell with bars made of maple wood. "Marchavious, is that you?" Theo said, looking at the rabbit-like figure slumped on the floor in the next cell.

"Yes, Theo, this is quite a mess we are in." Marchavious was not happy about being a rabbit, or the fact that she had said he was mad as a March Hare.

"What happened to you, Marchavious?" Theo inquired.

"The queen turned me into a March Hare after I pleaded for your release," Marchavious said, standing up and tripping a bit on his gigantic feet.

"Well, I thank you for your pleas, but they are not going to help us now," Theo said.

"Why did you sing that ridiculous song, Theo? Those were not even the words," Marchavious said, scolding him.

"I could not remember the words to any songs. The words were a jumble in my mind. I just sang what I could. I figured it would be better than singing nothing after I volunteered," Theo explained.

"Well, we are going to be killed and the queen said they are going to eat me for dinner," Marchavious said, sitting down.

They could hear the metal door to the building open and then slam shut. "Here they come now. We should think of something quickly, Theo." Marchavious looked desperate.

Theo and Marchavious looked at each other, but neither of them had any idea what to do. They could see a shadowy figure coming down the stairs. "Which one of you is Theophilus Hatmaker?" a voice demanded.

Neither one of them spoke up. "I said, which one of you is Theophilus Hatmaker, and be quick about it."

"I am Theophilus Hatmaker," Theo responded, his head slumped down.

"Well, well, Theophilus. You have committed a great crime indeed. Killing time is not an offense I take lightly," the man said, peering through the cell door. "I do not think death is a fitting punishment, though. If someone had killed you, would you not want them to suffer the maximum you could inflict on them?" The man opened the door to the cell. "Since the queen has no jurisdiction over time, I must sentence you myself, as it was me you killed with your horrid singing. As punishment, you will be in a state of perpetual time. I think six o'clock will do. No sleep, no wake, just an eternity at six o'clock. That would be enough to drive anyone mad for eternity," the man said, taking Theo by the hand.

"What about me?" Marchavious said, looking over at the man, who was dressed in a grey suit and holding a pocket watch made of solid gold.

"What about you? You have not committed a crime here. I have no reason to punish you," the man said, looking over at the rabbit in the next cell.

"I wish to be sentenced with him for eternity, sir," Marchavious pleaded with him.

"Well, since you are wasting me, I will do you the luxury of this. As someone who has all of me in the world, you are hereby sentenced to share the same fate," the man said, opening the cell and placing watches on the wrists of both Theo and Marchavious.

"Who are you?" Marchavious asked curiously.

"I am Time, of course, and I have gone quite mad myself," Time said. He turned each watch to precisely six o'clock. The watches moved forward, and Marchavious and Theo disappeared.

When Theo and Marchavious regained consciousness in their new surroundings, they were sitting at a large table set for tea, and a small, blonde-haired girl in a pretty blue dress was skipping down the dirt path toward then.

## *Thank You*

To those who made this possible:

Alan Stice- – Thank you so much for your support.

Wayne Williamson – my mentor, and his awesome niece Izzy,

who has shown us that strength resides in the smallest of God's people.

Dawn Oshima – Your support has made a dream reality

Jennifer Babbit – My dearest cousin and your family –

enjoy reading this to your kids.

I have enjoyed the time we have taken to rekindle our friendship!

AgentJLM – My brother in arms

Tim "FatElvis" Konkle – You, sir, have not left the building.

Lisa Yee – Thank you for the unconditional support!

You will always be a dear friend.

| | |
|---|---|
| Dave Beatty – BentBeat Productions | Matthew Ryan Robinson |
| David Freeman | Isaiah – I-Dizzle |
| Mercedes Thornton | Jesse Marinacci |
| Jean-Baptiste | Thomas J. DeCarlo |
| Vickie | Hakan Yuatsu Chang Gilhooly |
| Doriane | Brittany Miller |
| Jacob B. Carpenter | Charlie |
| @jaf0 (Daniel Weigh) | Anna Nicole Ureta |
| Mark and Kimberly Fiester | Sascha |
| Nathan Olmstead | Charles M Brown |
| Laura D. | Julie |
| Ross A. Mauri | Damien Swallow |

The Spencer Family

Mr. Dancer

Dan Higgins and Family

Lunchtime Studios LLC

(www.lunchtimestudios.com)

Illicit Cookies

Corie L. Jurisch

Dennis Beatty

Vickie Tate

Andy Brokaw

Doug

Jordan

Amanda Kennedy

Steph and Eric

Robert Harrington

Susan Gordon

Rachel DiPaola

Tomomi

Megan

Radda Family

Trinda Burch

Lyric Halterman

Alexei

Steve and Kira Lee Kramer

Kevin

Audra Lemke

Mark Bowers

Helen

Randi Himes

Margaret M. St. John

Achim

A.K. Tosh

Roy Sutton

Melissa Beher

Amanda Plaugher

Tonya Brewton

Ashleigh A.

Eric Moeller

Pia Briseño

Brian Goubeaux

Ron & Emily Hayes

Carsten Insertcoin Propach

Carolyn Mariot

Amanda Sanders

Diana J Peters

Rylan Cottrell

Joy, Kyle, Mia and Nathan Dickinson

Ryan Durney Illustrations

Chris and Kelley Adams

Steffen Bach Thorbjørnson

| | |
|---|---|
| Fred Patton | Greg |
| Pete Duchak | Adam Marks |
| The Dowis Family | John Kneeland – Last Man Standing |
| Brian Tucker | Bruce Beatty |
| Brian Wiegele | Jessica |
| Wayne Yeager | Reaper Media |
| Jennifer Steen | N.L.Cobb |
| Daniel Abigail | Erin Cashier |
| Casey Clark | Linda Jefferies |
| Matt Fox | Michelle Runde |
| Nora | Surrey |
| Susan B. | Kimberly Daviner |
| Diane Flores | The Newnham Family |
| Patrick Havens & Boys of the Napa City Zoo | Animal Store Alphabet Book |
| | Rubiee Tallyn Hayes |
| Devin L. Michaels | Charlie McElvy |
| Majorie-Ann Lacharite | |
| Mary Lingel | Clarice Williams |
| | Stephen Mercer |
| Melissa Reid | Thomas Giles |
| Emily Cox & Stuart Fullmer | Ben Combee |
| Joe Martino – Creator of Shadowflame, Ripperman, and The Mighty Titan | Shannon O. |
| | Karl Foster |
| Sarah Boisvert & Jed Curtis | Scott Foster |
| Jevin Hernandez | Scott Jimmo |
| Ruth Elizabeth Gerhard | Cara Lee Adams |

Jenee Hughes

Harry Steinman

Ari Bailey

Rocco Haase

Steven Ready

Daniel Camp

Jennifer Rodriguez

Scott GrantSmith

Jac Camara

Buddha

Cerity-la Tradewind

Art Dahm

Anonymous

Ellen Fleischer

Torgamous

Ken Brosky

Jonathan Fesmire

Christine B. Penley

Shane Zeagman

Remsey Atassi

Silvernis

Przemyslaw Tomaszewski

Peter Morrison

Timothy Schwader

Edmond Aggaboa

Johnson Hor

Noah H Bayindirli

Braden Schlosser

Michael Tervoort

Greg

Michael Mullin

Chuq Von Rospach

Cameron TifaLita Jones

Beth Basilius

Chris Heslop

Karen D. Taylor and Zoe!

Maggo

Peter Polivka